T0367548

THE PIONEERS
COMMENCEMENT

BEN OWENS

authorHOUSE®

AuthorHouse™
1663 Liberty Drive
Bloomington, IN 47403
www.authorhouse.com
Phone: 833-262-8899

Published by AuthorHouse 02/09/2024

ISBN: 979-8-8230-1526-4 (sc)
ISBN: 979-8-8230-1525-7 (e)

Library of Congress Control Number: 2023918305

Print information available on the last page.

Any people depicted in stock imagery provided by Getty Images are models, and such images are being used for illustrative purposes only.
Certain stock imagery © *Getty Images.*

This book is printed on acid-free paper.

CAST OF CHARACTERS

The Owens Clan – from Pennsylvania; mortal, immortal and perished.

<u>Mortal</u> – survived the tribulation and will enter the Millennial Kingdom.

- Irene Owens* – matriarch
- David and Vera Owens* – her son and daughter-in-law
- Joshua Owens* – their son, born at the start of the 7-year tribulation.
- Michelle Sandahl* – Irene's granddaughter from Maryland

<u>Immortal</u> – disappeared before the troubles began.

- Daniel Owens – Irene's husband
- Dennis Owens – Daniel's brother
- Irene's Daughter Katherine Owens and husband Stephen Engle and four children

<u>Perished - took the mark of the Beast</u> - from Maryland.

- Irene's older daughter Abigail Owens and husband Michael Sandahl and two sons (Michael Jr and Merlin). Their daughter Michelle survived with her grandmother in Pennsylvania in the bunker.

The Freeman Clan – bunker mates; long-time friends and employees of Stephen Engel

- Russ Freeman*
- Kim Marshall*

Michael and Sylvia Cohen* – Jewish neighbors rescued by Avi Sharon. Fellow bunker mates, survivors of the tribulation.

Avi Sharon* – An Israeli missionary and bunker mate who was sent to warn them of the pending tribulation.

Characters they met after the tribulation.

- Angela – a neighbor's 6-year-old daughter who was born during the 7-year tribulation but is orphaned when her parents do not return from Israel.
- Walter Petersen – a friend of Irene Owens whom she meets on the trip to Israel to be judged by the King.

*Those who survived in the bunker

PROLOGUE
Kingdom Year 1010
New Columbia

It was once called Pennsylvania, one of the United States. When the Kingdom began the North American leaders reorganized the continent into six new countries, and it was absorbed into the eastern seaboard nation of New Columbia. From that location they connected across the Atlantic Ocean to what had been Europe and the King's homeland in Israel.

Only those who survived the troubles remembered that ancient time and the old order of things, groups like three pioneer clans – the Owens in New Columbia, the Freemans in Cascadia in the Pacific Northwest, and the Sharons in Israel. They were bound by a common history of refuge and survival, and at the end of earthly time they could reflect upon an amazing millennium as they witnessed the end of it all.

The Owens clan clustered in a circle around the holovision in their dwelling's viewspace, focusing on the 3D satellite images projected before them. Neighbors drifted in and the group quickly swelled to twenty people. Some sat, others knelt or stood. Irene Owen's son David held the controller, taking suggestions to zoom in or out, alternating between twenty-kilometer-high views of the King's land in Israel, or swooping down to mob level to scout individual faces.

Shortly they were virtual-linked with another clan – their friends the Freemans in Cascadia in the Pacific Northwest, with an even larger crowd in their dwelling's viewspace. The Freeman clan blended in with their virtual crowd, visible but immaterial, specters wandering around the viewspace, drifting through people and material objects. The Owens clan did the same in Freeman's viewspace, creating simultaneous jumbles of material and virtual humans at opposite ends of the continent.

Cascadia's clan leader Russell Freeman introduced his group, many already familiar, and said, "Think of it, David. We began this long adventure in your dwelling. A thousand years, and it's come to this."

"It has been a wondrous journey," David said, a chorus of clan members voicing agreement.

Before the troubles, before the Kingdom, they lamented their chaotic world: the lack of equality and justice, plagues and natural disasters, peace was elusive, violence everywhere, and much of their world existed in poverty and ignorance. The King responded by cleansing the earth of ungodly elements and then presented the survivors with the ideal they desired. He gave peace, abundance, prosperity, health, and longevity that had now reached a thousand years. And to aid their chances, he bound Satan and his minions. They were free to exercise their God-given talents, to succeed in whatever they might become, to make their world as perfect as possible.

The King kept his end of the bargain, but human nature reverted to form. As generation followed generation in the millennium, by degrees they forgot the primal truth – to fear the King and keep his commandments, for this is man's all, and that the King would bring every work into judgment, including every secret thing, whether good or evil.

As portended, the inevitable happened. As the millennium lapsed, rising tensions erupted into open rebellion: the King had released Satan and his minions from their imprisonment for one final test of humanity.

The wise knew what was coming, which made the anticipation at once terrifying and fascinating. Both clans sensed the climax was at hand. They stared at the living images before them, hordes of rebellious humans teeming into Israel, encircling the King's Temple Mountain. Instigated by Satan himself, they were ready to attack with whatever weapons they could muster: lasers, sound stunners, ancient ammunition guns, tanks, hand rockets, explosives. Their resolve was clear: they would no longer have this King rule over them. They had become weary of his rules, his standards, and his discipline over their lives.

Up close they could hear the chaotic shrieks of the rebellyers, with noises of machinery and discordant music spurring them on. Zooming out, the din coalesced into a dull roar, and they saw a panorama of the whole invasion, masses of humanity swarming the King's holy land like a plague of locusts. To their horror, they knew some of their own descendants were among the throng, stumbling on as lambs to the slaughter.

David Owens used the controller in face scanning mode to focus on the crowd from a few meters view, searching for anyone familiar. Several descendants, five generations removed, had joined the underground rebellion movement and had traveled to Israel to join the fight.

David's wife Vera was first to spot them. "Oh my God," she said, gasping as she held her hand over her mouth, pointing at two men of indeterminate age, mouths agape, perfect teeth, in obvious rage. "It's our kinsons Drystan and Gwyn. Look at them. They bear weapons and cheer on the rebellyers."

"Many times we warned them," David said, shaking his head. "They fight the King himself. They cannot succeed."

"Look for more," Vera said.

Their mates from the Freeman Clan also scanned the crowd virtually from their viewspace in the Pacific Northwest. "See there. Look," Russell said to his wife and pointed, "The man. Red headband. Angry. He is from our area. Recognize him, Kim?"

Russell's wife peered more intently at the spot. "Yes. It is him. The McLaren kin. Joseph I think his name was. He worried us. Tried to seduce our Leah. We have kinson Thomas to thank for saving her," casting a glance toward the Clatsop Indian descendant that married their great granddaughter.

They watched helplessly as this disaster tsunami unfolded before them. A low voice had been narrating the holovision scenes with a running commentary on the events. David let the holovision scan on automatic and it withdrew to a twenty-kilometer-high view again, giving a panorama of the entire nation of Israel with the rebellyers approaching from all directions, in mobs many kilometers deep.

Irene Owens voiced concern for her own granddaughter, married and living in Israel. "What of our friends Avi and Michelle and their descendants? Think they are safe?" she said.

"Michelle signaled me," Vera said. "They moved all family into Zion City on the Temple Mountain. The King will protect them," Vera said.

"Their beautiful home on the ocean. All gone," Irene said.

"It will not matter Mother," David said. "After this...the eternity. New homes."

"Eternal homes," his wife Vera echoed, savoring the concept.

No one could take their eyes off the holovision. From that height it looked like a flood rising toward the Temple Mountain. Through the Millennium they had seen the power of angels and the King's intervention in national disputes. Why the delay now? What is supposed to happen?

As the tip of the flow reached the base of the Holy Mountain on three sides, they held their breath.

There was a flash of orange-red light, matched with screams in horror and agony.

It was over.

"For behold, in those days and at that time, When I bring back the captives of Judah and Jerusalem, I will also gather all nations, and bring them down to the Valley of Jehoshaphat; And I will enter into judgment with them there on account of My people, My heritage Israel, Whom they have scattered among the nations..."

Joel 3:1-2 NKJV (ca. 835 BC)

Then I saw another angel flying in the midst of heaven, having the everlasting gospel to preach to those who dwell on the earth—to every nation, tribe, tongue, and people—saying with a loud voice, "Fear God and give glory to Him, for the hour of His judgment has come; and worship Him who made heaven and earth, the sea and springs of water..."

Then a third angel followed them, saying with a loud voice, "If anyone worships the beast and his image, and receives *his* mark on his forehead or on his hand, he himself shall also drink of the wine of the wrath of God, which is poured out full strength into the cup of His indignation. He shall be tormented with fire and brimstone in the presence of the holy angels and in the presence of the Lamb. And the smoke of their torment ascends forever and ever; and they have no rest day or night, who worship the beast and his image, and whoever receives the mark of his name."

Here is the patience of the saints; here *are* those who keep the commandments of God and the faith of Jesus. Then I heard a voice from heaven saying to me, "Write: 'Blessed *are* the dead who die in the Lord from now on.'"

"Yes," says the Spirit, "that they may rest from their labors, and their works follow them."

Revelation 14:6-13 NKJV (soon)

CHAPTER 1

SPRING - YEAR ZERO

By late March, their first robin had ventured north to the mountains of northeastern Pennsylvania. Through the bombardments, the wariness, and the wonder if the turmoil would ever end, the bird's annual arrival hinted at calmer times and the hope of peace at last. It rustled through puddles of dead leaves blown against old cars and machinery scattered about the junkyard, scratching for seeds and the crumbs the humans tossed discreetly from the door of their bunker.

David Owens stood in the doorway and made a cautious scan of the surroundings before stepping outside. With four years of practice, he methodically checked the security cameras covering the unexposed areas around the building and up the hillside behind them, and then visually scanned the junk yard in front, the road beyond, then down through the valley below and onto the low hill to the south.

No movements.

A wisp of smoke drifted up from the remnant of a barn that had been hit by a fireball, but otherwise all seemed at rest. If their building ever possessed an outside thermometer, it was lost years ago. He estimated the temperature to be in the forties, but the morning sun softened the chill.

There were no sounds of small planes or helicopters or drones, so satisfied that it was reasonably safe, he slipped outside with his lawn chair and laptop computer and set up under the entrance canopy shielding them from satellite surveillance. It was more secure when leaves filled the bushes surrounding the entrance, but they were all anxious for any news, so it seemed worth the risk.

He booted the laptop and continued to stare around while it cycled through its startup routines. He took several long, deep breaths to flush the mustiness of the bunker from his lungs while the computer searched for its home page. The browser finally gave the date, March 24, but the page's information was merely a memory. There had been no updates for several weeks now. He tried a few other browsers, but the response was the same. They either would not load at all, or the information was stagnant.

While he was distracted with his search, his son Joshua spoke up from behind him. "Anything, Dad?"

"Afraid not."

"Can we come out?"

David turned around to see his mother, Irene Owens, standing in the doorway next to his son. They were leery of having too many people exposed to view at any one time, and he instinctively turned back for another quick scan of the valley and the hill beyond. Still no movement.

"Check the security cameras. If they look good, I guess it's okay."

In a few seconds Joshua dragged out another folding chair and set it up next to his dad. Irene stood behind her son, hands on his shoulders, scanning the valley herself in the surveillance pattern they had all come to use.

Joshua had plugged into his iPod with earplugs, and David asked him, "Anything on the radio?"

"No. I can't get any stations."

"It's been over a week now with no bombardments," Irene said.

"Ten days," David said.

"Do you think it's finally over?"

David shrugged. "Don't know. The time's about right...almost four years now. Seems like this should have ended a while ago."

"I imagine these prophecies are inexact."

"Maybe, but they should be close enough if they're true. It reads that there should be forty-two months of this...whatever it is. This tribulation?" David said.

"With build-up time, and some time afterward, maybe it runs longer," she said.

"Do you ever think this will never end, Dad?" Joshua said.

David Owens reached around his son's shoulder and stroked his arm, still staring across the valley, ever vigilant. "Josh, if the prophecies are true, it has to end. I'd like to tell you I think it will end soon, but, yeah, I wonder. It's scary. I don't know how much longer we can all hold out. Ten people? What if someone gets seriously ill? And sooner or later we'll run out of food and have to make some trips out of here. Or move. Then we'd be vulnerable...more vulnerable, anyway."

Irene massaged David's shoulders and said, "We all feel that way, but you've been a rock through all this. I don't know what we'd have done without you."

"Everybody's pitched in, Mom. The others know more about technology than I do, and Avi's the go-to guy if we're in any danger."

"Yes. I know. But you're my steady force. I used to think it was your sister Abby, but I think this really forced you to the front."

David reached up and patted his mom's hand. "It's hard Mom. Wish we knew what happened to her and the rest of her family."

He felt his mom's hands tighten on his shoulders. "I have to accept the fact that your niece Michelle may be all that's left."

"At least she's safe with us. Or, as safe as we get, anyway," David said.

With no browser available, David clicked through the computer shut down routine to save on battery time. Finally, he folded it closed and let it sit on his lap as they stared ahead across the valley. About half a dozen vultures had appeared, soaring in the thermal currents, circling over the ruined farm buildings in the valley below.

"I hope they're just enjoying the morning," Irene said.

"Don't like to think they've spotted more carcasses," David said.

"I don't mind animals. It's the dead humans that bother me. Unfortunately, it's not as unsettling as it used to be."

Joshua had been fumbling with an old computer game on his iPod, and looked up at his grandmother, as if wondering what she was getting at.

"We should go inside and let some of the others have a turn out here...if you think it's safe," Irene said.

"Looks okay," David said, still scanning the scene for movement. "Getting so I really hate going back inside."

Irene gave him a hug as stood and they ducked back inside with Joshua.

CHAPTER 2

VISITORS

Their bunker mates Kim Marshall and Russ Freeman took the last turn outside that morning and had only been gone about five minutes when they burst back in and announced that two men were walking up the driveway, heading toward the bunker door.

The bunker group dropped their reading and craftwork and Joshua's studies and looked to David Owens. Had they been finally discovered? The only one of the group with any military type experience was Avi Sharon, the Jewish missionary who had been sent from Israel before the troubles began in earnest. David looked at him and without hesitation Avi suggested that they should lock themselves in the back room while he and David manned the security cameras and tried to defend the entranceway.

"Did you lock the bunker door?" Avi asked Russ.

"Yeah…used the deadbolt, and we put the bar across," Russ said.

With collective sinking hearts Avi ushered the rest of the group into the back rooms. Before he closed them in, he said, "We knew it might come to this. You know how to use the shotguns if a break in occurs. Be strong and use them if necessary…if these men get past us and into the building. Remember the guns will be very loud in this enclosed area. Perhaps they will not have time to report our position to the thugs, but if they do, may our God bless and protect you. If you survive, stay with each other, and flee to some abandoned location. If not…we will meet in God's time in his presence. Many martyrs have gone before, and they will welcome us."

The noble words were hollow. David's wife Vera was quivering, clinging to Joshua, and David lingered to hug them both, and then Irene before closing the door and joining Avi in front of the security cameras. Avi handed him one of the pump shotguns and they stood still, listening intently for any sounds outside the door. There was no movement in the monitors covering the sides of the building, nor on the uphill, backside of the property. It did not appear to be an organized raid.

Avi pointed to the monitor covering the front yard, where two men walked directly toward their door. They didn't have any visible weapons and didn't look like the typical thugs the Beast had deployed during the early days of the troubles when he first took power. They were casually dressed in light jackets worn over slacks, colored tee shirts and casual shoes.

"Have you actually been in combat, Avi?" David said.

"A few times...in the early days after the Christians all disappeared. When the Arabs were attacking us in Israel."

David tensed as the two men closed in on the bunker door.

"What was the first time like?" David said.

"Very scary," Avi said. "Probably like what you're feeling now."

"How'd you handle it?"

"I remembered why I was doing this. My homeland. My family and friends. I might be killed, but there was something more important than my life and my fears. So, I wasn't going to die without a fight."

"And that worked?"

"It got me through the first battle. After that combat came more naturally. Maybe automatically is a better word." Avi paused and pressed his finger to his lips and pointed at the monitor covering the doorstep. The two men stood directly outside, looking around the doorframe, and finally directly at the security camera.

The men stared at one other in silence, as if communicating on some non-verbal level. David shifted his feet slightly so his knees wouldn't lock up, waiting for their next move. If this tension lasted much longer, he knew he would begin to shake and feared he might do something rash and give away their location.

Finally, the man on the left looked directly into the camera and said, "David Owens. Avi Sharon. We want you both to know there is no longer a danger. We mean no harm to you and your group. The rebellion is over, and we have come to give you further instructions."

With that the man dropped his gaze to look at the other man, and they turned and strolled to the edge of the canopy, clasped their hands behind their backs in full view of the camera, and stared off across the valley.

David relaxed his arms and lowered the muzzle of the shotgun toward the floor. He glanced at Avi and whispered, "Could this really be it?"

"It must end sometime," Avi said.

David stared aimlessly around the bunker and then said, "But how can we know if they're alone. Or telling the truth?"

Avi peered up at the monitor again. The men hadn't moved, and the other monitors showed no movement.

"Can we test them?" David said. "I mean if they're friendly, would they mind that? And if God sent them, wouldn't they know we'd be wary...or scared?"

Avi shrugged and said, "Probably."

"Who is God supposed to send? I can't think straight."

"Angels," Avi said.

"Angels? Well, if they're angels, they could float through the door or something. Right?" David said.

"I think so. Yes."

David looked up at the monitor again. The men still hadn't moved.

"So, what do you think our options are here?" David said.

"We can pretend we are not here, but they seem to know we are. How would they even know our names, and that it's just you and I standing here. Not some of the others."

"Right."

"So that leaves opening the door…or asking them to walk through it," Avi said.

"Suppose they're really human. That through-the-door thing won't work."

"True. Which leaves opening the door."

"At which point we're committed," David said.

"But we have shotguns. We can shoot them and dispose of the bodies," Avi said. When he peeked up at the monitor, the men glanced at each other and seemed to smile.

David and Avi stared at their feet for another minute, pondering their next step. Avi looked up to see the inner door crack open and Russ Freeman look a question silently: what was going on? Avi shrugged and gestured to close the inner door again.

"I think we have to open the door," David said.

"You are probably right. The timing is good. No bombardments now. No thugs roaming around. Someone is supposed to come and get us. Had to happen sometime."

As Avi leveled his shotgun, just in case, David took a last glance at the monitor. The men still hadn't moved. So, he took a deep breath, slid back the cross bar, twisted open the deadbolt and swung open the door.

CHAPTER 3

THE NEWS

As the door swung open, the two men turned to face David and Avi, dropping their hands to their sides. The one on the left looked at the shotguns and said, "Weapons are no longer necessary. The rebellion has ended."

"Yeah, right. How do we know you're telling the truth? The thugs may have used that line to sucker people out of their hiding places," David said.

"It is immaterial whether you trust us or not. We have been sent to give you specific instructions. You have no choice but to trust us, so it will be easier for you and your friends if you follow the instructions voluntarily."

Avi and David glanced at each other, then back at the two men, still holding their weapons pointing at the two strangers.

"Time is important. We have other groups to visit as well, so I must ask you to place the weapons aside before you hurt someone," the man said.

"Like you?" David said.

"You cannot harm us," the man said as he stepped toward David, who became immobilized, unable to move his arms or hands. The man pried the shotgun out of his grip, casually bent it in half like a piece of hose, wooden parts splintering and spraying about, and then tossed it aside. Then he turned to Avi and said, "Must I repeat the demonstration with you as well?"

"Er, no. You have made your point." Avi handed the other man his weapon, who pumped it enough times to eject all the shells and tossed it into the bushes.

"Are you...angels?" Avi said.

"Yes. We do not know you but are familiar with David Owens and his family."

"How do you know us?" David said.

"We requested this visitation because we watched your sister Katherine and her family before they were removed. Before the troubles started."

"You know Kathy and the kids? And my dad?"

"And her husband Stephen."

David wandered in a circle, muttering to himself. "This is really freaky. We didn't know what happened to them. Where are they now? They just disappeared," David said. "Kim and Russ are here. They used to work for Steve."

"All in good time," the angel said. "Incidentally, it will be easier if you call me Al, and my partner Matthew. These are not our real names, but they are easier for you to pronounce and remember. Now, please call out the rest of your group. We prefer to explain this message to everyone at once."

In ten minutes, David and Avi had coaxed the rest of the group out of the bunker. As they emerged into the bright sunshine, they shielded their eyes until they adjusted to the light. Vera Owens stood by her husband David, keeping her arm around their son Joshua's shoulder. Irene Owens stood next to her son David, and beyond him their senior friends, Sylvia and Michael Cohen, completed the line. Avi led Irene's granddaughter, Michelle, to the other side, and finally Kim Marshal and Russ Freemen fanned out to complete a semi-circle around their visitors in front of the bunker door.

The angels waited until they all had settled and then the one called Al asked, "Are there any more humans in there?"

"No," David said. "Just the ten of us."

"Very well. There is much to explain, but we cannot relate everything at once. We will have time before your visit to Israel to fill you in on the details."

"Visit Israel?" Michael Cohen said. "Why would we want to visit Israel?"

"We will come to that," Al said. "Let me begin by stating something very basic: the world you have known has disappeared forever. You must adjust to that thought. You now have a King who has conquered and destroyed his enemies in the great rebellion."

"King? Who's our king? This is a democracy," Michael said.

"Don't be so impatient. Just listen to the man...or angel, Michael," Sylvia said.

"I'm not impatient. He's talking crazy."

Al responded and said, "Your Messiah is your King - the Lord Jesus Christ. He has returned to earth and is setting up his throne in Israel. He will reign from there for the next thousand years."

"When did this happen?" Avi said.

"Nine days ago," the angel called Al said.

"About the time we lost the Internet signal," David said.

"What about this trip to Israel?" Russ Freeman said.

The angels, Al and Matthew, stared at each other for a few seconds, and then Matthew took the lead to explain what would happen.

"As Al mentioned, the King will soon begin his formal reign here on earth. It is unfortunate, but not every human will be able to enjoy the blessings of his reign. Only those who have believed in him and have proven their faith by their actions. Your King knows each of you personally, and you will go before him to be judged, to determine whether you are worthy to enter his kingdom.

"And if we are not worthy?" Avi said.

"You will be banished and will proceed no further," Matthew said.

"Meaning what I think it means?"

"If you are asking whether you would be slain, the answer is 'Yes'."

The group looked around at each other, as if gauging whether they all had a similar reaction to the enormity of the angel's reply.

"That's cruel, considering the four years of hell we just went through," Kim said.

"No. It is just. Remember what I said. The world you have lived in is gone forever, and you are now subjects of the great King and God. His judgments are perfect. If you are worthy before him, you have nothing to fear," Al said.

"So, when is this trip to Israel?" David said.

"We believe within the next month or two. And there will be two trips for your group. How many of your number are Jewish?"

The group stood motionless for ten seconds, staring around or down at their feet.

"Is there a problem?" Matthew asked.

"Of course there's a problem," Avi said. "That's the first question the thugs would ask. They were looking to kill of the Jews first."

Al the angel studied the group and said, "I see. But to be a Jew now is a very good thing. Once the Lord's kingdom is established in Israel, all the nations of the earth will serve her. All Jews are invited back to repopulate the country and share in the blessings promised to their fathers centuries ago."

"But what about all those Arab states?" Michael Cohen said.

"There are no longer any Arab nations. They were all destroyed. There are no other religions, only the worship of your Lord and King. You will dwell there in perfect peace and safety, in abundance beyond your comprehension. Therefore, I ask you again, are there Jews among you?" Al said.

This time Michael and Sylvia Cohen, and Avi Sharon raised their hands. Vera Owens was slower to respond, prefacing her response with a question. "I was raised Jewish, but I married David here, and he's a Christian. And we have our son, Joshua," she said, hugging the boy close to her.

"This becomes a little more complex, but let me say that there are no longer Christians, as you have known them. All Christians were removed prior to the start of the troubles that you have survived. Henceforth, you will be known as followers of the King, either as Jews living in Israel, or as gentiles in these other nations. In your situation you will have the choice of taking your family to Israel to live or remaining here in this nation."

"So that's the only reason to know if we're Jewish?" Michael Cohen said.

"No," Matthew said. "The other reason is that you will be judged separately. You will travel to Israel in the first wave, and if deemed worthy, will be resettled in Israel as your new nation."

"Will it not be crowded?" Avi said.

"Not at first. Very few of your fellow humans have survived the troubles, and so it will be your task to resettle and repopulate the earth in the Kingdom," Matthew said.

"Also, the new nation of Israel has been greatly enlarged," Al said. "There will be much more space."

The group began to murmur among themselves, and then Avi Sharon spoke up and asked, "If we are not sure if we are even coming back here, what are we to do between now and these trips to Israel?"

Matthew said, "For the moment you should gather your belongings and travel back to your homes. You can assess the damage and join with other survivors to begin rebuilding your communities. It will be interrupted by your trips to Israel, but you can get started."

"Do you have transportation?" the angel called Al said.

"We have a large passenger van stored in the garage, and we had hidden some gasoline, but we're not sure how reliable it is," David Owens said. "It's got a roof rack, so if it runs okay, we can probably get most of the stuff loaded. We don't have a lot."

"Very well. But I must warn you that you will see much destruction. You have chosen this location well; those in more populated areas were not so fortunate," Matthew said. "You will see very disturbing scenes; dead humans lying about. Do not stop to bury them. There will similar scenes in your own communities, and you will help there."

Al added his benediction. "Remember that you have done well. You are the first generation. The pioneers. If you are worthy, only you will have known the old world, and what the world was like before your King conquered his enemies. You will keep the truth for each new generation. It is a great honor, one that you alone will share. You have survived and will live with the King for hundreds of years and experience the blessings of his reign...if you are judged worthy."

CHAPTER 4

RELIVING THE MYSTERY

The group stared at their two visitors for a minute, digesting the enormity of their explanations before slipping off into side conversations.

"Do you have any further questions at this time?" Al asked.

"Many," Avi Sharon said. "But we do not know where to begin."

"We will visit again tomorrow before you depart this location, and then in your home locations as you begin to rebuild. We must visit other groups now," Matthew said.

Before they could turn to go, all four of the Owens clan members drew them aside to ask the questions that had haunted them the past four years. "When you first talked to Avi and me, you said you asked to come here because you knew my dad and my sister Kathy and her kids," David Owens said.

"That is correct."

"And my mom and dad, Abby and Michael," Michelle said. "They were in Maryland when I came here to Pennsylvania with Gran Irene. Do you know how they are now? Or where they are?"

"No. We know nothing about them," Al said.

Irene had trouble framing the question, but finally said, "Where did my husband Daniel and my other daughter, Katherine and her family go? They just disappeared with all those other people. It was awful. We

were so confused and panicked, and then all these…troubles started. Are they safe?"

"They are very safe. They are with their Lord in Paradise, as you will eventually be if you are judged worthy," Matthew said.

"You keep bringing up this judgment thing. Is that to frighten us?" David said. "Can't you just tell us if we'll be okay?"

The angel called Al looked out at the valley below, then turned back to David and said, "The judgment, yes…know that you should *always* fear your King, because he is the one who can declare eternal life and death. If you are worthy, you will want to serve him and enjoy his blessings. However, we are unable to determine how you will fare in the judgment; only the King knows your heart. For the moment we will help you learn about this new world, but at an assigned time you will all have to stand before him."

"What are my husband Dan and my daughter and grandchildren doing now?" Irene said.

Matthew addressed this question. "This becomes more difficult to explain. Their Lord, the King, has already judged them. If you were to see them now, they would look much the same, except the children have become the adults they would have been if they had remained physically alive. They may also serve in this new kingdom. They are able to pass between paradise and this physical earth."

"So, my cousins aren't kids anymore?" Michelle said.

"No. They matured in an instant," Al said.

"Would they know us?" Michelle said.

"I believe so, but I would not expect to meet them," Al said. "They could be serving anywhere. You must begin to think in terms of a new world and a new life. You will potentially be alive, on this earth, for the next thousand years."

"My God," Irene said. "That is a long time to be retired. What could we possible do for a thousand years?"

"You will not be retired," Al said. "You will begin productive service for your King, to rebuild your communities, and to support his nation of Israel."

"What sort of service? You mean careers?" Vera Owens said.

"Some careers will no longer be necessary, and new ones will be needed. That is a subject for later, once you have undergone the judgment."

"So, we wait," Vera said.

"You have much to do now and will be fairly safe now that the rebellion is over," Matthew said.

"Fairly safe?" David said.

"Until the judgment, you must beware of those who are unworthy. They will not survive, but they can be dangerous until that time."

"Won't you protect us?" David said.

"If we are present, yes. If not, you must unite against them. They have no organization. There is no Beast for them to serve. It will strictly be their evil natures."

"We didn't need to know that," Vera said.

"It is always wise to understand your fellow humans," Al said. "We must visit other groups now. You are not alone in these remote areas. We suggest that you prepare to travel to your homes in the morning."

This reminded them of the others, and they glanced back to see that the group had dispersed, apparently back inside the bunker. When David looked back toward the two angels, they had disappeared.

CHAPTER 5

RETROSPECTION

Avi Sharon stood alone in the doorway as the Owens clan walked back in. They passed by wordlessly, managing only a shrug to answer his unspoken question. Michelle Sandahl remained outside and stood next to him.

"What did you talk about?" Avi said.

"They knew...know...my aunt Kathy and her kids, and my granddad... Irene's husband. And Kathy's husband Steve. Kim and Russ used to work for Steve. I think they're in heaven or something."

"Your grandmother looks pretty upset."

"Well, yeah. I mean, it was a big shock when they all just disappeared like that before all this started. We had no idea. My parents thought they were in some cult or something and were hiding. Nothing made sense."

"Your parents are what...in this family?" Avi said.

"My mom is Irene's daughter...uncle David's sister."

"Do you have siblings?"

"Two brothers."

"You mean they were not taken? Do you have contact with them? Where are they?"

"I have no idea. You weren't here when we snuck up here to hide out. It wasn't long after this Beast guy took over with the 666 mark on the hand, and his thugs started rounding up people. And then those voices from the skies started and the earthquakes and things falling out of the sky. Like God and this guy were getting it on. Things were really weird."

"Where were you then?"

"Back home in Maryland. Near DC."

"How did you get up here?" Avi said.

Michelle didn't answer right away, staring instead across the valley.

"Is that a bad question?" Avi said.

"What? No, it's just painful. My dad wanted us all to get this mark on the hand. My brothers and my mom went along with him. I think Dad thought this Beast was a good guy who was going to straighten everything out...like all that fighting over where you come from in Israel."

"But you did not agree?"

"I didn't know anything about politics and war much, but somehow it didn't seem right. And he was pressuring me, so I made up an excuse that I wanted to check in on Gran and drove up to Philly. And once I got there, they had some really bad stuff happen in DC, so Mom suggested I don't come back right away."

Avi studied Michelle's face as she paused again, watching her eyes well up while she stared out at the valley again. He put his arm around her shoulder and held her silently for a minute.

"You never heard from them again?" he said.

"No. I left cell phone messages, but no one called back. Uncle David and Aunt Vera and Joshua had come down from Boston and started talking about this bunker thing. And he told me not to call anymore because they can trace the calls."

"They?"

"These thugs...the ones the Beast guy was using. He didn't trust anybody."

"David had been planning this bunker hideout?"

"I think so. Over a couple years." Michelle said.

"Why? How did he know to do this?"

Michelle flopped her arms open and said, "I asked him that and he didn't really know for sure. Once he heard the voices and became a believer, he started to read about what was supposed to happen before this Messiah returned. Said it seemed like we didn't want to be anywhere around other people, and Gran knew the folks who own this place. They were going out west to Montana or someplace to get away, and it would be vacant. And we didn't want to move that far away."

"Are you still hoping to find your family?" Avi said.

"Of course..."

"But not too hopeful?"

"No. I guess I'm not. Not with all the bombings or whatever God or whoever's been doing for the last four years. I guess it'd be a wonder if anyone is still alive down there."

"Have you accepted the fact that you might not find them?"

"Yeah, well, I guess I have. I mean, I was really torn up for the first six months here. Weeping half the time. Scared out of my wits. Thank God for Gran and for Dave and Vera. They're concerned about them, too. After all, it's their family as well."

"It sounds like you are prepared for whatever happens," Avi said.

"I'm emotionally numb by now. Like how much of this disaster scene can you take without going crazy or something?"

Avi continued to hold her shoulder, and when she lapsed into silence, they both just stared at the remains of the hill across the valley.

"You know, when we first got here, that hill was twice as high," Michelle said. "Things were shaking so hard, I thought this place would fall down on top of us. But we made it. Must be stronger than it looks," she said, looking around behind them at the ugly gray cinderblock front wall.

"God protected you," Avi said.

She looked up at him. "Would he do that?"

"I think so. He knew where you were even if the thugs could not find you. Think about it. How did those two angels know where to find us today?"

She stared up at his face for a few seconds, and Avi nodded his head slightly and dropped his arm to his side and stared ahead once more. Michelle followed his gaze, but stood in place, shoulders still touching.

"Do you have family back in Israel?" she said.

"My parents. A sister. Some cousins. I am not sure they are alive now. One of the reasons I was chosen was because I had no close family."

"I never did catch that whole story. Why are you here?" Michelle said.

Avi crossed his arms, exhaled, and paused for a minute before answering. "I cannot say I really understand all that happened...but the voices in the sky came to Israel first and warned us that the Messiah was coming back soon. So, a lot of the Jewish leaders became believers, and then one day I was summoned to my local synagogue and the rabbi told me that I had been chosen to be one of twelve thousand witnesses from my tribe."

"Tribe?"

"The tribes of Israel. Families forgot what tribes they belonged to a long time ago. And they intermarried, so no one knew what tribe he belonged to. But evidently God did, because I found out that I am from the tribe of Benjamin."

"So why did they pick you?"

"I guess God told them. I never understood. They said someone gave them a list of names, and mine was on it. Maybe it was one of these angels. Angels do things like that. And I was a believer, and I was single. You had to be single."

Michelle had been watching Avi's face as he labored through this explanation, and as he looked down, he stopped short.

"What?"

"Why were you single? You seem like a good guy. I would have thought that you would have wanted a wife and children and all that. The Jews I knew back home were really into family stuff."

Avi chuckled to himself at the thought. "I suppose you are correct. Many of my friends were married and were starting families. But...I was in the army, and the wars with the Arabs were on again, and I never really found the right woman. A lot of reasons, I guess. But it did prepare me for this assignment."

Michelle smiled at him and put her arm around him this time. "Well. Just think. You got to travel to the States. You got to tell people about being a believer. And you brought the Cohen's here. They would have been toast if the thugs found them. You saved their lives."

"Toast?"

"Er.... our way of saying they would have been killed."

"Interesting. Then, yes. I suppose so."

"But you still miss the family stuff, right?"

"Yes."

Michelle watched his face for a few seconds and then crossed her arms and stared ahead with Avi. "So how did you know about this place?"

"Well, I was in your grandmother's neighborhood, and I met the Cohens at a secret meeting. Older Jews are usually stubborn about new things, but it seemed like God had helped them to understand that the Messiah was coming soon, and they cornered me because I had come from Israel, and I knew what was going on there. You have seen how curious Mr. Cohen is."

"He's not bashful," Michelle said.

"Not at all. And he asked whether it was safe in their neighborhood, and I said probably not, so he said, "Where can we get away?" I didn't know, but the leader overheard us and had some prior arrangements with your uncle David. He had directions and said you could take three or four more people. Even had a special way to approach the bunker here, and three passwords. So here we are. You remember the day?"

"Yes. Uncle David had gotten some signal on a blog, so he knew someone was coming. He was on the lookout for a couple of days. Like spy stuff or something."

Avi looked down again and said, "Your uncle saved your lives. It could have been a lot worse. The location, the security cameras, the food rations..."

"I know. I'm just weary of it all. I hope these angels are right and it's all over."

Avi looked thoughtful, and then said, "When we get back to your grandmother's home area, if you would like, I will travel with you to try to find your family. I am not familiar with driving here in the United States, but I can keep you company."

Michelle stared at him for a few seconds. "Thanks. I'd like that."

CHAPTER 6

THE BUNKER

The bunker was meant to look abandoned. The grey steel doorway opened into a cinderblock workspace that formed the foundation for a frame second story that could be a home. The foundation was wedged into the side of a sloping, rocky hillside, with only the front wall fully exposed to the outside world. Two steel-framed, industrial-looking windows faced out across the valley, protected by security grating, and backed by black plywood to prevent light from escaping, and for weatherproofing once vandals broke the glass.

The building sat in the middle of a five-acre junkyard, several miles from the nearest town. It was originally a large open shop where John Foster, the owner and Owens family friend, had his greasy office desk in one corner, and where he could dismantle auto parts out of the weather on hot or cold days. When the troubles began, and he decided to move west to Montana to be with his daughter for the duration. David Owens and Russ Freeman framed out the lower level into six makeshift bedrooms and a common area. To reduce the heat signature from prying satellites or drones, they over insulated the interior, upstairs and down, so it could be warmed with body heat alone. That only ten people eventually moved in was a blessing; space was tight as it was.

Early in the troubles the thugs cut the chain on the stockade fence and invaded the property, looking for believers who might be hiding out.

But they had tossed food outside so that bears and rodents roamed the property, and the bombardments and earthquakes disturbed colonies of rattlesnakes looking for prey. After several of the thugs were bitten, they avoided the area and the group remained invisible to other humans until the two angels arrived.

It was a relief to leave the steel door open, admitting fresh air in more than just the usual brief burst through a cracked door. As David Owens and his family stepped back inside, the rest of the group stood in the middle of the common area, staring around at the forlorn scene.

"It's sour. I didn't notice how much it smells," Kim Marshal said.

"Funny how you get used to it," Russ Freeman agreed.

Sylvia Cohen added, "I haven't been comfortable in years. And to think I lived at Bloomingdale's in the old days. And we've been wearing these jump suit things or whatever you call them for four years."

"What are you talking about? You spent too much money then. This is God's way of getting even," Michael Cohen said. "You should be thankful the thugs didn't get us and we're alive."

"I am, Michael. Don't be grouchy. I'm just saying."

"Is he new? Have we seen him before?" Kim said, pointing at a mouse nosing around the open doorway of their makeshift bathroom and shower area.

"I used to be afraid of them. Now we're fellow survivors," Sylvia said.

"Joshua's only pets for four years," Russ said, putting a hand on the boy's shoulder.

Still, no one moved, soaking in the memories of four years of subsistence living.

Their home.

They scanned their common room with its cast-off tables, chairs, couches and other stuffed chairs, the industrial sink with its water-logged plywood drain board, electric hotplates, stockpiled propane tanks for the gas plates during the frequent power outages, the old refrigerator and the hand-cranked power generators for emergency use.

They saw the back stairwell that led upstairs to several extra rooms: a bedroom, a tub where they could bathe once they heated some spring-fed water, a room with their hand-cranked washing machine with its drain hose running into the bathtub drain and into the septic tank, and a larger room with the treadmills and bicycle powered generator for exercise, and where they could string clothes out to dry. It wasn't much, but they survived if what the angels said was true.

David and Vera glanced at each other, and he slipped his arm around her shoulder. "How about a picnic? Outside," Vera said.

"It's still chilly outside," Irene said.

"Who cares?" Michael Cohen. "I don't care if I have to eat wrapped up in blankets. I don't want to spend my last day cooped up in here."

"Is this really our last day?" Kim Marshal said.

"Yea. It's unreal," Vera said. "This morning...confused and then these guys show up out of nowhere and say, 'all done'. You can go home now."

"So where do we go?" Kim said.

Russ shrugged and said, "Back home...if anything is left. Three years of bombardments with those beach ball size hailstones, firestorms, drought...could be pretty messy. What if we're just lucky up here?"

"We'll find out soon enough," Irene Owens said.

David Owens poked Russ Freeman and said, "Give me a hand and we'll see if we can get the van to run."

"What is happening inside?" Avi Sharon asked David Owens as they stepped back outside.

"Not much. We were having a moment," Russ Freeman said. "We're going to see if we can get the van running."

Avi swapped glances with Michelle for a few seconds, and she nodded toward the two men as they walked off. Avi took the hint and said, "Let me help you."

The van was stashed in a storage shed fifty feet from the bunker. As close as it was, they seldom walked in the open, fearful of meandering thugs, drones and satellite surveillance. While there was no certainty of being watched from the skies, once the Beast took access to the military cameras, David felt it was best not to risk unnecessary exposure.

In his heart David was only half convinced that the immediate danger had passed and was wary of any movement around them as they walked. It was still too cold for the rattlesnakes to be a danger, but startling a rabbit or dove could still paralyze him for a few seconds. However, as he ambled he relaxed, and it was invigorating to walk in the open space.

The shed was a dilapidated wooden building with a shingled roof, only slightly larger than the van it held. It hadn't seen a coat of paint in twenty years, an advantage if you wanted to be anonymous. To look uninteresting, the twin door panels were not chained - only propped closed by two small stakes jammed into the ground. Since they last visited, durable weeds had sprung up, and the three of them had to yank hard to pull the doors open.

A large tarpaulin covered the van, and David and Russ grabbed the front edge and dragged it over the roof and out of the way into the junkyard. The van had been backed in, easier to drive out in case of a quick getaway, and a scan revealed that the tires were all low on air, and the left rear was almost flat. They had left a tire pump just inside the door, and while Russ began the arduous pumping task, David took out his small flashlight and checked around the wheelbase for snakes, finding only one rattlesnake that was torpid from the cold weather. He used an old pair of fireplace tongs left for the occasion, lifted the serpent and carried him outside and tossed him into bushes near the edge of the property.

"I will never get used to those things," Avi said.

"Me either, and here's hoping we don't have to. Maybe he'll get himself a stray thug for old times' sake," David said.

In another ten minutes of pumping, they had managed to inflate the tires enough to nudge the van onto the hard dirt in front of the shed. The key was in the glove box, and David slipped inside and said, "Here goes."

Nothing. The ignition made a slight clicking sound but did not activate the starter.

"Does it have gas?" Russ said.

There was enough current to run the gauge, and David said, "Yeah. We're okay there, but the battery's dead."

"Open the bonnet," Avi said. "Let me check the connections."

"Bonnet?" Russ said.

"The hood?"

"Better. We'll have you speaking American yet."

David searched around but there was no release inside, and hopped out again to check above the grillwork in front until he found the lever and was able to pop the catch and prop up the small hood. As they peered in, Avi pointed down on the lower suspension where another rattlesnake had taken refuge.

They waited until David extracted this next serpent and checked for any additional strays, until finally Avi felt free to start checking connections, which was further complicated because they could not find the battery. After tracing the wire from the starter, they concluded it was inside the vehicle and finally found it under the passenger seat.

"Everything seems tight, so it must be the battery," Avi said. "It has liquid in the cells, so we can hope it just discharged."

"Do we have a charger?" Russ said.

"Forgot about that one," David said. "Tried to plan for everything, but sometimes you miss. Mr. Foster may have one around here somewhere… if the power stays on."

"Is this a manual transmission?" Avi said.

"Yes," David said.

"We can try the easy way first. The yard goes downhill. We could push you down and you engage the clutch."

"Never did that," David said.

"Me either," Russ said.

"Then you two push me," Avi said.

David and Russ looked at one another for a few seconds. "What can go wrong?" David said.

"If it does not start, we locate your battery charger and take the battery out and bring it up here," Avi said.

David caught Russ's glance again, then said, "Not that much worse. Hop in."

With Avi manning the wheel, and the ignition on, Avi cranked down the window and said, "Begin to push."

Russ looked over at David and said, "Ready?"

David flicked his eyebrows. "I guess. Well, here goes," he said, and after a few rocking movements, they got the van started down the hill. It took on a life of its own, and after each thirty-foot run, Avi popped the clutch. The first three times it jerked and failed to start, but on the fourth attempt it shuddered to life with a small cloud of black smoke as it sneezed out unused fuel. Avi revved up the engine to keep it running, and then let it sit and idle.

When David and Russ walked up, Avi said, "God bless American vans. We let it idle to charge the battery. Want a ride back?"

"Sounds good, but only after David does his snake check thing inside the van," Russ said.

"You tell me this now?" Avi said.

David spread his hands out in humility. "I don't think they can get up inside. But just in case…"

In twenty minutes, they checked the temperature gauge to make sure the engine wasn't overheating, backed the van up the hill and parked it in front of the garage, still pointing down the hill.

Avi checked his watch and said, "Thirty minutes. Shall we give it the test?"

Once David and Russ nodded in agreement, Avi switched off the engine.

They stood in silence for a minute, awaiting the moment of truth. Finally, Avi leaned forward, twisted the key, and the engine sprang to life amid applause from the group."

"Perfect," Avi said.

CHAPTER 7

THE PICNIC

While the men revived the van, Joshua Owens and his cousin Michelle lugged the folding chairs, the smooth wooden doors and sawhorses outside, setting up two tables for their ceremonial picnic. Their threadbare tablecloths had been cut into cleaning cloths long ago, so they flung clean sheets over the tops. Flowers, iced tea, a grill for hamburgers and hot dogs and barbeque chicken or steak would have been ideal, but everyone knew that their lentil stew mix, food bars and powdered juice mix would have to suffice. It was enough to be outdoors, in the sun, in the chill air of late March.

Midway through their preparations, they heard the faint sound of a vehicle approaching on the road outside their stockade fence, and everyone ducked behind the nearest large object to shield themselves from view of the road. Kim Marshal instinctively reached inside for the shotgun over the doorway, then stepped outside and closed the door, maintaining the abandoned look.

The volume grew as the vehicle neared the front entrance gate, and everyone froze with four years' accumulated wariness. As it reached the entrance it passed by without stopping, and from their fleeting view, they could see it was a van not unlike their own, perhaps the first of many reclusive colonists to venture out and head toward wherever they called home.

Sensing this wariness could be nerve wracking, Irene Owens suggested they shift the tables out of view of the road entrance, and completed the strategy just as the three men drove the van up and nosed it down toward the entrance gate.

"It lives!" Vera said, gesturing at the van.

"Looks great," David said, surveying the picnic tables.

"Invitation only?" Russ said, pointing at Kim's shotgun.

Kim looked embarrassed, and as she propped it against the front wall, she said, "Sorry. Forgot to put it back after the van passed."

"What van?" Avi Sharon said.

"Folks like us, I think. Stuff on the roof. Maybe heading home. Maybe the angels talked to them yesterday," Vera said.

"So it begins," Avi said.

"That sounds ominous," Irene said.

"Maybe, but for now we celebrate and eat."

As a token of honor, David Owens was asked to sit at one end of the table and Avi at the other: the creator of the bunker, and the refugee from Israel. When all were settled in place, David stood and said, "For a man who wasn't particularly religious before these troubles began, I think it's safe to say I've come a long way."

Vera sat next to him and reached out to squeeze his hand.

"Earthquakes and firestorms and bombardments with humongous hail stones that could have squashed us like bugs…and yet we're all still here."

"Amen," Michael Cohen said, and Sylvia stroked his back.

"So how about I say the blessing, on this our final day here," David said.

As they all bowed their heads, David closed his eyes and tilted his head toward the heavens. "God. Father. I hardly know what to say to you. We hope this whole thing is over and done with at last, and yet we're nervous about going home, and whatever we're going to find here. And about this judgment thing your angels are talking about."

He opened his eyes for a few seconds and stared down across the valley. When he closed them again, he added, "None of us thought much about you before all this started, and so we thank you for thinking about us, and for helping us to understand who you are and who Jesus is. A great king these angels said. A monarchy. Strange. Sounds like we really have a lot to learn...if we make it through this judgment. I ask that we all will, and that you'll help us cope with what's going to happen." And after a pause, he added, "Thank you for this food, and that the old van runs, and I guess that's all. Amen."

"Amen," the group echoed and looked up at David.

"Well, I really wish I could ask who wants white meat and who wants the drumstick, but the old stew never looked better than it does in sunlight."

They began to eat slowly, pausing often to tilt their heads back and savor the sunlight and the chilly breezes that drew no complaints.

"Since I am not from America, what have you missed...being up here?" Avi said.

They looked around at each other as if to say, 'what haven't we missed?' and then began to toss out personal favorites.

"Sports," David said. "Playing them. Sports on TV."

"My family," Michelle added.

Irene looked at her granddaughter, nodding in agreement.

"Golf with friends," Michael Cohen said. "Especially Irene's husband, Dan."

It was a memory that cracked the surface, and Irene's eyes welled up as she said, "Yes. And my daughter Katherine and her children."

"And the boss. Her husband Steve," Kim added, stroking Russ Freeman's back.

As if sensing too many painful memories, Sylvia Cohen said, "How about a nice dinner at a good restaurant. After shopping at the mall."

"I knew you'd work that in," Michael Cohen said. "You can keep the mall, but I could really go for the perfect steak about now."

"Me, too," Vera said. "But only after a very long and hot bath, and some new clothes."

"*Avant garde* jump suits not good enough anymore?" David said, breaking into a broad smile.

"More like Chinese peasant," Kim said. "And how about all of us in a hot tub?"

Irene raised her eyebrows and said, "Before this all started, I'd have been shocked at the suggestion. Now…it sounds pretty good."

To a person they sensed the moment. Avi, the outsider, threw out the sentiments for the group when he said, "I cannot thank Irene and David and all you people for taking in Michael and Sylvia and myself three years ago now. And no matter what, we will always have the memory of this time together. I am thinking, if we suddenly start to live long lives like these angels say, and like the scriptures say, we will be the first generation. 'Pioneers', I think you would say." He paused for a few seconds and then said, "If we make it through this judgment, no other generation will have seen what we have seen."

Avi looked down at the tabletop as he added his thoughts, and the group followed his lead. They struggled to consider the enormity of his statement, but the thought was too heavy to carry the moment and they could only shrug.

"Perhaps. With time," Michael Cohen said.

"What?" said Sylvia.

"We'll understand what Avi means."

In the silence, Kim said, "What about you, Joshua? What have you missed?"

He fiddled with the edge of his plate, and without looking up he murmured, "A friend."

Before anyone could offer a platitude that they were *all* his friends, Vera Owens stroked his neck, pulling him toward her so she could kiss his hair. "I'm so sorry, bud. Maybe there will be some kids at your grandmother's place. And we can get you a better pet than the local mice."

"I know, Mom. It's not your fault. But I miss having friend just the same."

"You will be one of the first-generation children, Joshua," Avi Sharon said. "In years to come, you can bore little children with stories of your pet mouse and the bombardments. Just think, they will all be saying, 'yeah, yeah, we know all that'."

"But they won't know, will they?" Joshua said.

"No. They will not. But *we* will know. And you will know all of us."

They dawdled at their food, drawing out the afternoon, no one eager to go back into the bunker, even if they could leave the door open for once. As they ate in silence, Sylvia and Michael Cohen became more animated, nattering at one another quietly, and finally Michael got up and walked inside the bunker.

"Is he alright?" Irene said.

"He's fine. You'll see," Sylvia said. "And by the way, Avi, we haven't heard what you missed from Israel."

They turned to face him, and he stared at the tabletop for a few seconds. "Not any of these material things you mentioned. They are all nice. I am not being critical. We just did not have them. I cannot even say I miss living in peace in Israel because we had no peace. Just surviving was good enough. If it was not the crazy Arabs, it was the Beast and his unpleasant policies, and then his thugs. You know, I have never known a land without threats and without warfare. Israel is a beautiful country, and I think what I miss most, is actually something I have never seen: my nation in peace, enjoying our God. Does that sound strange to you?"

David spoke and said, "A little, maybe, Avi, but then maybe we were all spoiled."

"I more than most," Irene Owens said. "But this time has been a great equalizer. And, believe me, I am very grateful to have had the chance to share it with you all."

"Perfect timing," Michael Cohen said, walking up to the table with three bottles of wine. "We've been hoarding these for a special occasion, and this is certainly an occasion."

He set the bottles on the table with a thump and carefully opened all three with a corkscrew he had handy. As each opened, he passed the bottle amid smiles from the whole group. They each dumped the remains of their powdered fruit drinks on the ground and refilled their mugs with a generous portion of the Cabernet Sauvignon, now aged six years.

Once everyone filled their cups, with a small portion for Joshua, Michael remained standing. When they finished, Michael said," I add my sentiments to Avi Sharon's. Thank you, from the bottom of my heart, for rescuing my beloved Sylvia and me...and for your friendship."

"A toast," David said.

"To what?" Kim said.

"L'chaim," Avi said.

"To life," Michael said.

CHAPTER 8

PACKING UP

David Owens awoke at two in the morning, disoriented, wondering if he had been dreaming of angels and rescue and the time to leave their sanctuary and drive back home. And if there was a home anymore. Vera breathed softly as she lay next to him, and he considered waking her to ask if she remembered the same things. But in the end, he decided it would be best to let her sleep. If it were a dream, he'd find out soon enough.

He lay awake for half an hour, unable to recapture sleep, and finally got up and slipped outside into the chill night air for a view of the night sky, undiluted by background light. When they had first arrived, the mountain opposite held a cell tower, with its blinking white nightlight, but that had been knocked down several years ago, leaving not a single distraction. As he stepped out from under the canopy, the one constellation he could normally see, Orion, had slid below the horizon, but the Milky Way was clearly visible in the clear, moonless sky, dredging up memories of family times at their cottages is Maine, now likely gone forever. Then again, it could be just as dark back home if all the lights were out.

Back home.

They had paid a dear price for such nostalgia. The years of anxiety, bordering on terror, with the aerial bombardments, the roving bands of thugs, the deprivations of bunker life. And perhaps the loss of his sister

Abby and her family...Michelle's family; they were possibly the only family she had now.

And Joshua.

Such a simple thing he wanted: a friend. David had plenty while growing up, and couldn't imagine life without them. Would he ever see *them* again?

The thought of the uncertain day to follow finally outweighed the need for nostalgia and he slipped back inside and slid under the covers next to Vera. After a few minutes he drifted off into a sound sleep until awakened by the movement in the common room outside their door.

He had grown accustomed to the near pitch-black interior. With the lights out, even in daylight they could only see the security monitor. From the crack under the door, he could see clear white light, not the dull glow of battery-powered lamps used during their current power outage. He checked his glowing watch face: almost seven o'clock.

As Vera shifted position to flip onto her left side, away from him, David slipped out of the room and saw that the bunker door was cracked open. He automatically checked the monitor to see two men standing under the canopy, backs to the door. He recognized Avi Sharon and Russ Freeman and stepped outside to join them.

"Morning," David said, scanning the area. A milky layer of clouds had drifted in to shroud the dawn twilight. "Any movement?"

"Nothing so far," Russ said. "And it looks like the van tires are holding air, so we're wondering the best way to pack. It's got that big roof rack. If it doesn't rain, we may not even have to wrap stuff in a tarp."

"How long will this drive take?" Avi said.

David shrugged. "A normal day, with light traffic, I'd say under three hours. But who knows what the roads are like. We've got some good maps, but with all the destruction from earthquakes and missiles or whatever those things were, we might be backtracking. Probably best to double or triple that time."

"We have enough gas?" Russ said.

"Should have. I don't know if goes bad after four years, but we have six of those military jerry cans," David said. "We can filter it through some cloth."

They watched silently, staring out across the low valley, perhaps for the last morning ever, each harboring their secret concerns. They stood for several minutes until distracted by the bunker door drifting open and soft footsteps behind them. They turned as one to see Michelle and Kim step out to join them.

"How's it look?" Michelle said, stepping up next to her uncle David, who put an arm around her shoulder and said, "Man, you are lovely as ever...and the day doesn't look to bad either."

Avi watched the scene with obvious interest as Michelle smiled and gave David a playful jab in the ribs before circling his waist to hug him back. David was over six feet tall, and she was only slightly shorter than him. She looked up at him and puffed out a blast of air to blow the long blond hair from her face. "Thanks. Good to know you still got it."

"You both do," Russ said, encircling Kim's shoulder as well.

Kim put her arm around Russ and said, "Time is important. Michelle and I called ahead to schedule our spa and makeover day tomorrow, so we need to get home early."

That word again. Home.

"Anyone else up?" Avi Sharon said.

"I thought I heard the Cohen's," Kim said. "Maybe Irene."

As they spoke the words, Vera stepped out to join them. She looked and the group and said, "We stay another day, we're going to need a bigger porch."

There wasn't much to pack. They had pared down to subsistence living and could fit their entire worldly possessions into suitcases and duffle bags. By ten o'clock the roof rack was loaded and strapped down, including the extra jerry cans of gasoline. They stuffed their monotonous food supply in the back along with several cans of water.

While the others wandered in and out, checking and double-checking the inside of the bunker for left items, Irene Owens drifted down the hill toward the entrance gate, then turned to stare back up at their sanctuary. David trailed her down and stood alongside, staring at the anonymous cinder block foundation, tucked into the hillside, the bare trees surrounding it like a shabby mantle. The wooden superstructure, where they would sneak up for more sunlight and hang their clothes to dry, had miraculously survived damage from the fire or hail bombardments.

"Will you miss it?" David said.

"Not the place, really. I'll miss the…camaraderie. Surviving with you and Vera and Joshua and the others. Your father used to talk about his combat experiences in the Granada War, and I'd smile and pretend I understood. Now I know."

"Yeah. I remember those stories. Funny…"

They suddenly heard the crunch of gravel behind them, and after years of wariness, the adrenaline rush jolted their systems, and they swung around to see the two angels walking up the driveway toward them.

"Oh my God. Don't do that," Irene said.

"We try to be sensitive. Sometimes we just materialize and then humans faint dead away," the one they remembered as Al said.

"It appears you are almost ready to depart," the angel called Matthew said.

"Just about," David said. "We don't have much that we can leave behind."

"Good. We should meet with your group before you begin to travel. There are things you need to know."

Remembering their remarkable visit yesterday, the group stopped all activity to watch Irene and David and the two angels as they approached the front of the bunker. Joshua drifted next to his mom and Vera put an arm out to draw him close. Michael Cohen did the same with Sylvia, and Russ hugged Kim as the visitors drew near. Avi had been checking the oil on the van engine, and he wiped his hand on a rag and joined the others. To a person, they knew the time had come.

They clustered around the angels, anxious for advice on the next step of their life's journey in this strange new era. The angel called Al spoke first and said, "It would appear you are ready to begin your journey, and the journey will take much longer than you anticipate because of the road conditions...plus other considerations. But you must begin sometime, and so we would suggest you do so as soon as possible."

"What other considerations?" Avi said.

The angel named Matthew glanced at Joshua, paused a few seconds, and then said, "We hesitate to mention this in front of the boy, but perhaps it is best that he be prepared."

Joshua looked up at his mother, then at the angel.

Matthew continued and said, "As we spoke yesterday, you have been sheltered in this remote area, but you will encounter populated areas on your journey home where you will see much destruction."

"Including dead humans who have not yet been collected and buried," Al added. "These images will be disturbing, but we ask you to keep moving until you reach your home...wherever you choose to go on this first stage."

Irene looked around at the group, and said, "I would assume my home as a first step. Is that agreeable to everyone?"

The group nodded and murmured their assent, and Al added, "You will find similar destruction and death in your own neighborhood. So, you should be prepared for that. When you arrive and settle in, you will join with other survivors to begin the cleansing process."

"What about this judgment thing?" David said.

"That will happen in the King's own time," Matthew said. "Until then, you must begin to reclaim your neighborhood. It will take some time until you fully comprehend this, but you now live under a monarchy, and you must trust in your great King and work accordingly."

"A king..." Michael Cohen muttered.

"Shush, Michael," Sylvia chided him. "Listen to the man. Or angel."

"We have known the Son as Lord for millennia. It is a very good thing. Trust us," Al said.

It was obvious to all that they had no other choice, so they just stared.

"Will you go with us?" Avi said.

"No. We have other groups to visit. You will meet other groups traveling home as well. You should band together when you find them."

"Why?" Avi said.

Matthew answered and said, "The Beast is gone, but there are still evil people left, and will be until the judgment. There will be other angels about, and we will do what we can to protect you."

The group stood silent, staring alternately at the angels, each other and the cluttered junkyard that was their sanctuary. Finally, David spoke up and said, "Should we just start then?"

"Yes. That would be best," Al said.

David looked at the group, raised his eyebrows and said, "Well. Let's do it."

"May God go with you," Matthew said, and the two angels evaporated from sight.

CHAPTER 9

HOMEWARD

As they settled on seating arrangements, Avi Sharon started the van and let the engine idle for ten minutes to check for oil and water leaks. Having the most experience with a manual transmission, Avi agreed to drive while David Owens would ride in the front passenger seat with the maps. He confided to David, "We drive on much damaged roads in Israel, but I do not own an American driver's license."

"I doubt anyone cares. Just go slow. These large vans tip over easy," David said as they eyed the load for their packed vehicle.

"Slow it is," Avi said.

Avi checked the engine temperature gauge to see that they were not overheating, and then peered underneath the van for leaks. Seeing nothing unusual, he gave the signal to David that they could board and begin their trek.

"Everyone ready?" David shouted to the group.

Following a chorus of assenting murmurs, he said, "Did we lock the bunker?"

"Done," Russ said.

"Good. We'll probably never have to come back, but we should leave it shut for Mr. Foster and his family."

"And keep the snakes out," Kim reminded him.

"Won't miss them," David said. "Tell you what, though. Let me pray for a safe trip...and to get ready for whatever."

Wordlessly, they gathered in a circle and held hands while David prayed. "God and Father…and now our King…thank you for protecting us here and give us a safe trip back to our homes. And we ask that our homes might be there when we get back."

"And our families," Michelle added.

"Yes," Vera whispered, squeezing David's hand.

"Father," David said, "you know us all. You saved our lives so far, and we ask you to keep us safe today. Amen."

"Amen," the chorus echoed, and with a lingering look back and their sanctuary, they loaded into the van and closed the doors.

Avi slipped the van into gear and drifted down the hill to the entrance gate with the crunch of gravel under the tires, a comforting sound not heard for years. At the road, they checked both ways, saw no traffic, and turned left to begin to retrace their journey home. All heads turned for a last glance at their sanctuary, and then it was gone.

The initial stretch followed a stream east for ten miles where they would reach a larger road that could take them south. The asphalt surface was cracked and crumbled in after years of earthquakes and missiles and general neglect. Trees had been snapped in half by flying objects, branches and whole treetops broken off, littering the ground. Vegetation had been burned or withered by drought. A few hardy daffodils had emerged from hibernation in gardens of abandoned houses where they could be spotted above the brown, wilted grass that had been left uncut for years. Most houses were damaged and uninhabitable, and the few that were left relatively intact showed no signs of life. A ghost countryside.

Avi kept a slow, steady pace to accommodate the cracked road surface, steering around the assortment and rubble and tree parts that littered the road. Then just before they reached the larger road to take them south, they saw their first bodies lying in a lawn near the road. They gave each other knowing glances, but no one said anything. Without their slow pace and the time to scan the terrain, they could have been mistaken for two piles of rubbish. From glimpses of parched skin that were once live hands, they could tell it was probably two adults, and had apparently lain there so long their bodies had turned hard and leathery like a roadkill deer no one bothered to clean off the highway. For this one at least, Vera was thankful that Josh had been looking the other way.

David checked his watch at the intersection with the main road: over half an hour to go ten miles, almost three times the expected pace. There was no traffic on the larger road, and David motioned Avi to turn south and head toward the Allentown area. There were more abandoned vehicles littering the northbound side of the road, perhaps hoping for an escape route. Some died on the road so Avi had to maneuver around them like a slalom course. Bodies appeared more frequently, some in cars, others strewn along the roadway or in the yards of houses like refuse blown off a trash truck. They tried to look away at first, but soon found themselves desensitized to the sight.

"My family could have ended up like that," Michelle murmured.

Irene sat next to her and patted her leg. "Let's hope for the best."

The scenes of destruction intensified as they neared the more populous Allentown area: buildings squashed, trees pounded into submission by falling objects, more bodies strewn about. A musty, noxious smell of destruction and decay began to permeate the interior of their van, even with the windows closed.

"Does this have air conditioning?" Michael Cohen said.

"We'll try," David said, "but it probably lost its coolant long ago." He fiddled with the controls and held his hand over the air vent to detect any change in temperature. After about five minutes, he said, "Nothing. It's not working."

"At least you tried," Michael said. "Maybe you can crack the windows open in the back. It will still stink, but at least the air will be moving."

Occasionally they would see live people in front of homes, looking at the sky and staring around much as they had done just yesterday. Avi would beep the horn, and they would wave, but they kept moving.

As they neared the east-west Interstate 78 they encountered the first vehicle heading in their direction, but still none in the opposite direction. Avi pulled up a stop behind it and they waited while what appeared to be two local policemen or fire auxiliaries spoke with the driver in front. Finally, the car ahead pulled away and turned down a side road off to their right.

Avi pulled up and stopped next to the two men. As he rolled the window down, one of them asked, "Where are you headed?" Since Avi was not familiar with the geography, David waved him around to the passenger side of the van.

"We're headed south, to the Philadelphia area."

The men wore badges that appeared to be local police force, and the taller of the two said, "What route were you planning on?"

"We'd hoped to take I-78 west and then take the Turnpike extension south."

"That probably won't work. We've heard reports that a lot of the Turnpike overpass bridges collapsed onto the highway, and they haven't been cleared yet."

"So, what can we do? Any suggestions?"

They glanced at one other, and then he said, "The information is kind of sketchy so far. Our radio is just starting to come back, and we've got a few volunteers scouting the area to open routes. The big problem is bridge collapses. That bridge ahead of you over Route 22 is gone, so you'll have to take the side road down there and pick it up at the next exit. The bridge over the river is still holding. Then I'd try Route 309 south. Though I have to warn you...you been up here before?"

"Yes?" David said.

"Darndest thing. You know that big hill heading south past Emmaus?"

"Yes."

"It's pretty near gone. The whole mountain was flattened in one of those earthquakes, and the roadbed is pretty bad. But if you go slow, you can probably make it through."

"Have others come this way?" Avi asked.

"Very few people. Two today. One yesterday. I don't know where everyone is. But nobody's come back this way, and we haven't heard of disaster stories. Beside this one," he added, gesturing at the scene around them where a series of small strip malls, fast food places and gasoline stations lined the roads as you near a major highway.

"I don't see any bodies here," Avi said.

"We've been burying them for the past five days. Tough to look at. Well, good luck, or Lord bless, or whatever," the man said, slapping the side of the van. He looked behind them and David checked his mirror to see another vehicle pulling up behind.

"Thanks guys," David said, and rolled up his window. He pointed ahead for Avi and then directed him to the right, following the route on the topographical road map he held in his lap. The rest of the group had been silent, straining to hear the men's words; those in the second seat passed the words back to the third and fourth seats.

"I hate to ask this," Vera said, "but do you think there's any chance of a bathroom around here?"

David and Avi looked at one another, pondering the question. Then Avi pointed to a battered home ahead, among the many seemingly abandoned dwellings. He pulled into the driveway, got out and walked up to the front door and knocked. They watched as he waited, then knocked again. With no response, he twisted the doorknob, but it was locked. He stepped back, looked left and then walked over to a gaping hole in the wall and disappeared inside. In a minute the front door opened, and he reappeared from inside.

Instead of waving them in, he held up his palm to wait and disappeared back inside, only to reappear a few minutes later and walk up to the van. "All clear," he said.

"All clear of what?" David said.

"Bodies. And the toilets flush."

In twenty minutes, everyone had used the facilities, wandered around the van, stretched and were ready to head south again. Russ and Kim had gone foraging and found some very old snack food in a basement panty area: potato chips, pretzels, even a case of soda in cans. "Think they'd mind?" Russ said to David.

David glanced at Irene and said, "Probably not. May not be coming back."

"People may have done the same with my place. Looks like we were the fortunate ones," Irene said.

Amid the telltale whoosh of aluminum can lids popping open, Avi backed out of the driveway, and they resumed their trek. Plain brick and frame houses lined the road on both sides, most damaged heavily by hail missiles or fire. The body cleaning crews had not reached this stretch yet. They had become hardened against death, looking on with dispassionate curiosity.

In a few miles small businesses replaced the houses as the road approached the next interchange access road Route 22. The traffic lights were dark, so Avi stopped and then eased left onto the larger road and stopped behind another occupied passenger vehicle that had stopped at the entrance ramp. He and David got out and walked up to car and found a man and woman with two children puzzling over a road map.

David startled him by knocking on the window. They both looked nervous, but cracked the window open slightly so David could ask, "Where are you going?"

The couple glanced at each other, as if wondering whether to trust these strangers with any of their life's details. David smiled and waved at the two children in the back seat, a boy and a girl perhaps a little younger than Joshua. The children waved back with tentative gestures and continued to stare at him and Avi.

"We're driving south toward the Philadelphia area," David said, trying to pry out conversation.

The man checked his rearview mirror to peek at their van, stopped behind them, and finally rolled the window all the way down. "Sorry," the man said, "but we're pretty nervous. We were told to head home, but all this destruction, and these bodies, we're pretty upset."

"Know what you mean," David said.

"We're headed down that way, too," the woman said. "To Oakville."

"I know it well. My sister lived there," David said.

"Is she with you?" woman said.

"No. She and her kids and her husband disappeared before this all started. Our mom's with us, and her niece, and a bunch of others. There are ten of us."

The man and woman both craned their heads around to peer at the van, roof laden with all sorts of items.

"Why not follow us," Avi said. "Maybe safer in a caravan."

The couple looked at each other and nodded in agreement, and then the man said, "Sounds good. We're Cooper's, by the way. But we have a problem. We're low on gas."

"Ah," Avi said. "That is one problem we can solve."

Avi retrieved a jerry can from the roof of the van and topped Cooper's gas tank, then the van's, while David filled the group in on what was happening. With a loud clunk indicating the can was back on the roof, Avi Sharon climbed back into the driver's seat, drove around the car in front to lead them, and then eased down the ramp onto Route 22, heading west.

For the first time, they began to encounter traffic, though still at a pace like an early weekend morning. The roadbed was frequently cracked and crumbled, and they could tell that bulldozers had gone before them to clear away the debris from overpasses that had collapsed onto the highway. When they reached the bridge over the Lehigh River, policemen halted them and had them drive across one at a time. It looked reasonably solid, but they were taking no chances.

After ten miles they reached the larger interchange for Route 309, and were able to swing off onto the cloverleaf and finally start south. After a mile the road would normally have passed under an underpass where it would merge with Interstate 78, but the overpass had collapsed, and they had to wait while a bulldozer darted back and forth across the road to clear a space. While they waited, several other policemen walked up and asked where they were headed, and repeated the caution about road hazards and to be aware that the familiar terrain had changed so that hills were flattened and that driving would be slow and treacherous at spots.

Yet a third vehicle pulled up behind them, an SUV with a heavily laden roof rack. Avi and David walked back to meet them and discovered another family, the Gravers, heading into Philadelphia itself. Mr. Cooper got out to join the conversation. This last car had two sets of walkie-talkies, and they agreed to coordinate rest stops and keep in contact on the drive south. Once the policemen gave the go-ahead signal, their caravan of three began their slow trek south again.

They passed the ruins of the roller coasters at the Dorney Park amusement center, collapsed from the earthquakes or missiles, and off to the east in the distance they caught glimpses of the ruins of the taller buildings in Allentown. Ahead, as forewarned, the low mountain that bordered the city had sunken to perhaps a one-hundred-foot elevation, but the passage was that more difficult because of the severely crumbled roadbed. At times they were forced to ease past rubble on the dirt berm of the road but managed to make it through.

They changed order after the first caravan stop since no one could see around their larger van, and David took over as driver as they moved to third in line. As they neared town centers, they could see men in white jump suits with face masks loading bodies into trucks, and road crews would appear, clearing off their stretch of Route 309. They pulled over frequently to chat and get any news of the road ahead. During these breaks, the three cars used abandoned restroom facilities in stores and homes as needed; the few people they met did not seem to care.

The local crews seemed glad for any human contact, since no one had much news from the outside world, save what the angels might have told them in their areas. They swapped survival stories, and everyone was concerned about this judgment to come, but shared the same instructions: work to clean up in the interim.

In the end, it took six hours to reach the turn off area for Irene's house. The Cooper's had left their caravan an hour earlier to head for Oakville, and the Graver's in the SUV would continue on into Philadelphia. At each parting, the vehicles would empty, and all would shake hands, hug, give thanks for their company, swap phone numbers and e-mail addresses, and feel comfortable enough with the idea of forming a circle to pray for a continued safe journey and the strength and courage to meet whatever may come.

It was the beginning of a new age.

CHAPTER 10

HOME

It was already dusk when David turned off Route 309 and began to ease the van through the maze of neighborhood roads, backtracking as needed when roads were blocked by fallen trees, rubble, or abandoned vehicles. With the daylight fading, and no streetlights, the group strained for what they could see of the damage in their familiar neighborhood. They had seen it elsewhere, but this was personal.

One of the magnificent old oak trees that dotted the neighborhood had toppled, blocking one end of Irene Owens' Street: Pendragon Way. Her house was at the far end, so it was just one more frustration, but David circled the block and with a collective sigh of relief, they saw the other end was still clear, so he turned up in the street and nosed the van into Irene's driveway.

Dark by now, they could only see that the house was still standing, but with a lot of fallen tree clutter and perhaps some rubble from damaged sections of the house strewn about the yard. One of the giant white ash trees had been snapped off halfway up the trunk, but the section fell harmlessly into the front yard.

"Well, we made it. This far, at least," David said as he cut the engine. The words brought a round of applause from the rear of the van, and Irene spoke for the group when she said they had done magnificently.

As they climbed out for the last time, Avi Sharon said, "I believe the men should go in first. There may already be guests in there."

After a few seconds to consider the suggestion and recalling all they had seen on the drive down today, Michael Cohen said, "We Jews can be suspicious, but I think Avi's right. Let's go."

"Do you want to wait outside, Mr. Cohen?" David said.

"I'm not dead yet, David. Let's go in."

"Don't even start with him, David," Sylvia Cohen said. "Just let him go. But hurry up. It's cold out here."

As they spoke, Avi and Russ dug four flashlights out of the rear storage area, and Avi brought one of the shotguns. He had never been there before, so when the four men were ready, Avi said, "Which way?"

"There's a rear entrance. No one uses the front door," David said.

David led the way to a rear door, and they saw that it had been smashed open. Avi took the lead and nosed the door open with the muzzle of the shotgun, stepping through a mudroom and then into the kitchen.

Whoever had been there had ransacked the kitchen for any foodstuffs, just as they had done to abandoned houses on the drive down. There were dirty dishes on the breakfast bar, unclean pots and pans, cans and packages littered about, plus a large number of dead flies lying on the floor and flat surfaces.

"I don't like the looks of all those flies," Michael Cohen said. "Let me go ahead."

They found them in the den area at the far end of the house. A family of four perhaps: two adults and two older children. They had been dead long enough for the stench to mostly evaporate, and like the corpses they had first seen that morning, they were stiff and leathery looking. Michael Cohen was a doctor by profession and kneeled down carefully to get a closer look. They all had severe looking sores on their faces and other exposed skin, and he checked the hands of the two adults and noticed that they both had an unusual logo design seemingly branded onto their skin.

"Can you see this?" he said to Avi. "I forgot my glasses."

Avi knelt down next to him and leaned in for a closer look. "Oh my

God," he muttered. "It's that 6-6-6 mark...in a black and red design." He shifted over to examine the two children, who seemed to have been teenagers, and they had the same mark."

"It brought the curse of God on them," Michael Cohen said. "You see this? These sores. Just like it said in David's Bible reading. Not AIDS. Something God was going to do. Where was that again?" he added, kneeling erect again. Then he reached over and clasped Avi's arm, and gesturing at the four bodies said, "That could have been Sylvia and me if it wasn't for our Avi Sharon. Or our heads chopped off. The bastards... pardon my language."

David patted Michael's shoulder and said, "That's the way we all felt about those thugs. And the Bible reading was in Revelation. The Apocalypse."

"Yes. That's right. I remember you read that to us," Michael said.

"What do we do with them?" Russ Freeman said.

As Avi helped Michael to his feet, David thought for a few seconds then said, "Mom has a patio area out back. We can carry them out through the French doors and stack them somewhere until tomorrow. Maybe there are others in the neighborhood who will know what's people are doing with them."

"Want me to check the rest of the house?" Russ said. "I kind of remember the layout."

"Yeah. Check the basement, too," David said.

They found no others, and in fifteen minutes they had carted the bodies to a back tennis court, swept the kitchen clean of dead flies, and stepped back outside to give the all clear signal. To their surprise, an older couple and a young man had joined their own. As they walked up, Irene called to David and said, "Do you remember the O'Neill's from the other end of the street? They made it through with us."

"Yeah. Wasn't your daughter Sharon in school with my older sister Abby?"

54

"That's right," the man said. "This is her son, my grandson Chris."

"Is Sharon here?" David said.

The young man spoke up and said, "She divorced my dad, and she and my kid sister were taken away."

"The thugs got them?" David said.

"No. They disappeared. I guess like your dad did."

Irene clutched David's forearm at the reminder.

"How about your dad?" David asked Chris.

"We don't know what happened to him. We kinda lost contact once this all started. We weren't that close anyway."

"I'm sorry," Irene said.

"It was difficult," Mrs. O'Neill said. "And now we've only got each other. But anyway, I'm glad you folks are all back. It's cold out here. Get your things inside and maybe we can talk tomorrow. It's not like we have a lot of neighbors now."

"Any word on electricity?" David said.

Mr. O'Neill said, "I told your mother. Two policemen were around, and they thought they might have something in another week or so."

Vera gave Michelle a hug and said, "Well, looks like you and Kim will have to hold off on the spa trip."

After the O'Neill's had started back toward their house, Irene said, "Well, David? What did you find?"

Michael answered first and said, "Irene. You have a lovely home. It needs some work right now. We were hoping for electricity to run the vacuum cleaner. And we removed some unpleasant things, but we can settle in for the evening."

"Meaning?" Vera said.

David held up his hand with four fingers extended.

"Oh my God," Irene said.

"My sentiments exactly, Irene," Michael Cohen said. "And there's more to the story. But that's for the morning. Let's just be thankful we got this far."

CHAPTER 11

MORNING

Everyone chattered as they straggled into the kitchen the next morning. Not about how they slept or about mustiness or dust or dead flies or litter strewn about from the squatters. In fact, no one lingered in bed; they wanted everyone else's take on the phenomenon. They awoke to *daylight*. No more artificial blackouts with security cameras, but sunlight streaming in through windows. They could stare out a window unconcerned about who might peer in to see them.

It was a down payment on their new age.

By unspoken consent, the kitchen was already their meeting room while the group still held together. With a flagstone floor, it was easiest to keep clean. The house had a large living room, but it had been desecrated by all manner of dirt, stains and debris that would require electricity to properly power the vacuum and steam cleaners. But with no electricity, there was no heat, and so everyone stayed bundled up.

David Owens waited until everyone had some sort of food for breakfast, then scheduled a meeting for ten o'clock to gain consensus on where they would go from here. Everyone knew that the group might begin to split up, probably sooner than later, and their final gift to each other would be an orderly transition to recover some semblance of life before the troubles, and to prepare for their trip to Israel.

When they had all gathered, he leaned on the breakfast bar with a pencil and pad of yellow lined paper and said, "Give me your ideas. What do we have to do today, and the rest of the week?"

Kim Marshall jumped in first and said, "Try to find out about our families."

"And transportation. We can't all use the van," Russ Freeman said.

"Go and see if our house made it through this mess," Michael Cohen said.

"See if there is any local authority left," Avi Sharon said. "Like those policemen we saw yesterday. And do they need our help?"

"Good," David said. "So far it's only us and the O'Neill's around here."

"Check for damage outside, and clean this place up, inside and out," Irene said. "For those of us staying here, that is. And you're all welcome to stay as long as you want, by the way."

"Thank you," Avi said. "I really have no place to go until my trip to Israel."

"Food," Vera Owens said. "We should see if anyone is selling anything. Like any supermarkets open."

"And gasoline. Anyone selling fuel."

"Is money any good?" Kim said. "And who would be around to sell anything?"

"Good point," David said. "If we find any, maybe the police will know. And by the way, we may have a working fireplace so we can at least build a fire to warm up. Should be plenty of wood lying around outside. Anything else?"

The group stared at each other for a minute before Michael Cohen said, "I think that's probably enough for one day, David. Just do the most urgent things first."

"Okay. Looking at the list, I think we can check for food and fuel and whether there's any local authority left. Mom, can you lead us to the township building or whatever it is?"

"Of course," Irene said. "But Michael, your home isn't that far away. We can go there first."

"Thank you. We've been worried about it. It's best to know," Sylvia Cohen said.

"Then when we get back, Russ and Kim can take the van and drive up to their homes. See if they can find their families. How's that sound?" David said.

"I'd really appreciate it," Kim said. "Do we have enough gas?"

"For a few days yet," Avi said. "That's why we should check around this area."

"Sounds like a plan. Let's do it," David said.

When the group disbursed to get dressed for the morning, Joshua Owens wandered into the front living room to stare at his new world, and noticed movement out front, and called to his father on one of his trips from the kitchen.

"What Josh?" David said.

"There are men in driveway."

David walked over next to him and peered out to see four men looking at the house, taking notes.

"Be back in a minute, buddy. Maybe they're the local authority," David said, and walked out through the kitchen and around to the front of the house.

"Morning," he said to the man holding the clipboard.

"Morning to you," the man said. "You squatting here?"

"Squatting? We live here."

"Well, no more. We want you out by tomorrow morning."

"Excuse me?"

"You see our sign there?" he said, pointing to a red and black symbol painted on the side of the house. "That means we claimed this place. We want you out by tomorrow morning."

"Who are you supposed to be?" David said.

"We're in charge now."

"In charge of what?"

"Everything. We're it. Nobody's left that matters, so we're taking over. We're taking over all these houses," he said, gesturing at the homes along Pendragon Way.

David stepped back to take in the four men: three white guys and one large black man who stood with his arms crossed, staring with that blank look he used to see with the old rap music group CD labels. The clipboard guy was his height and age, but outweighed him by forty pounds, and wore a pair of sunglasses with vibrant yellow frames suspended from his neck with a red cloth lanyard.

David's response was visceral: he looked at the clipboard guy and held up to fingers. "Two words: get lost," and turned around to walk back inside.

"Tomorrow morning, pal," the clipboard guy yelled after him. "Or we throw you out."

Vera and Avi Sharon met David in the kitchen and said, "Who were those men?"

David waved aimlessly and held up his hand to ask for time to gather himself. When he could finally speak, he recounted the whole episode, shaking his head in disbelief when he had finished.

"Vultures," Avi said.

"What?" Vera said.

"Like scavenger birds. We had them in Israel, too. They come in after the battles and try to take over the areas. Warlords. Vultures."

"What did you do with them?" Vera said.

"Some people gave up. We shot them," Avi said.

Vera stared at him for a few seconds. "You didn't really do that, did you?"

Without hesitation, Avi said, "They were vultures. They were...what do you call them? Scum. Of course we shot them. Anyone else with those ideas gets the message."

Vera started to react, but David held his hand up to silence her. "Do you think it will come to that?"

Avi shrugged. "Who knows? But I would not give an inch," he said, jabbing his index finger into his palm.

CHAPTER 12

THE NEIGHBORHOOD

To calm down, David left his wife to set up an itinerary for the morning and joined Avi Sharon and his mother outside to survey the state of any external damage. For the most part the house had weathered the hail and rock attacks with only minor damage to one corner of the building, and some of the rain gutters were torn off by fallen tree limbs, minor compared to some of the homes in the neighborhood that had roofs caved in and walls totally collapsed.

A large tree had fallen across the back wall of her patio garden, and the barrier at the far end of the tennis court was flattened by a large rock that still lay on the grass. Irene wanted to examine it further, but David discouraged her because they had stacked the squatters' bodies there last evening.

David took notes all the while, and by the time they returned inside, Vera Owens had the morning lined up. They would take Irene to guide through the township streets to find the local authorities if any still existed, then to take the Cohen's to their home, and finally to a supermarket if any were open.

"I have money," Irene said.

"You may not be able to buy anything, Irene," Sylvia Cohen said.

"Well…we'll see what happens."

"David. Should we bring all our things?" Michael Cohen said.

"I don't think so. Take what you might need for the day. We can make a second trip if your house is livable."

"I'm nervous about being there alone, what with these thugs David spoke with this morning," Sylvia said.

"I can stay with you," Avi said.

"Let's just see how it looks first, Sylvie," Michael said. "Then we can decide."

Her husband, Daniel Owens, was an inveterate map collector, and Irene found a township map in a kitchen drawer. "I know how to get to the township building, but not how to backtrack if we get stuck or lost. It's been four years, you know."

David and Vera, Irene, Avi Sharon, and the Cohen's piled back into the van and the trip to the township building went smoothly for a change. As they parked in front, next to a lone police car, David switched off the engine, looked at Avi and said, "What did we do wrong? That was too easy."

"God knows we need a break."

David stepped back to survey the building, which also seemed to have weathered the troubles fairly well. A rock missile dug into the parking lot, but it otherwise seemed intact.

They checked to see that the main entrance was open, though the glass in the door had been smashed, replaced by an ill-fitting piece of plywood.

"Hello," David yelled once they had stepped inside.

"Down here," a voice replied, coming from the hallway ahead of them.

They moved like a pod and wandered down the hall, passing three open doors for unoccupied offices until they reached the far end of the hallway. In the last door on the right, they found two men in police uniforms, plus two civilians: a middle-aged woman and an older man who could have been in his sixties.

"Come on in," one of the officers said. "We like company these days."

"Thanks," David said, speaking for the group. "We just got back last evening, and it's been a weird experience."

"Weirder than the past three years?" the older man said.

"No. I guess not. We didn't know if there was any government left here. Or in the state."

"Or in Washington," Michael Cohen said.

"Well," the older man said. "I can't speak for the state...or Washington, for that matter. We haven't been able to get any news yet. The Internet isn't even up for the moment. But we had these fellows calling themselves angels show up and tell us to keep at it and set up some sort of order as folks filtered back in. Did you meet them?"

"We met some," said Avi. "Maybe not *your* angels. Probably a lot of them around."

"So, what *is* the government?" David said.

"We're about it," the older man said. "I'm Frank Patterson, by the way. I was one of the township supervisors before this all started. There's another one, Al Harris, but he's not here yet. And this is Ginny Hartman, and our only patrolmen here are Doug Peters and Gene Kelly."

After a round of introductions and handshakes, David said, "We have some serious questions."

"Like food and gasoline?" Frank said.

"Yeah."

"Nothing's open. So, the best we can tell you for food is, if you find a building you can get into, take what you want. Ordinarily that would be looting, but chances are the owners are gone or dead, and there's no one to pay anyway. And we can spare you some gasoline until we run too low. I figure we're all in this together until this judgment thing gets sorted out."

"You heard about that?" Avi said.

"Oh yeah," one of the patrolmen said. "The angels made that clear enough. In fact, they said we might not have much to do because they would kind of take charge of things in the meantime."

"Are you getting paid?" Michael Cohen said.

"None of us are," Frank said. "We're just doing our bit."

Michael stared at the four officials, looking at their hands and foreheads. "We carried out four bodies when we arrived at Irene's house last evening. They had been dead a long time. They had sores on them, and a mark on their hands."

"Black and red design? The number 6-6-6 in the middle?" Frank said.

"That's it," said Michael.

"We've seen a lot of them," the patrolman called Doug said. "The mark of the Beast. They probably had a really painful death. Saw a few of them in progress while we were hiding out. We've been taking them to the township maintenance building. We try to identify them, but often we can't."

"What do you do then?" David said.

"We dug a pit behind the building and there's a common grave. About all we can do," Frank said.

They were silent for a minute before David asked, "We have one other...situation. This morning a group of men came to our house and told us to get out. Said they were the new local authorities and were taking over everything. You know anything about them?"

Frank reached behind him and picked up a large photograph and handed it to David. "This him? The leader?"

"Yeah. Who is he?"

"His name's Gerry Brophy. Thinks he's a bush-league warlord or something. We've had some other complaints, and Gene and I have even talked with him, but he figures this is his great opportunity to clean up and become a big-time landowner in the new world."

"Was there a big black guy with him?" the other patrolman said.

"Yeah."

"That's Antwon Williams. We think he was a thug from north Philly and somehow got hooked up with Gerry."

"Are they dangerous?" Irene said.

"Could be. Gerry keeps collecting lowlifes that survived the troubles. He's making himself a small army."

"Don't they know about their judgment in Israel?" Avi said.

"If they do, they're ignoring it," Frank said.

"He said he would be back in the morning to throw us out," David said.

"You never mentioned that David," Irene said.

"I didn't want to worry you, mom."

"So, you were going to tell me this tomorrow morning when these men show up?"

Doug jumped into the conversation and said, "Tell you what. We don't have a working phone system, and the cell service is still out. But take one of these walkie-talkies. They have about a five-mile range. Call if you need help."

It was an unexpectedly genial time, and Frank capped it off by taking a roster of everyone's name and where the local people lived. While he was writing, Michael Cohen spoke up and said, "Tell us what we can do. I'm a doctor if you need my service."

"Good to know. You should take a walkie-talkie, too," Frank said, digging another one out of a box and noting the label to identify the recipient, and handing it to Michael. "For the rest of you, we need help with everything. Burial duties if you're up to it. Plus, we have to do a census of all the houses to see who survived. And who didn't make it. Could get pretty grim. Especially tough when kids are involved."

"We'll do what we can," David assured him. "I think some of our group will move on, but we're ready to help."

Taking a recommendation for food sources, the next stop was an unoccupied supermarket that they had to loot for non-perishable foods, charcoal briquettes, cleaning products and paper towels and toilet paper. A few other people were foraging as well, and after swapping some brief survival stories, they wound their way through cluttered township streets to find the Cohen's house.

It had not fared as well. It, too, had been tucked under large trees, and one of them had fallen across one end of the L-shaped structure. The three men went in first and found two squatter bodies, and also some anti-Semitic symbols and slogans written on the walls.

"Fools," Michael said. "They thought hating Jews would save them from the Beast. And now look at them. They're like roadkill. I don't even rage at them anymore. It's so senseless."

After they had carted the bodies out back and covered them with a sheet, Avi said, "Michael. You can't stay here like this. I think you should bring Sylvia in and show her the place, and once she sees what it looks like, you should go back and stay with Irene until we can fix it up. Then you can move back."

Michael looked around, then patted Avi's shoulder and said, "When you're right, you're right. Sylvie will want to see it, but you and Irene are godsends."

CHAPTER 13

CONFRONTATION

Russ Freemen and Kim Marshall wanted to take the van and search for their families but insisted on staying around because of the local warlord threat that was supposed to come in the morning. And so it was that David and Russ fired up the charcoal grill to at least heat some of the items they had been eating cold.

David slept restlessly, and the sunlight was not as welcoming when it burst through his window at seven o'clock the following morning. Evidentially the others felt the same because they were up about early, not mentioning what might happen. No one spoke specifically about the warlord; after all, he might not even show up. But the threat lingered.

The morning dragged on until eleven o'clock as David and Avi and Russ wandered around outside, cleaning up fallen brush, cutting tree limbs with old bow saws, until the fateful moment when three pickup trucks pulled up the street and stopped in front of their house.

"Go talk to them," Avi said, and took Russ inside with him.

David was confused with the departure but trusted that Avi would not abandon him and walked over to meet the man he now knew as Gerry Brophy. At a quick count, he seemed to have about a dozen men, including Antwon Williams and what appeared to be two teenage boys.

"You're still here," Gerry said.

"We live here," David said.

"So, you've gone stupid. Or deaf. Challenging our authority?"

"You have no authority. This is our house. And we spoke with the township people yesterday," David said.

"Really. How many did you count? Four? Five? Look around, pal. How many of us are there? We're in charge now."

"It doesn't matter. We live here," David said again.

He could see that Gerry looked over his shoulder to something behind him, and the men behind Gerry tensed up. Before he could turn to look, Avi breezed past him, and before Gerry could react, Avi had poked his sawed-off shotgun into Gerry's stomach. Russ stood next to David, holding a shotgun, and passing one to him.

"Whoa. Easy, dude," Gerry said. "You see the weapons behind me? You're outgunned."

Avi didn't take his eyes off Gerry, staring through him. "Do not flinch. It does not matter what your thugs do. If anyone raises a weapon, you will be the first to go, with a large hole in your stomach. It will be very painful," he added, jabbing the muzzle into Gerry's stomach for emphasis. "Understood?"

Gerry looked tentative, not knowing how to deal with this man he had not seen the day before. But he didn't move, and Avi looked over his shoulder and spoke to the men behind him.

"I've spent ten years fighting crazy Arabs in Israel. Three years surviving the troubles. These good people took me in and saved me and my friends, and I am not about to let a bunch of thieves steal their property."

"Who you callin' a thief, man?" Antwon Williams yelled back, not backing down. "We're in charge now. We just takin' what's ours. We on top now."

"Don't listen to that man. He's a fool. You are thieves. You will soon be judged before your King in Israel. Have you no shame? No fear? You may not even come back here."

It was an uneasy standoff, no one quite knowing what to do. Gerry made to turn his head to see how his group was responding, but Avi poked him in the stomach again and repeated, "Do not move."

Unthinking, Irene Owens had walked up behind them and announced that she had radioed for the police. Antwon Williams looked at her and decided his course of action.

"This is nonsense. You shoot Gerry, I shoot the old lady," he said, raising a large pistol to point towards Irene. But before he could aim, two shotgun blasts hurled him back into the other men as David and Russ fired simultaneously. He crumpled into a heap on the ground, two gaping wounds in his chest.

The severity of the response stunned everyone, David and Russ the most, and the other men began to take stock of what they had gotten themselves into. Their leader was being held captive at gunpoint, and their main enforcer was a bloody heap on the ground at their feet.

As the uneasy standoff dragged on, the O'Neill's drifted down from their house at the next corner, and both Mr. O'Neill and his son were carrying pistols. At the same time, the police cruiser with Doug and Gene pulled around the corner and the offers stepped out, hands on their weapons.

Finally, Gerry Brophy spoke to Avi Sharon and said, "Okay, dude. You've won this one, but we'll be back with more men. And don't count on the two loser cops over there. Like I said, we're in charge now."

"I told you not to move," Avi said.

"So, shoot me in the back then," Gerry said and turned and walked back to his men. He started to order the men back into the vehicles when a voice from behind Avi said, "No one is leaving for the moment."

David and his group were as surprised as the others, and watched as the two angels, Al and Matthew, walk between them and face the group of thugs. Al pointed at Gerry Brophy and said, "Walk up and stand here," pointing to a spot in front of his group of thugs.

Gerry didn't argue, but he didn't move either, looking as if he was weighing his options. He was slightly taller than this new arrival, so he opted for the intimidation approach and ambled up to try to tower over him with his menacing stare.

"Who else stands with this man?" Al said.

The thugs looked at each other and seeing that Gerry was taller than the other man, all but two men and the two teenage boys walked up to stand behind him for moral support.

"Are you all in agreement with this man?" Al asked again.

Gerry did an eye roll and said, "Look. Dude. I don't know who you think you are, but you can see who's here. You and these other toads are outnumbered, and like I said, we'll be back."

Al stared at Gerry, then scanned the group and said, "Last chance."

Perhaps it was something in the phrasing, because one man slipped away in the back, and stood with the teenagers and the other two men.

"So be it," Matthew said, and it began. As their friends looked on in stunned horror, Gerry and all the men who stood with him began a rapid decomposition, their skin and flesh dissolving and seemingly evaporating into thin air. The process continued soundlessly for a full minute until their clothed skeletal remains cluttered to a heap on the ground before the assembled group.

When it was done, and the group was released to look around, Avi and Russ turned their faces away and held a hand over their eyes, while Irene Owens clutched her son, burying her face in his shoulder. The two policemen and the O'Neill's just stared in amazement, but the two teenagers and Gerry's men who failed to stand with him drifted over to a hedge and began to vomit.

No one wanted to be there, but no one felt free to leave either, so for the next five minutes all present looked at each other or wandered around in a circle. No one spoke until the two angels finally called the group together.

The angel called Al spoke and said, "We take no pleasure in destroying lives like that, but you must remember that you are now subjects of the great King in Israel. Never more will such rebellion be tolerated. Not this week. Not this year. Never. Is that understood?"

The angel stared around and the assembled group, searching for reactions. Slowly everyone nodded 'yes', glancing at the pile of bones as reinforcement.

Al then spoke to the man and the two teenagers who survived and said, "You must understand that you very nearly met their fate. You still have an opportunity to repent and call upon your great God and King before you are judged. And if you have any other acquaintances with similar plans about robbing others instead of contributing to the welfare of this community, you will explain to them what you have just seen. If they fail to listen to you, they will meet this same fate. Do you understand?"

To a person the head nods were more vigorous.

"Which vehicle belonged to your former leader?" the angel Matthew said.

One of the men pointed to the lead pickup truck.

"Very well. You will load these remains into the other two vehicles and leave. His vehicle will remain here."

One of the men started to protest, and Matthew pointed at the bones.

"You got it," the man said, and he and the two boys started tossing skeletons into the back of the two remaining trucks, eager to depart as fast as they could.

Once the thieves had left, the two policemen, the full O'Neill family and the entire Owens household emptied out into the driveway to discuss the event.

"Is everyone here now?" Al said.

David Owens looked around and counted nine people beside himself. "Yes."

Al and Matthew glanced at each other, and by some unspoken consent Matthew began to speak this time. "This was an unfortunate situation, certainly for those men, but it was necessary demonstration of life in the kingdom. As I explained to those men, rebellion will not be tolerated." Looking at the two policemen, he said, "You have served a necessary function in the past, but in the future we will establish and maintain order in your society. You would be free to select another useful profession. And for now, the message will spread that it is not permitted to rebel against the King, and that you should cooperate to reestablish order in your communities."

No one said anything in response, and finally Al said, "Are there any questions?"

"Probably a lot," Michael Cohen said, "if we could think of them."

"Are we even needed, then?" the policeman named Doug said.

"For the moment. Until the judgments are over, and you receive further instructions, you will help establish an orderly rebuilding process," Al said.

"Do we really keep this truck?" Russ Freeman said.

"Of course. The owner has no use for it. And you may find other abandoned vehicles as well. If you cannot locate the owners, or if the owners are no longer alive, you may take them and use them. I believe you will find that very few people will return to their homes."

"What happens after that?"

"We do not know for certain," Matthew said. "But if you enter the kingdom, your lives will undergo a remarkable change. There will be time then to discuss such things."

"Are there other questions?" Al said.

No one spoke for a few seconds, and finally David pursed his lips and shook his head slowly, side to side, and said, "Russ and I actually just shot someone and killed somebody. How am I...are we...supposed to react to that?"

Matthew answered and said, "You had the natural response of someone defending your family. The man would have killed Mrs. Owens if you had not shot him. I would not suggest this as a habit, but in the moment, you exercised your right of self-defense."

"He would have ended as a skeleton anyway," Al said. "That may sound casual, but the Lord is quite clear about good and evil, and those men were evil and unrepentant. That is not an attitude that will be tolerated in the kingdom.

CHAPTER 14

NEW LIFE

Irene was up early, wandering the back yard alone, surveying the state of her property in the morning fog. The scene was disheartening, but amid the destruction new life was appearing. Intrepid crocuses and daffodils were popping up and beginning to bloom, and small buds were forming on the trees that had not been damaged in the bombardments. As a feast for the ears, she heard serenades of chattering sparrows, Carolina wrens, cardinals, robins and even crows. She'd missed that in the bunker these past four years. Birds flitted between trees and bushes, some of them carrying straw and twigs, sure signs of nest building and the blooming spring to come. No doubt they'd suffered in the bombardments, but their resilience shone through as they resolutely began the process of securing the next generation.

One by one the bunker refugees emerged, congregating in the kitchen again. As they considered what to do next, finding their families was the highest priority on everyone's list. Vera's parents were in Connecticut, and Michelle's near Washington, DC, making travel difficult. Vera was an only child, and her parents had accepted the Beast's mark early on, so she harbored no illusions that they were still alive. The Cohens had two married sons and grandchildren, and they had also taken the Beast's mark when the troubles began so their fate was sealed.

Only Russ and Kim had family nearby, and so after yesterday's confrontation with the warlord they took his truck and retraced their way out of the neighborhood and then northeast toward New Hope. They had met when they both worked for Irene's son-in-law, Steve Engel, where he had his business. As on their trip from the mountains, there were several checkpoints and re-routes before they reached the outskirts of New Hope. At the last checkpoint they asked for the latest information.

"Can we get across the bridge to Lambertville?" – the twin town across the Delaware River.

"The bridges are out," he said, "but you can cross up at Stockton. It's about five miles north and then double back."

"I'm familiar with the area. How is New Hope?"

"It's in pretty bad shape. Can't get down the main street. Where are you heading?"

"I had an apartment on the water. And my folks live on the hill above town."

"I doubt your apartment is still there. All those buildings were demolished in the bombardments. Your folks' place may still be there. Take the back road up there. Don't try to go through town."

"Okay. Thanks," Russ said.

As he slid the window closed, he checked the rearview mirror to see another car pull up and he edged their truck ahead and pulled over to the side of the road.

"What do you want to?" Kim said.

Russ considered his options for a few seconds and said, "Let's check on my parents. Sounds like the apartment's a waste of time; I don't need anything from there. Then we can check on your folks' place."

"Sounds like a plan."

Russ checked the mirror again and slipped out onto the road down the hill into town, turning right onto the winding back roads that gave access to the homes on the hillside above New Hope. Most of the houses had been demolished, destroyed by the beach ball sized hail or the rocks that had splattered the earth during the bombardments.

Kim had been there several times and saw that his house was among those destroyed. Russ pulled into what little space the driveway afforded and they climbed out to search the premises. They couldn't crawl inside the house; under the collapse it was too cluttered and probably dangerous. So, they peered in where they could but saw no signs of bodies. A quick survey of the outside property gave the same results: nothing. No bodies. In fact, none of the other properties seemed to have bodies either, which was odd. Unless they were buried inside.

"You seen enough?" Kim said, once they'd wandered the property for fifteen minutes.

"I guess. I didn't expect to find them, really. None of them were believers and they were all ready to take that mark of the Beast. I figure they probably went off with the rest of the neighbors to hide out somewhere when all hell broke loose that last year."

"At least they're not lying around here like roadkill."

"Right. That would have been tough to take."

Russ wandered off by himself for a few minutes, catching the view of the town below before spring leaves would once again block the view. When he came back to Kim he said, "Do I seem too...casual about them? Like I don't really care what happened?"

"A little."

Russ paused a moment to look around. "I was happy to work for Steve..."

"We all were."

"Yeah, but when I mentioned that he had this strong Christian faith, they used to take shots at him. Not to his face...they hardly ever met him, really. But, like, when I told them he didn't agree with the gay marriage idea, they really went on about it."

"Especially here in the gay center of Bucks County, I would think. Was one of them gay?"

"No. Just 'evolved', or whatever the word was back then. Couldn't imagine how primitive Steve was. They were so stupid. It wasn't pleasant to be with them toward the end."

"But they were still family," Kim said.

"That's the hard part. We never came to any resolution about the whole thing. And when you and I decided to escape, they thought I was an idiot. Said as much. I tried to warn them that they were making a big mistake and said I'd try to keep in touch, but once we got to the bunker and David warned us about the government tracing calls and finding our location, I never heard from them anymore. Nothing even on my brother's Facebook page. They may have been tagged early on."

"It could have been different..."

"Can't go back. Just accept it I guess."

After a lingering look around, Russ said, "Well, nothing more here. Let's go and see what your place looks like."

Russ backtracked down to where they met the patrolman and asked him whether they could take the river road on the Pennsylvania side of the Delaware River north to the next crossing bridge at Center Bridge.

"Can't go that way," he said. The bridge over the canal towpath is out. Best to head inland and pick up the road to Center Bridge that way. You know the way?"

"Yeah. I'm okay with the roads up there."

"Good luck."

It had been four years since Russ had driven this way, but the route was familiar enough once and he reached the bridge from Center Bridge to Stockton in less than an hour, allowing for the now common easing around obstacles and the crumbled road surface. There were fewer houses and those they did see had the usual damage, but with no bodies lying about. Maybe they had already been cleaned up. Once across the river into New Jersey, they saw that Stockton had only moderate damage. They turned south at the end of the main street and started toward Lambertville on the other side of the bridge from New Hope. It was only five miles, but the trip took half an hour. Kim's family lived in the north end of town, and on approaching the outskirts, they recognized heavy damage. It looked like a tornado had ripped through and leveled the whole north end.

"My God," Kim said, holding her mouth.

"Good thing your folks were taken away before the troubles," Russ said.

Kim slowly shook her head in wonderment. "We had no idea. I thought things were bad up there in the bunker. God must have really been protecting us."

"We could have been flattened like that," Russ said. "Your street was one of the worst hits. Do you want to get out and look at anything?"

Kim was still distracted and suddenly realized Russ had asked her a question. "What?"

"Do you want to get out and look around? Any personal stuff you want to look for?"

She thought for a few seconds, and finally said, "No. Nothing here I want. I know my folks are with Steve and his family. Let's just get out of here."

They rode in silence on the slow drive home, lost in the moment, until Kim reached across and took Russ's hand and gave it a gentle squeeze. He knew the meaning. All links to their old world had been severed forever.

"We've known each other for, what, ten years now?" Russ said.

"About that long."

"We could be living another six hundred years or more if what those angels say is true."

"Yeah. That's the plan," Kim said, "if we get through this judgment thing."

Russ paused for a few seconds and then said, "If we do get through it, together, how'd you like to spend the next six hundred with me?"

She looked at him with a soft smile and said, "Is that really a proposal?"

"Sure is. I should have made it a long time ago. We've been good buds, but I really do love you and can't think of going on into this new…world without you. I really need to know you'll be there with me."

He looked over at her. "You feel like that?"

She squeezed his hand again, eyes misting over. "Of course I do, you dope. I can't imagine life with anyone else."

"So that's a yes then?"

"If that's a question, of course it's a yes."

Russ slowed and glided to a stop in the middle of the road. "Need to seal the deal," he said, leaning across the console to pull Kim close for a lingering kiss.

"Perfect," he said as they started up again. "Now I wonder who does marriages these days."

CHAPTER 15

PROSPECTING

Avi had no relatives or friends in America and knew he would only stay until the call to return to Israel. His only obligations were to his 'family' from the bunker. And with the warlord threat removed he felt safe to leave the family to themselves during the day to help the Cohen's clean up their house and repair some of the minor damage. He borrowed a chain saw from the township maintenance building and cut up the large tree that had fallen across the end of their house while Michael and Sylvia cleaned up inside. He could tell from Sylvia's expression that this was a painful time. The smashed pictures he'd seen inside of her children and grandchildren were a metaphor for what was probably their fate. They had perished, and for someone who took joy in her home and family, this was devastating.

"I have a hard time keeping Sylvie going," Michael said, wandering out to check on Avi's progress. "She's inconsolable at this point. This house and the family were everything to her."

"I sensed that."

"You think we can ever get it fixed up nice again?"

"I would think so," Avi said, "but have you considered that it may not matter?"

"What do you mean?

"Think about it. Assume you both will pass through this judgment in Israel and be accepted into the Kingdom. What happens then…since you're a Jew."

Michael stared at him for a minute, considering the riddle, and then it dawned on him. "Our old prayer. Next year in Jerusalem."

"Exactly. Our people have prayed for that for centuries, and now it's here. You and Sylvie would be with your King. All the gentiles will honor you. They will send you off from here with valuable things…their money and jewelry and silver and gold. And at last you and Sylvie will have a brilliant future in a new land. God's land."

"So, we won't want to come back here…"

"This house will not matter at all. You can give to whoever you want. Or just let it be. Some other survivors will need a nice place. Let them fix it up."

"I don't know if Sylvie can accept that," Michael said.

"You think she would want to keep it as a holiday home or something? Once you live in Israel with the King and see the new Temple and the land blossom again, this place will be meaningless."

Michael pondered the thought while Avi continued with the chain saw. He walked out to the street and scanned the house in panorama. It was special to him as well, and the idea that it could just fade from memory was not an agreeable thought. But like the angels said: they were the pioneers in a new age. They could tell the next generations what it was like in their day: what passed for luxury, and how it paled by comparison with what they knew in Israel. Maybe it was important that they cling to the memory of this present age, a crazy and chaotic world where any peace was an illusion at best.

As he stared at the house, the truth of this swept over him, but convincing Sylvie would be another matter.

There was so much to do in the neighborhood it was hard to know where to begin. The township staff was most concerned about an inventory of houses and properties, and to discover if anyone else might still be alive, returning from a distant hiding place. They had lists of properties but didn't know who might have lived in any particular house. For this they depended on the knowledge of neighbors who could tell them about life on their street. Armed with this information, and a township map, they divided the area into sections and David volunteered to reconnoiter in their area. Irene and the O'Neill's knew almost everyone in their neighborhood, and made out a list, house-by-house of who they would be looking for.

When they worked in their home area they would break and come back to Irene's house for lunch, sharing stories and the latest news. David had come back from the township work and reported that the early population estimate was that only about of the tenth of the population had survived and returned to the neighborhood, and an almost unbelievable development.

When Avi and the Cohens returned, they noticed Chris O'Neill had joined them, the grandson of their neighbors. He was huddling with Michelle in the corner of the kitchen. Vera caught Avi staring at them, and with her typical brashness took Avi aside and said, "Checking out the young people?"

"He's the neighbor boy, right? Is he helping out at their house?"

"I think so. But I think Michelle is better scenery for lunch if you know what I mean."

Avi looked at her, realizing her meaning, then back at the young couple.

"Is there a problem?" Vera said.

"What? No, I guess not. They are probably the only people around here her age."

"Her age?"

Avi looked at Vera and after a few seconds said, "Can I talk to you outside?"

She looked around, and everyone seemed occupied. "Sure. Let's go out on the patio."

There was enough clear space to wander around as they spoke, and it took a few minutes for Avi to open up. "I am not familiar with your American ways in these matters," he said.

"What matters?"

"I think you would say, 'matters of the heart'".

"You mean romance? Who? Michelle?"

"Yes."

"What about her?"

"She is a lovely girl."

"Gorgeous would be a better word. No wonder Chris stops down to see her. What's your interest?" Vera said.

"I would like to marry her."

It was difficult to flummox Vera, but Avi managed the effort with that confession. "Are you serious?"

"Yes. Does that seem so strange?" Avi said.

"Well, it's not strange for a man to be attracted to a tall, blonde Nordic beauty queen. I'd be more concerned if you *weren't* attracted. I just didn't know you had feelings for her. Have you talked to her about this?"

"No."

"Okay, then. This could get a bit weird."

"You think this is a bad idea?"

"Avi, I don't know what to think. You're catching me cold here. How old are you?"

"I'm thirty-five."

"So that's about five or six years older than Michelle, give or take."

"You think that is too big an age difference? And do you think she likes me?" he said.

Vera put her arm around his waist and eased him to the far end of the patio where the original wall had collapsed. Once there she turned to face him, arms folded.

"Like you? I can't say. I know she admires you; we all do. Along with

David, you two were our strength during the years in the bunker. You may seem more like a warrior hero to her than a marriage prospect."

Avi didn't respond. He just studied her face.

"Not that a warrior hero wouldn't make a good husband. And keep in mind I've never been to Israel, but I have an image of shorter, dark haired women like me. Michelle would be kind of different if you know what I mean. Can you catch the image? Warrior hero with tall, blonde Nordic queen?"

Avi was beginning to look a bit disheartened by the direction of this conversation.

"However, I'm just trying to prepare you for some of the 'downsides', as we Americans say."

"Down sides?"

"Disadvantages. Awkward things. Negatives. Stuff bound to come up."

"What about the age difference?" Avi said.

"I don't know if that's really an issue. Even six years isn't much difference. And if these angels are giving us the straight story about long lives, when you're seven hundred years old, she would be six ninety-four. Hardly make a difference. Right?"

"Right," he said, and seemed to perk up a little. "So, what is your advice? Should I ask her?"

Vera thought about the question for a minute and then said, "Let me give you a little background on Michelle first. I don't know her very well; I only have passing impressions from some family times together. And...stories. We lived in Boston, and they were in Maryland, so we didn't see her much."

She paused for a few seconds, and Avi said, "I'm listening."

"I know. And don't misunderstand me here. You can ask David or Irene later if you want. I'm not trying to be catty."

"Catty?"

"Er...bad gossip. Anyway, when Michelle was younger, she was really into herself if that makes sense. Came with being gorgeous."

"You mean proud?"

"That's it. And if she were still that way, I'd suggest this is not a good idea. I don't think she'd be a good wife for you. But that time in the bunker seems to have matured her a lot. She's not the same girl we knew back then."

"I understand. I knew girls like that back in Israel. And now that I have been with you people for three years, and I have seen how good a helper she is to Irene and the rest of us, I do not see the selfish nature you speak of. I think that is why I like her so much."

"And the fact that she's a real beauty doesn't figure in?"

Avi smiled and put his arm around her shoulder. "Of course it figures in. I am a male after all."

"Then, you don't know if you don't ask. So I'd say go ahead, talk to her."

"When would be a good time?" Avi said.

"Well, not now with Chris in the house. Say, weren't you going to go down to Maryland with her to see if she can find her family?"

"Yes."

"Perfect time. You'll be cooped up with her in the car for about a day. Just pick a romantic spot and pop the question."

"What?"

"Ask her to marry you."

"Ah. Yes, that might work." And as an afterthought, "I value your opinion. Would you be happy to have me in the family...whatever relations we would be?"

Vera thought over the family tree for a few seconds and said, "You'd actually be my nephew-in-law by marriage. That's a bit weird. But yes, I'd love to have you in the family."

"As you people would say, you have made my day."

CHAPTER 16

THE NEWS UPDATE

The threat of impending judgment had come to occupy their imaginations, and the busyness of surveying houses and damage cleanup was therapeutic. The township staff gleaned information from other districts in the area, trying to determine when utilities like electricity and water and natural gas would be restored. Apart from the equipment itself, destroyed in the bombardments and earthquakes, they could barely locate qualified personnel to work on the projects. When limited power was restored, it was localized, and the survivors had to content themselves with communal laundry and bathing facilities if they wanted hot water.

Without working markets, the township set up distribution centers for food, clothing, gasoline, bottled water and the like. Money was useless at this point, so survivors exercised self-discipline and took only what they needed. Not that there were severe shortages. With only ten percent of the population left, even their limited supply exceeded demand.

Radio transmission was the first to return, but not with sports or music or call-in shows. It was strictly news on one AM and one FM station, and it generated as many questions as it did answers. They could learn of road outages and power restoration areas and supply centers, but nothing of state or national news.

The most pertinent news they received came via the angels - Al and Matthew on their sporadic appearances. At lunch on the day after Avi and Vera's conversation they appeared to provide an update.

"We have a lot of questions," David said.

"We thought you might," Al replied. "We will explain what we can."

"We're getting some idea of what's going on locally, but what about our state government? And what about the federal government in Washington?" he said.

"There is no state or national government. They were all destroyed for cooperating with the Beast."

"Who's in charge, then?" Vera asked.

"We are and will be until you return from Israel. Then we will work with the survivors to establish a new national government. Remember that you are now under what you would call a monarchy, under the King in Israel. You are no longer a democracy or republic as you might think of it."

The group glanced at each other, considering that concept.

"And there will be no separation of church and state...as your leaders insisted upon in the past when they wanted to justify their ungodly behavior," Matthew added.

"Would that really work?" Russ Freeman said.

"Of course it will work," Al said. "It is an unfamiliar idea to you now, but we can assure you it will be the perfect government for your lives. Your generation will have the most difficulty adapting to it, but the generations that follow you will find it natural."

"And other peoples from different governments will face the same difficulty at first. You will not be the only ones," Matthew said.

The silence extended and finally Avi Sharon spoke up. "We can deal with that later. I think the most important questions now are about this judgment to come. Can you tell us any more about that?"

Al took the lead and said, "All we can say at this time is that the King has already started to judge Jews from nations that are physically closer to Israel. We do not think it will be much longer until the Jews in your area will be summoned. And after that, you gentiles as well."

"Do you have any idea how long now?" Avi said. "A few days? A week? A month"

Matthew and Al looked at each other, communicating silently. Then Matthew spoke and said, "We are uncertain, but our estimate would be in about a week. Does that help you? And then the gentiles a few weeks after that. The King desires that the Kingdom start as soon as possible."

Avi glanced at Vera, and she responded with a subtle head nod. If he was going to travel to Maryland with Michelle, there was now a deadline.

"Thanks. That gives us something to work with," Michael Cohen said, now more certain than ever that he must speak to Sylvie about emigrating to Israel. 'Mazel tov' he muttered.

"What?" Sylvie said.

"It's nothing. I thought I was going to sneeze."

"Are there any other questions," Al said.

"Ah...should we be going to church or something?" David said. "The subject hasn't come up."

Again, the angels conferred non-verbally and this time Matthew spoke. "This may be even more difficult to understand than the idea of a King. There is no more church."

"What do you mean?" Irene said.

"As we said before, the church left with the believers before the troubles started. Your daughter Katherine and your husband Dan and those who...disappeared...were the last church members."

"So, what's now?" Vera said.

"This will take more detailed explaining, and it will become clear very soon. You will continue to worship the King, who is God's Son here on earth, but you will be under the Law."

"Really? I thought if you believed in Jesus, and he saved you, there was no more law?" David said.

"No. That is not correct. Your Lord Jesus Christ satisfied the demands of the law for your salvation, but the law was not discontinued. It is eternal and is still God's most perfect government for you humans, but only under a benevolent ruler like your King."

"Does that mean that we will worship on the Sabbath like Michael and Avi?" David said.

"Yes, once the Kingdom starts. For the moment, we would suggest scripture reading in your group until you travel to Israel. The prophecies speak of the judgments and the Kingdom to come. You will know the future before it happens," Al said.

The group glanced at one another, seemingly unsure about this answer. "Okay," David said. "I guess we can do that. Anything else we should know?"

Al responded and said, "I believe you are working with the township surveys. Our...associates have spoken with your authorities as well."

"You mean other angels?" David said.

"Yes. We have instructed them to collect any gold, silver, and jewelry they find in their surveys, and be prepared to send them to Israel with the first wave of Jews who will be emigrating."

"Really? Isn't that people's property? Or the government's?" Russ Freeman said.

"Again, the King is the government now, and he has decreed that when his people return to Israel, they should bring along the wealth of the nations."

"That doesn't seem fair."

David looked at Russ and said, "It is fair. It's a prophecy. I'll explain it later."

Russ still looked puzzled, and just said, "Whatever. It's been a rough week."

"Matthew and I have other appointments, so if there are no further questions, we must go," Al said.

"I think we're good for the moment. It'll take a while to digest all this," David said.

With that the two angels evaporated before the assembled group, and Sylvia spoke for them all. "This will take some getting used to."

As the group began to look at whatever they could find for lunch, Vera pulled Avi aside and said, "Okay. It's now or never. You have to schedule this trip as soon as possible. Have you asked Michelle yet?"

"No. Tomorrow?"

"That would be my thought. You go ask her and I'll see if David can get you a good car."

She could see that Avi looked uneasy with the time pressure, which was odd considering his decisive actions during their periodic emergencies. But he did wander over to Michelle and while they huddled in the corner, she took David aside.

"I need a favor."

"Sure, babe. What do you want?"

"You know that Avi is going to drive down to DC with Michelle to check on her family, and it looks like he has to do it soon before he gets recalled to Israel. Probably tomorrow. So can you get him a really nice car for the trip...from your motor pool or whatever you call it?"

"Well, yeah, probably. What kind were you thinking about?"

"Oh, a Mercedes or a BMW, maybe. Something like that," she said.

"Wouldn't a Jeep or an SUV be better? You know what the roads are like."

"As usual you are my voice of reason, darling, but you'll have to trust me on this one. A Mercedes or a BMW would be better."

David studied her face. "You're up to something, aren't you?"

"I'm not at liberty to divulge the information quite yet. A Mercedes or a BMW, okay?"

"As you wish, my princess," David said with a mock bow.

"And none of the Jewish jokes. Remember, we're in charge now," she said, giving him a big hug.

CHAPTER 17

THE PILGRIMAGE

David managed a compromise: an all-wheel, low mileage BMW SUV that had survived the bombardments and earthquakes. It seemed to run well, and he topped up the fuel tank for the trip. Washington DC. It would normally be about 150 miles, but with backtracking David thought it could be more like 200 miles. The fuel range for the car was about 450 miles, so they should make it round trip, but to be safe he strapped a small can of gasoline onto the roof rack.

As Avi and Michelle made final plans, David took Vera aside and said, "You sure he'll be okay driving down there. He doesn't know the roads. We could maybe ask Chris to go along to navigate..."

"No," she cut him off. She tapped his arm. "They'll be fine. He made it from Israel, right?"

"I'm sensing an intrigue here," he said.

"All will become clear."

"Well, okay, but let me at least go over the maps with him."

"That's my hero," she said.

David gathered Avi and Michelle and spread out the road maps they had available on the kitchen bar. Using a green highlighter pen, he traced out the route from Philadelphia to College Park, Maryland, just north of Washington, following Interstate 95.

"Okay. This will be the most direct route. But my guess is that some of these river bridges will be out, like this big one over the Susquehanna River at Havre de Grace. And maybe overpasses collapsed on the highway. You'll have to hope for patrolmen like we've seen to give local advice. And look, there are parallel routes if you need them."

Avi nodded and glanced at Michelle. "You have driven these roads before?"

"Lots of times. We'll be okay I think," she said.

"And make notes on the map on the way down," David added. "You'll be doubling back the same way. You should be able to make it down and back today, but if you have to stay overnight somewhere, I'd say give us a call, but there's no way to do that. We'll just commit you into God's hand. He'll watch over you."

"He already has," Avi said. "I have an appointment back in Israel, so I know we will be safe."

"Right. Well, give me a hug, kid," David said to Michelle. "We can only hope for some news about your family. Irene would like to know about Abby, one way or the other. It's hard not knowing."

"I know Uncle Dave. We'll hope for the best."

"You like the car?" Avi said as they started out of the neighborhood.

"Pret-ty nice. How did you get this?"

"Your uncle has influence with the township people, I think. They did say to take whatever we needed if no one claimed it."

She smiled as she looked around the inside and stroked the dashboard and leather seats. "I could get used to something like this."

Local Philadelphia reports indicated that the Interstate 95 bridge over the Schuylkill River had collapsed, so they headed west on a circular route around the metro area and picked up Interstate 95 a few miles above Wilmington, Delaware. They approached their first checkpoint near the Maryland border and Avi drifted to a stop.

"Where are you heading?" the patrolman said?

"College Park, Maryland," Michelle said.

"Man. Long trip under these conditions."

"We expected that. What can you tell us about the roads?" Avi said.

"I can tell you that the big bridge at Havre de Grace is out, but you can get over the town bridge on the old Route 40. We've had a few overpasses collapse, but we've been able to bulldoze them away. And the road's a bit rough in spots but looks like you have big tires and four wheel drive. Should be okay."

"Thanks," Michelle said.

The man said, "No problem." His gaze lingered on Michelle, and as Avi put the car back in gear the man nodded toward her, gave a thumbs up and winked at him.

Michelle caught Avi's smile and said, "What's up?"

"Oh...nothing. Just a pleasant day."

The day was cloudless, warm enough for early April to crack the windows open for fresh air and so she bought the response. Then, armed with this new information, she directed them off onto a side road to pick up Route 40, and they headed south again. As usual, there was almost no traffic. The road surface crumbled in spots, slowing them to a crawl, but they made steady progress. Michelle gazed around, and Avi peeked at her from time to time, wondering about an opportune moment to propose. Probably on the way back north, once she found out about her family.

Houses and buildings had collapsed, cars were crushed, trees were toppled or broken off, but they didn't notice any dead bodies. The cleaning crews must have already been over this area. It was amazing that this surreal landscape had begun to seem normal, a testimony to human adaptability.

As they eased into Havre de Grace, they could see that the lower Route 40 bridge was still intact, and they could cross with ease. Off to the right, the center portion of the Interstate bridge was missing, and the harbor, normally full of boats, was almost empty. A few fishing vessels or other utility boats lay at anchor, but no pleasure boats were in sight.

They weren't talking much, just staring around, so finally Avi said, "So tell me again about your family. What are their names?"

"Oh. Yeah, I forgot you don't know them. My mom's name is Abby. She's Uncle David's sister. My dad is Michael. Uncle David's other sister, my Aunt Kathy, was taken away with her whole family before this all started. I guess that's what they called the rapture. And you've heard grandmom Irene mention her husband Dan and his brother Denny. They went, too. And Kathy's husband Steve. He owned the company that Russ and Kim worked for. So, except for the Cohens, everyone you've met is connected.

"I see. But your family stayed."

"Well yeah. My parents are progressive. They don't believe in this religious stuff. When that Beast guy came to power, they bought right in like I told you before."

"Ah, yes. You mentioned that. Up at the bunker. It must have been a difficult decision for you to leave your family like that."

Michelle didn't respond, so he said, "I am sorry. I think you told me that before as well, but with everything going in I forget the facts."

"That's okay. I don't mind telling you again. The decision was sort of made for me. Once I drove up to Philly, I couldn't get back, and then Uncle David took me up to the bunker."

The next checkpoint was just north of Baltimore where they found out that the harbor tunnels had been destroyed, but miraculously, the Key Bridge was intact so that they could avoid the long, counterclockwise route around the city. Once over the bridge, the road was good enough to reach Interstate 295 and the last twenty-five miles directly south toward College Park. As they drew close, Michelle folded the map and took over with visual directions.

"Right at the next interchange, then we'll go left in a mile or so on Route 1."

"Going home. You know it well?" Avi said.

"Yeah. Very well. But not like this. These buildings were crushed. All this debris. It's gonna take a lot of work to clean up this area."

"From what the angels said, this may not even be your capital area anymore," Avi said. "Would that bother you?"

"I don't think so," she said, still looking around. "Right on this next street. We're just a few blocks up."

"You do not care about the capital?"

"Oh. It's not that. I was never into politics. We were here because dad taught at the university. I don't feel any real connection. Friends, maybe, if any of them are still around. Slow down now, it's the next left."

Avi turned where Michelle pointed, and looked at a street with damaged houses, but not worse than many he'd seen.

"We're number 115, on the right ahead. The tan house with brown shutters."

He slowed to a stop at the curb and checked his watch. Four and a half hours. And the fuel gauge indicated a little over half a tank. So far so good.

Michelle slid down the window and stared at her house: a two-story colonial with a garage on the right end. The front yard looked like a meadow since the grass hadn't been cut in years, and maple saplings were growing around the lawn. The left side corner had been collapsed by a rock missile that still lay in the weeds next to the building, but otherwise it was intact. They saw no bodies lying around; either they had been cleaned up or they were still inside. Or hidden in the weeds. She scanned the street but didn't see any other human activity.

"Shall we go in?" Avi said.

"Yes. But I forgot my key."

"We can probably climb through that hole on the end."

"Oh. You're right. Forgot about that."

They climbed out of the car, stretched a bit, and finally Michelle said, "Let's do this," and they walked over to the front door. There was no need to worry about the key; the door was sprung open.

"Listen," she said. "Would you mind going in first and checking around the place? You know what I mean?"

"Bodies?"

"Yeah."

"Certainly. But even if I find any, they may not be your family. There are a lot of squatters. Who might I find?"

"Well, mom and dad, and I have two brothers – Mike is older than me, and Merlin is younger."

"About your height?"

"All of them are taller than me," she said.

"Give me a few minutes then. You want to scout around the outside?"

"Maybe. Let me think about it," glancing at the weeds for unpleasant surprises.

Avi pushed the door fully open and stepped into a foyer and living room that was littered with furniture debris and glass from both broken windows, picture frames and a chandelier that had crashed to the floor. He stooped down to pick up a family portrait: a lake scene with Michelle plus two adults and two boys. As she noted, they were all slightly taller than her.

There were no bodies in that room, so he continued along through all rooms on the first floor, each with varying amounts of destruction. There were garbage relics in the kitchen area, so either the family had failed to clean up or there were squatters around. That answer came on the second floor where he found two bodies in one of the bedrooms. One was a woman, much shorter than Michelle, and with her a child. Both had the red and black mark of the Beast and had been dead at least a year he would guess.

Judging by the pictures on the wall, this was one of the boy's rooms, so he just closed the door to seal off the scene and went back downstairs. When he stepped outside again, Michelle was speaking with an older man and a tattered track suit.

"Avi, this is Mr. Stone, one of our neighbors," she said.

"How do you do?" the man said, extending his hand. "Didn't think I'd find anyone from her family left. The others took off somewhere about two years ago. Never heard from them since. She filled me in on your bunker hideout up in Pennsylvania. Pretty clever. And you're from Israel?"

"That's right. Just a tourist in a way," Avi said, attempting some humor. "Picked an odd time to visit."

"I expect it was a lot worse back home," the man said. "We were in western Virginia. Just got back here ourselves. We never took that red and black mark, so we didn't want to hang around here any longer. We have a cabin in the hills."

"We?"

"Oh. My wife and I."

"I am glad that you survived."

"We are too, of course. But now we have this judgment thing. Know anything about that?"

"We get briefings every few days from angels of all things," Michelle said. "They don't really tell us much; only that it's coming and get ready to travel to Israel."

"Well, then I guess we'll see you there. Have a safe trip home now," he said as he ambled off through the weeds and on up the street.

"At least you know something," Avi said. "I was going to tell you that there are two bodies inside, but I could see neither one was from your family. They are in one of your brother's rooms upstairs, so I closed the door. You can check out the rest of the house now."

"Thanks." She took his arm and said, "Come with me and I'll give you the tour."

CHAPTER 18

THE PROPOSAL

Back inside the house, Michelle took the same route through the living and dining rooms and into the kitchen, staring around at the devastation and clutter from accumulated dust and debris, pictures and paintings toppled on the rugs, their China cabinet toppled over, and dishes broken on the table and floor. Her mom's silverware cases open and empty. Stolen? In the kitchen empty food cans and cartons, refrigerator door open, pots and pans piled up in the sink, dishwasher door broken off, cupboard doors open and nearly empty. Someone must have had a dog because there were scattered piles of feces on the floor along with empty food and water bowls.

She ran her fingers over the counter and looked at them with what looked like years of accumulated dust, idly rubbing them together to flick off the dirt.

"This must be very difficult for you," Avi said.

She reached out to take his arm again. "I'm stunned. I used to see pictures on TV after tornados or hurricanes or whatever. People wandering through ruined houses. I couldn't really relate to them. This is awful."

After another lingering scan of the kitchen, she took his arm again and said," Come upstairs with me."

There were fewer items to crash to the floor in the bedrooms, but there was enough clutter lying about to mimic the scene downstairs. When they reached the end of the second floor, there was a gaping hole in the ceiling and corner walls where the rock missile they saw outside had crashed through the roof. The end of the carpeting was mildewed. "This is my room. Or was anyway," she added, slowly shaking her head.

"Would your parents have left you any kind of note, telling you where they were going?" Avi said.

She looked up at him and shrugged. "Maybe. But where?"

"Did you have any special hiding place where you kept things. A place that only you would know about?"

She cleared some debris from her bed and sat down, patting the place next to her for him to sit. They settled in for a minute as she stared around the room. "I used to keep a diary and keep it in the bed table there, but I took it with me when I drove up to Philly."

Avi looked at the table and slid open the drawer. Empty. Then he took the drawer all the way out and flipped it over. Nothing. He stooped down to peer inside the drawer opening, then reached in and fumbled around for a few seconds and pulled out a business letter envelope that had been taped to the underside of the tabletop. He handed it to Michelle and said, "Is this something you put there?"

She shook her head 'no' and took the envelope from him. It was sealed, so she held it up to the light to see where the contents ended and ripped off the end. Avi sat back next to her as she read the handwritten note aloud:

Dearest Michelle,

If you find this letter you will be safe. Please know that we miss you very much and are confused that we have not heard from you. Things are bad here. We all took the mark. We thought things would be better, but it has not turned out that way. There are bad people in the town now – vandals. The government is vicious and corrupt. Now we have these voices and the bombardments. People with the mark are getting sick. We don't know what to think. It's no longer safe here, so we're going to our special family place, and if you find this in time you can join us. Again, we're together here, and we love you. Love, Mom.

Michelle dropped her hands into her lap, staring at the letter and then glancing idly around the room. As she absorbed the words her eyes slowly filled with tears, and she leaned into Avi and put her head onto his shoulder. As he reached around to hold her near, she began to cry silently, moaning with primal despair. She slowly slumped across his lap and wept for ten minutes, at times convulsing for breath. He stroked her back and shoulders, offering the touch of an empathetic soul until her misery ran to ground.

Once the grief had exhausted itself, she lay still for a few minutes and then sat up. "They're really gone," she said.

"I am so sorry," Avi said.

"I'll never see them again. Ever. Not even in Israel at this judgment thing."

Avi kept silent. She spoke the truth, but it would serve no purpose to reinforce her conclusion. "The letter mentions a special place where they went. Do you know where that is? And would you want to go there?" Avi said.

"I'm not sure where she means. We used to go to the family place in Maine, but that was more special for Uncle Dave and Aunt Kathy. She may mean the beach house in North Carolina. We didn't own it though. Maybe she thought they could just hide out there. Must have been desperate."

"Is that far away?"

"Yeah. It is. And we haven't seen anyone with that mark that is still alive. I think they are really gone, so that would probably be a useless trip...if they even made it."

Avi leaned over against her.

"So, what do I do now?" she said.

"There is nothing you can do. You will have to adjust to the idea that you are starting over in a new world. I am not a psychologist, but I think you will need time to deal with this sadness about your family, and with time the wounds will heal."

She glanced at the letter again without reading it, and then starred out through the whole in the wall.

"You have people who love you and will help you. You are not alone," he said.

"Am I supposed to do something with this house? Do I own it now?"

"Maybe you do own it. I would not know your laws. Unless you want to come back to live here, there is nothing to do. No one to sell it to. There is not even any money now. And after the judgment, who knows? No, I think you will just forget about it. Take some souvenirs maybe. Anything special for you?"

She smiled at him and gave him a soft punch on the arm. "I'm really glad you're here, guy. Don't know what I'd do without you. I feel exhausted. This is so confusing."

Was this the time to propose? Avi held off for the moment, thinking he'd choose a place on the way home. Let her take some time to calm down. He glanced at his watch. They had been there an hour now. He was concerned about unfamiliar roads and if they started back now, they could be home before dark.

"If you have seen enough, I think we should start back now," Avi said. "Take the note with you and give it to Irene. And look around to take any special items since you may never be back here. Perhaps something from each of your family members. Then leave a note on the door or somewhere telling the local authorities that you have been here and what happened to your family. They are probably doing a survey just like your Uncle David."

She stood up and said, "Right. Sounds like a plan. Can you write out the note?"

"Certainly," he said, and while Michelle wandered around the house collecting items in a plastic bag she salvaged. Avi found some notepaper in what looked like an office and wrote down the date and said that one of the family members had come back, but the other four were gone and probably missing. To be more specific he numbered the lines but forgot their names, letting Michelle fill them in. Then he added Irene's address in Pennsylvania where Michelle could be reached. That done, he found some duct tape to fasten it on the inside of the front door. Perfect.

In ten minutes, Michelle was finished, so he had her sign her own name on the bottom as a witness. "Your family name is Sandahl," he said. "I never heard it. Odd we only use first names now."

"That does seem curious now that I think about it. Shows we're comfortable with each other I guess."

"Before we get started again, I'm hungry now," she said. "Vera packed some food in this cooler. She's been oddly helpful about this trip. Did you notice that?"

"Er, yes. Vera has been quite helpful."

"So, what would you like? Looks like peanut butter and jelly sandwiches, food bars and water. And some apples."

She looked at Avi for a response. Like most foreigners, peanut butter and jelly was a strange combination, but he had accepted the taste. "One of each, I guess. That should give strength for the whole trip."

As Michelle dug items them out and unwrapped the sandwich for him, Avi started the engine and drove up to the end of her street to turn around so they could get a fuller picture of the neighborhood devastation. She gave a last look at her house on the way back down and then directed him out of the neighborhood and back to Route 295 heading north toward Baltimore.

The afternoon had warmed into the fifties, and he said, "Do you mind if I roll down the window?"

"No. I enjoy the cool air."

As they crossed the Key Bridge again around Baltimore and wound their way back to Route 40, Avi began to tense up. Their infrequent conversation was mechanical at best, and he was running out of time to broach the subject of marriage. He glanced at her from time to time, each time struck by her beauty and the sinking feeling that she might never consider marrying him.

A silent despair was welling up, so he tried his own advice: do not indulge your fears. As they approached the bridge at Havre de Grace, he slowed and turned onto a side street, and wound his way down to the harbor. With a flash prayer for wisdom and strength, he looked over at her and said, "Can we get out and stretch for a few minutes?"

"Sure."

Avi led the way out onto the remains of a pier for a good view of the water, waves sparkling in the afternoon sunlight. There was a strong breeze, and he was concerned for her comfort. "Is this too cold for you?" he said.

"No. I'm fine. Thanks."

They stared out into the open bay for a few minutes, savoring the open air. Back in the bunker, they despaired of ever seeing such sights again.

"I wanted to speak with you about something," he finally said. "And please forgive me if I seem awkward. This is very new for me."

She studied his face for a few seconds. "What is it?" she said.

He paused before continuing, and then said, "In a week maybe, I will be returning to Israel. I know I will make my home there. I was one of the chosen ones who were to be a witness and will help to rebuild our nation."

"Okay..." she said as he paused again.

"There is no graceful way to say this I think." He looked at her, took her hand and said, "Michelle, you are a beautiful and gentle woman, and I think you will have a special life ahead of you in God's Kingdom. And...I would like you to spend that life with me."

Michelle just stared at him for a few seconds. "Are you asking to marry me?"

"Yes. I am. Does that seem strange?"

"A little. Yes. I had no idea you were interested. I mean, why would you want to marry me? Won't there be plenty of women in Israel when you get back home?"

Avi smiled and said, "Yes, I suppose there will be. But why should I not propose to someone I know now, a beautiful and sensitive woman who has survived trials with me and will be an example to the next generations? That is not strange."

She didn't respond, instead looking out over the water.

"Is that a refusal?" Avi asked.

"What? No. Look, I had no idea you were even interested. I mean, you call me a woman and I'm still calling myself a girl. Woman sounds so mature, and I'm so confused about life and future and what's going to happen and these judgments and what happens after that and...I don't know that after that. You seem so serious and I'm a ditz half the time. It's a lot to take in."

"Do you trust me?" he said.

"Oh yeah. You and Uncle Dave have been our rocks. And you've always been there...like today."

He pulled her close and gave her a hug. She was slower to respond but finally held him as well. He spoke softly near her ear and said, "I can be there always. I am not asking you to say yes or no right now. I wanted to ask now since I do not know when I will be leaving, and then it would be more difficult."

"Okay," she muttered over his shoulder.

"Talk with your family when you get home. Ask their opinion."

"Aunt Vera by any chance?"

"Yes, she would be good."

"Did she put you up to this?"

He stepped back and looked at her. "No. No. This is my desire. I only spoke with her to ask her advice."

"Does that explain the BMW?" Michelle said, grinning at him.

"Would not hurt, as you people say."

She stepped back to look at him again, full on. "You are certainly a good-looking man and can really take care of a girl in a tough situation. And we are natural friends, I think. So, if you're okay waiting a bit, I really have to think about this."

"Of course."

"There is the age difference."

"Your aunt and I discussed that. About six years, I think. That means when I will be 700, you will only be 694."

Michelle covered her mouth and snickered. "I forgot about that part."

She opened her arms again and flicked her fingers to draw him in, giving him a big hug. "You certainly know how to perk up a girl's...a woman's day. But I think we should hit the road again."

CHAPTER 19

DEBRIEFING

Avi and Michelle arrived back at dusk but had to park in the neighbor's driveway. David and Russ had been working in the front yard with scythes to get their meadow down to a manageable height for the lawnmower. They saw the SUV pull in and David walked over to greet them.

"What's with all the cars?" Michelle asked. "We have visitors?"

"No. We're borrowing them from the township. Just about everyone has one now. How'd the car run?"

"Perfect," Avi said. "Very impressive, and I understand it was your wife's preference?"

"True. She wanted something nice for you two. So how did the trip go?"

"The travel was not bad, but there is not good news about Michelle's family," Avi said.

"Did you find them?" David said.

Michelle handed him the note they had found, and he slowly read it twice. Then he drew her close to embrace her and said, "I'm so sorry kiddo. We sort of expected this, and now we know. Do you want to tell Mom, or do you want me to do it?"

She wept softly as the memory resurfaced. "Give me a minute," she said, wiping her eyes. "I'll do it." And taking the note from David, she walked around to the back of the house to the kitchen door.

David looked at Avi and said, "What did her house look like, and how did she handle it down there?"

"Michelle is a strong young woman. She broke down for a moment, as anyone would do when she saw the devastation in her home and that note from her mother. She knows she will never see any of them again. And yet she is able to accept the fact. I think she is stronger than she feels she is. Do you agree?"

"Yeah, I think so. I've seen a big change in her these past few years. She used to be kind of a ditz...came with being gorgeous I think," David said.

"What does this word mean: ditz? She used that term about herself."

"Wow. She really has come along. It's a slang term...means a girl who is sort of silly and scatterbrained. Not serious about things. Says dumb things."

Avi considered this; it was not the Michelle that he had come to know. "Thank you. That helps me. Now I should go in and see the family," he said as he wandered off.

David cocked his head and stared at his retreating form, then went back to help Russ in their meadow.

When Avi walked in, everyone but the Cohens and Joshua was huddled around Michelle as she described their trip down to Maryland and what they had discovered. As she ended the story, Irene hugged her, and they both wept once again. It was a personal moment, so by silent consent the group dispersed into other rooms. Avi was left staring, so Vera slid up and took his arm. "This way," she said, and led him out to the patio again where they were alone.

"Where is Joshua?" Avi said, missing him in the kitchen.

"He finally has a friend. A girl his age in the next street. He's over at her house for dinner. Now, you have to tell me everything."

"You really are a Jewish mother," Avi smiled.

"Of course. And think with hundreds of years of practice what I'll be like. But don't change the subject."

"Alright. Well…I did ask her to marry me."

"And?"

"She was not expecting the question and needs time to think about it. And she knows that I spoke with you, so she may come to you to discuss this. Are you prepared for that?"

"Of course. I'm a Jewish mother. So, what do you think she'll decide?"

Avi shrugged his shoulders. "I stopped halfway home to ask her, and we hardly spoke after that. I do not know whether that is good or bad."

Vera thought for a moment. "I don't know either, but I thought about it all day, and the more I think about it, the more sense it makes. I know Chris up the street is around her age, but he's really just a boy, and I don't know if he's just lonely. And she would meet other men eventually. But you're here now, and you're special."

"Special?"

"You're rugged and brave and serious about the future. And no one would be more protective of her than you would. She knows that which is why she agreed to go with you alone all the way to Maryland."

"That is true. I would protect her."

"Did you hit it off as friends?"

Avi shook his head slightly. "I think so. We seem comfortable together."

"Did you tell her you love her?"

He looked puzzled. "No. Should I have? I guess that sounds strange to propose marriage without saying I love someone, but I cannot say that honestly just yet. I think that would take more time. We like each other, and I think we have common interests, but love? Not just yet."

"Man. This is really old country or something. But it's so crazy it might work. I heard Big Bird say that once."

"Who is Big Bird?"

"Never mind," Vera said, and noticed Michelle watching them through the patio door. "This could be a bit awkward. How about you take a walk around the yard. Go help the farmers out front or something."

Avi followed her gaze to the door and said, "Ah, yes. Good idea. And remember, you are *my* hero," he winked as he wandered off.

Rats. The pop song with that title would now running through her head for days as she turned to wave Michelle out onto the patio.

"I can guess what that was about," Michelle said.

"Really? What?" Vera said, breaking into a broad smile. "Come over here and we can clear a spot on Irene's bench." Vera swept off the debris with her hand and then wiped it on her slacks. "To think I used to be neater than this. Bunker living makes you more primitive.

"Anyway...yes, we were talking about you two. And let me say up front that I was as surprised as you were when Avi brought up the subject. He wanted my opinion about asking you to marry him. I'm not sure why me instead of, say, Irene or Kim." Vera thought a few seconds and said, "No. That's not true. I do make more sense. We're related and Irene has too much on her mind right now."

"I'm glad he asked you."

"Oh, and by the way, Russ and Kim got engaged. Must be the season. Spring and nest building or something."

"That makes sense. They seem to have known each other a long time," Michelle said. "What did you tell Avi?"

A crow swooped low over the patio, chased by two noisy robins. When the sound died away, Vera said, "I didn't know what to tell him then. I think we went over the downsides – the age difference, the trip to Israel, how a tall, blonde Nordic wife would stand out in an Israeli neighborhood since I don't think he wants to live back here."

"I gathered that."

"But on the other hand, no one would take better care and protect you, and you would really be in the center of the world if you live in Israel, if what these angels say is true. And you would be there from Day One: one of the original settlers. And over time, the age difference wouldn't matter at all."

"Do you think he loves me?"

"Actually, we were just talking about that. He doesn't love you yet in a romantic sense. But that's a good thing, I think. It means he's looking beyond the fact that you're a beautiful woman. Although…he did confess that didn't hurt," she added, smiling and stroking Michelle's hair out of her eyes.

"Do you like Avi?" Vera said.

"Oh yeah. We're actually pretty comfortable together. We made a good team driving down there today. He had me navigate. The guys I've dated before wouldn't trust me with a map."

"Do you find him attractive?"

"Sure. But I've thought of him more like a warrior or something. It's hard to see him as a husband and father."

"I think he adapts," Vera said. "He does what he needs to do when the occasion calls for it. It's maturity."

Michelle thought over the day, and how Avi held her and stroked her back when she broke down…what the occasion called for. He could have taken advantage of her in a vulnerable situation and played on her feelings, but he let her work through the emotions on her own. She was the stronger for it.

"Hon, none of us knows what's really going to happen in the next month," Vera said. "Even if we all go to Israel and make it through this judgment okay, we'd still be coming back to a very uncertain situation. We know we'll be living a very long time, and that we'll have a lot of work to do to rebuild our whole country."

"I got that part."

"There may be a lot of guys you'll meet in the future, and trust me, you'll get a lot of attention. And not all of it may be from good guys. And over against that you have a really great guy that you can build a future with. And not all Jewish kids have to be brunettes, you know," Vera said, smiling again.

Michelle stared at the ground, saying nothing. "I'm sorry, it's just been a long day and like, really confusing. And that sounds like a sales pitch."

"It is, but a sales pitch isn't a bad thing if the product is great. Just making sure the customer knows all the benefits."

"I know, and thanks for talking," Michelle said, drawing Vera in and giving her a hug. "I need some time to think about this. What you say makes sense upstairs, but I need my heart to catch up. It would be easier if Avi wasn't leaving so soon. As it is, I feel like I need to give him an answer in the next couple days."

Vera stroked her back. "It would be nice, but maybe not essential. It's hard to believe I'm saying this, but maybe you should pray for wisdom or something. You mind if I mention this to David?"

"No. I trust his judgment, too."

"Get some sleep. Oh, and we found some wine. Maybe that will mellow things out a bit. Ask Irene."

"Thanks," she said, and wandered back into the house.

CHAPTER 20

A CONFIRMATION

In a group bred for office careers and homemaking, the shift to subsistence living had gone rather smoothly. To a person found they found it exhilarating, welcoming the lunch and dinner times when they could share their daily experiences, weary but contented. True, there was still no electricity, and the early April nights were cold, but candles and camping lights and propane cook stoves were sufficient after years in the bunker.

They had drifted into useful routines. In the morning David went off by bicycle to help with the township surveys, and lately for a body disposal detail. It seemed best to use mass graves since no one could identify the corpses with certainty or had time to track down burial plots. They selected an open field and a man who knew how to operate a backhoe dug a pit where they dumped the bodies in and sprinkled them with lime before closing over the hole. With each burial the township manager led them in a short prayer.

One worker commented that this seemed a cold process, like a holocaust body dump. To this older helpers said, "It is, but it's happened before in Philadelphia. Washington Square looks nice now, but it was a mass grave for Revolutionary War vets and blacks and the 1793 yellow fever plague victims. Sometimes it's all you can do."

Russ had expanded his resume by learning to drive a garbage truck, and Kim joined their crew as they began the slow process of collecting years of accumulated trash and driving twenty miles to the regional landfill.

Michelle was now looking for something productive to do, and at Vera and Irene's suggestion she went along with Avi to help the Cohens clean up their place. Vera had confided with Irene about Avi's proposal, and they both thought it might help to settle her thoughts.

"Is this awkward for you?" Avi said as they walked the two blocks to the Cohen's house.

"A little. And please know that I'm still thinking. Be patient with me."

"Of course I will."

"I mean, it's a big decision to spend hundreds of years with someone you don't know terribly well in a whole new country."

"It would be an adventure," Avi said, thinking positively.

"All my family is back here."

"You can visit them. And they can come to Israel to visit. In fact, someone has to come to Israel every year for a special feast."

"Travel is expensive."

"Maybe not. We really do not know what travel will be like in the future. It may be very fast and simple."

They were approaching the Cohens' house, and Michael was waiting in the front yard to greet them. Avi put his arm around Michelle's shoulder and gave it a squeeze as they walked up. "Thank you for not saying no," he murmured.

"You two look happy," Michael said. "But listen. I think I may have convinced Sylvie to give this place up. If she does, we can forget the fix up work and come over and help Irene."

As Michael turned around to look at the house, Michelle squinted at Avi, looking for a hint about what he was talking about.

Michael turned back in time to see her expression and said, "Ah. Michelle. Sorry for the secret. Avi and I spoke the other day, and he suggested that maybe it was unnecessary to fix this place up again.

"Why?"

"Because we're Jews, and we'll be resettling in Israel. From what we understand it will be such a beautiful place that we won't want to come back here. I mean, I'm fine with the idea. We have no family here anymore. Sylvie loves this place now, but I think she won't care at all once we get there."

"Yeah. Okay. That makes sense," Michelle said.

"We're almost there," Michael said, holding his thumb and forefinger close together. I've almost convinced her, but still need that final push."

"How will you do that?"

"Are you here to help her today?" Michael said.

"Yes. Avi invited me along."

"Then maybe if you mention how nice it will be in Israel...you know, hear it from someone other than me...that might help."

Michelle squinted at Avi, but he spread his hands out and shook his head 'no'.

As she wandered inside, Michael looked at her and said, "A lovely girl, but what was that about?"

"A private conversation. Maybe I will tell you later."

Once inside, Michelle called out. "Silvia? It's Michelle. Where are you?"

"Upstairs. Come on up," Sylvia yelled.

They had obviously made some progress since there was no clutter on the floors that she could see from the front hallway. They still had no electricity, but an old manual sweeper stood against the hallway wall.

Michelle climbed the carpeted stairs, and at the top said, "Where from here?"

"To your left. End of the hall."

Michelle wandered down and found Sylvia washing the windows. She had stripped the sheets from a double bed, and they were piled on the floor. This was probably a guest room. Bright, cream-colored walls reflected the morning sun.

"What can I do?" Michelle said.

"These sheets are terrible now, so you can tear off some pieces and clean those other windows, handing her a spray bottle. They're easy. They fold in so you can get the outside."

For the next two hours they moved from room to room and ended by tossing the bedding materials down the stairs in a pile to be collected for the communal laundry. "I'm not sure what to do with the trash though," Sylvia said.

"Well, that's easy. We have our very own garbage insiders."

"What?"

"Russ and Kim are now driving a trash truck," Michelle said.

Sylvia stared at her. "I know, hard to believe, isn't it? We bunker folks stick together."

"Listen, dear," Sylvia said. "Let's sit for a few minutes. It's almost time for lunch anyway."

They wandered into the kitchen and sat on stools opposite each other at the kitchen bar. "All I have to offer is water and some iced tea. Without the ice."

"Water is fine."

Sylvia retrieved two bottles from a cupboard and handed one to Michelle. "You've been a big help, dear. Can I share something with you?"

"Sure."

"When we met you and your folks in the bunker, you were all very... welcoming. Of course, I knew Irene for years, but it was just socially. Not intimate living. And had my questions about you."

"Really? What kind of questions?"

"Oh, I guess whether you would be able to handle the bunker lifestyle. I was sure you probably had a pretty good social life, and to be cooped up with this mixed breed of people for a long time."

"So, how'd I do?" Michelle said.

"Amazingly well. Very adaptable. I have a daughter, but you're nothing like her. I couldn't imagine her in bunker living. She'd be more brash than your Aunt Vera."

"Do you want to adopt me?" Michelle said, smiling at her.

"Hmm. That's a thought. Do you eat much?"

"No one does these days."

"But in Israel, there should be plenty from what we hear," Sylvia said.

Michelle looked at the countertop for a few seconds and then said, "I hear you may move to Israel permanently."

"Did Michael tell you that?"

"No. Avi mentioned it. Seems like all the Jews will have that option. Sounds like Israel will be a booming place once all these judgments are over. Or *blooming* place may be a better word. Center of the world and all that. Would you like to do that?"

"To be honest, dear, I'm torn. I grew up here and this house is special to me. It would be hard to leave it."

"What makes it special?"

"Well, the kids grew up here. We have friends in the area." Sylvia said.

"Are they still around?"

Michelle realized at once that the question was painful. Sylvia dropped her head and stared at the countertop. With a faint voice she said, "No. None of them are."

"It sounds like it might be more painful to stay, then."

Sylvia looked up again. "You're right, dear. There would be a lot of sad memories. I guess it's just the thought of change. I like routine. Familiarity."

"And the decision you make lasts hundreds of years," Michelle said. "But you can make new routines in a wonderful new place."

"Yes," Sylvia said, taking a deep breath and letting out a slow exhale. "Better even than moving to Florida," she smiled.

They went silent for a few minutes. With the windows open they could hear the early spring birds and snatches of conversation between Avi and Michael.

Sylvia reached across and patted Michelle's hand. "Thank you, dear. That was a big help."

"Oh, window washing is easy."

"I didn't mean that. I mean you helped my make up my mind to move. Michael said the same thing. I guess I just needed a second opinion." Then looking around she said, "At least this place will be clean for the next family."

"I'm glad."

"What about you? What are you going to do?"

Michelle looked around to buy time. "I'm still undecided. I can stay with Grand mom Irene and help her out here...assuming we both pass the test. Or I suppose I could move to Israel."

"Really, dear. You would consider that?"

"I've had an offer."

"An offer? What kind of offer?"

"Can you keep a secret?" Michelle said.

"Probably not. But don't let that stop you. What do you mean?"

Michelle liked this lady. She was brash like her Aunt Vera.

"Avi asked me to marry him."

Sylvia covered her mouth, and then said, "If I were Irish, I'd say 'saints be praised'. So, what did you tell him?"

"I said I'd need to think about it."

"What's to think about? He'd be a great match for you."

"Great," she thought. Now I have two Jewish mothers.

"You two would have beautiful children. They might not look too Jewish mind you. But that could work, too."

"That was mentioned," Michelle said.

"And you would kind of stand out in a group of housewives."

"That was also mentioned."

"So do you have any prospects back here?"

"Not really. It's a blank page."

"So, isn't the answer sort of obvious?" Sylvia said.

"I'm like you. Change is hard. But, come to think about it, everything is changing these days. Nothing is steady. There's not much to change… except leaving this country to live somewhere else. I won't know anyone."

"You'll know us for a start. And Avi. And I'll guess that you will be pretty popular…a beautiful woman like you."

There was that word again: woman.

"What do you think of Avi?" Michelle asked.

"My God, I love Avi. He saved our lives. Where would we have been without him? And he's been so helpful even around here."

She'd heard that before as well.

"But he needs a good wife. Or helpmate would be a better word. If you're going to live for centuries, you want to spend it with someone you love and are comfortable with."

"Like you and Michael?"

"Well, we've had a forty-year head start. But like that."

"Avi didn't actually say he loves me."

"Emotions are overrated, dear. That comes with time. Michael and I said we loved each other before we got married, and I think it took twenty years to realize what that meant. You have to climb the mountain together, and when you get to the top you look back and say, 'You know what. We've been through a lot, and I really love this person.' I would guess the seeds of love are there, but it's maybe too early to express it in words. It has to germinate and grow."

"What a nice way to put it," Michelle said.

"I amaze myself sometimes. I get poetic like that. Do you like him?" Sylvia said.

"Very much. I'm actually very comfortable with him."

"So, is that a yes, then?" Sylvia said.

Michelle made her 'talk to the hand' gesture and said, "I'm like you. I just need a little more time to think about it."

"You know those angels are coming any day now to collect us Jews, including Avi. No pressure…"

"Thanks," Michelle said. "I'm aware of that. But you've been a big help…and a good friend. Keep me in your thoughts."

"We call them prayers these days. And it will be my pleasure. I'd love to have you as a neighbor."

CHAPTER 21

THE FIRST PARTING

A cold front passed through overnight, and the morning was grey with a light drizzle that formed droplets on the bare branches. The house was not much warmer than the outside air, and those preparing for work outside bundled up, knowing they would suffer the chill.

Before they could disburse for the day, the two angels, Al and Matthew, reappeared, knocking on the back door to avoid spooking their human wards as apparitions.

"Is this good or bad news?" Michael Cohen said when they entered the kitchen.

They all sensed this might be a momentous event and looked for clues from the angels.

"We cannot say whether it will be good or bad, only that events are moving along. We have arranged for an airplane to transport the Jews from this area to Israel."

"When will that be?" Avi said.

"Tomorrow evening."

"So, it's finally here," Michael Cohen said. He looked around at the group and said, "Our first parting."

"May it be a new beginning," Sylvia said.

They didn't appear to take notes, and Al asked again, "How many here will be traveling?"

"Three of us," Avi said. "The Cohens and myself. Vera is Jewish, but she will stay with her husband David and come later."

"Very well. We will arrange transportation and pick you up here tomorrow afternoon. Prepare for three o'clock your time."

"What should we bring?" Michael asked them.

"Mostly just clothing and any personal items you would like to remember your time here. Books. Toiletries. In all probability you will not be coming back."

The group stared at the floor. This news was inevitable but disquieting nonetheless now that the time had arrived.

"And David. I believe your township has been collecting jewelry and gold items," Matthew said.

"Yes. We have a trunk full by now."

"Very good. Would you transport that over here and we will take it with us tomorrow."

"Sure."

"Thank you," Al said. "I know this is a difficult time for all of you… to be parting with your friends when you have suffered much together. But with God's grace it will not be a permanent separation. It will be the beginning of a new world that really will last forever. You are all very special people. Please remember that."

"We'll try," David said, speaking for the group. "Thanks for your help and your encouragement."

"It is what we do, as you humans say," Matthew said as they turned and walked out the back door.

"Well. There it is. It's our moment to shine, Sylvie," Michael Cohen said, taking her hand. "If you folks will excuse us, we'll go and start packing up."

Avi looked at Michelle, and she nodded yes. "We'll go with you," he said.

"Don't you have to pack?" Michael said to Avi.

"I travel very light."

Once they left, David spoke to the rest of the group. "I don't know how you guys feel, but this sort of helps me. Lingering around here when we know that this judgment is coming makes me tense. Now we know what the announcement will be like. And since we could be coming back, we won't have to pack as many things. Just like a week's vacation, maybe. I guess the best thing now is just to go back to work. Take our mind off things."

"Works for me," Russ said. "Business is picking up."

Kim gave him a punch in the arm. "That's a terrible joke."

"Ouch. That hurts. You're getting muscles tossing those trash cans. You know, they used to have husband and wife, over-the-road truck drivers. We could be a husband-wife trash team."

"Ordinarily I'd say 'be serious', but these are weird times," she said.

Joshua's friend Angela from the next block had wandered over to their house and he went off with her into the den to play some board games. Once he left, Vera said, "How are you doing, Mom? We haven't had much time to talk."

"I'm okay I guess. It's all so confusing. I wish Dan were here. He used to sort these things out. But David's a lot like him now. He's matured a lot. And Avi's helped him. I think Avi has given him a new outlook on life. He can look beyond the troubles to the opportunities we'll all have in this new world or whatever."

"Yeah. Avi's been great. And you heard he proposed to Michelle?"

"Yes. David told me."

"What do you think?"

Irene slid her hand over a countertop as if looking for dust. "It was a shock, I tell you. Not that anything's wrong with Avi...or Michelle for that matter. I just don't see them together."

"What *do* you see?" Vera said.

"I guess I thought she would go through this judgment thing, and then come back here and settle in with us until she found some nice young man...maybe like Chris O'Neill...and settle down and have children and grandchildren. Anyway, I thought she would always be around."

"She has her own life."

"I know. And I'm probably being selfish to want my family around all the time. It was bad enough with my Dan and her aunt Katherine and her family disappearing like that. But at least I will probably see them again someday. But now we know Abby and her family are gone forever and we'll never see them. It's hard."

"I don't think it's selfish at all. It's natural."

Irene looked at Vera and said, "What about you and David? Will you move back to Boston?"

"No. I don't think so. We were only there for our jobs anyway, and who knows what sort of careers will be needed when we get back. Or *if* we get back."

"Let's be positive," Irene said, patting her hand.

"Right. And I know my folks in Connecticut are gone, so you and Michelle are our only family."

"And Michelle would be in Israel," Irene added.

"Could be. But on the bright side, we'd probably have a great place to stay at the center of the world. And the Cohens will be there as well. It will be like old times."

"You're probably right, but it's still hard."

"I know Mom, I know. But we're with you."

It was one of those peculiar days where time seemed condensed. For every ten minutes you checked your watch, an hour passed, and as the daylight dwindled toward dusk the group reassembled for dinner for the last time in America.

"Remember our picnic in the junk yard?" Michael Cohen said.

"Who could forget," Irene said. "Was it really less than a month ago? We're survivors."

"And pioneers," Avi said. "Our God has been very gracious to us all. May I propose a toast?"

"You may, kind sir," Vera said, raising a wine glass in honor of their last night together.

Avi continued. "We cannot know the future, and we cannot know what joys and trials it will bring. But we know each other, and we know our great King and Lord. May we prosper and honor him now and in the ages to come. So, to the King..."

"To the King," they echoed in unison, sipping their glasses.

"As we Jews have said for centuries, 'Next year in Jerusalem,'" Avi added.

The meal lasted well into the evening as the conversation and dreams and ideas burned long past the usual bedtime. Candles were lit and the kerosene heater was ignited against the chill of the April evening. Eventually, one by one, everyone slipped away, weary from the day's labor and the emotional stress of the impending departure.

Michelle and Avi lingered to the end, each knowing they needed to talk. "Come on out on the patio," Michelle said, taking Avi's arm.

Once out there they stared at the sky for a few minutes to allow their eyes to adjust to the darkness. The rain had blown past, and it was a crisp, clear night with an abundance of stars visible, unhindered by moonlight or any ambient streetlights in the neighborhood.

He slid an arm around her shoulder as they gazed, and she wrapped an arm around his waist. "Avi, I'm about done thinking about your offer. As Michael would say, I'm this close," she said, holding up a dimly lit thumb and forefinger, almost squeezed together.

"And?"

She took a deep breath. "This is hard for me..."

His heart began to sink.

"I would like to accept your proposal."

"Oh my God…" he said, and grabbed her in a bear hug, pressing her head to his shoulder. "I am the most fortunate man in America. Maybe on planet earth."

"I wouldn't go that far," she muttered in his ear. "I'm still something of a ditz. I'm a work in progress."

"Ah, I asked your uncle about that word. You are definitely not a ditz anymore. You are a beautiful and gracious young woman, and by God's grace please know that I will always love and protect you."

"I know you will. I've learned to trust you."

"And you will love Israel."

She was silent for a moment, and then said, "There is still this judgment thing. I have to go through that."

"I will put in a good word for you."

"You can to that?"

"No, actually…but in case God asks my opinion. But I think our Almighty God knows how happy I am at this moment. I trust him to keep us together. Always."

"Always," she mumbled. Then aloud, "I guess that really means something now. Not just the 'until death do us part' line from weddings. Oh, and by the way, who does weddings nowadays anyway? There are no ministers."

"I have no idea. I will have to ask."

Avi stepped back and held her shoulders at arms' length. "You know, I just learned your family name, and have never even kissed you. May I kiss the bride now, even though you are not really a bride yet?"

"Of course," she said.

He was still tentative, and drew her face close to hers for a few seconds kiss, then backed up, studying her face.

She smiled and said, "You can do better than that," and drew him close again. This time they lingered for a full minute, the exhilaration of caressing this beautiful woman overwhelming the sadness of years of longing and loneliness.

When they broke apart again, he said, "I would like to make this a habit."

"It sounds like we'll have a lot of years to practice."

He pulled her face forward again and kissed her forehead, then drew her in again for a long embrace. "This is overwhelming for me right now. If I could, I would bring you inside of me so that you would never leave. Does that sound too...odd?"

"I don't think so. We both have feelings...emotional...physical. I don't know if either of us knows how best to explain them. This is new for me, too. I mean, I've had boyfriends, but it's never been serious enough to think about spending a life together. It's probably like Sylvia said, we'll be climbing a mountain together."

'What?' Is this anything to do with Big Bird?" Avi said.

"Big Bird? No. Why?"

"Okay. Never mind." Held her tightly for a minute and then whispered in her ear, "For as much as I can say this right now...I love you."

She looked up and stroked his hair, studying his face in the dim starlight. "I love you, too, my hero. And I guess it's in God's hands from here."

With one lingering kiss, they walked back inside and went their separate ways to bed.

CHAPTER 22

THE DEPARTURE

David and Irene were first in the kitchen. It faced east so the morning sun could brighten up the dark wood paneling and rust-colored stone tiles as flooring.

"I don't even know what day or date it is anymore," David said. "The only calendar we have is five years old. Looks like no one printed new ones after the troubles started. I'm not even sure on the year anymore... or whether my watch is accurate for that matter."

"And it's not liked we need any more confusion, is it?" Irene said.

He tried their portable radio, and scanning the dial he picked up one news broadcast. It was on the FM dial, so it must be a local station.

"Wow. Listen to this," he said, turning up the volume.

A male voice said, *"Today is Tuesday, April 25. The time is 6:43 AM, Eastern Time Zone. The temperature in the Philadelphia area is currently 38 degrees Fahrenheit. We estimate that it will be a clear day with no rain showers predicted...*

The broadcast continued to provide information on road conditions, food and gasoline distribution points, and the latest status of the public utilities: electricity, telephone, Internet and so forth, and ending with a schedule of trips to Israel. When the news finished, they played classical music until the next broadcast when the news repeated.

David synchronized his watch with the radio time and then stepped from the kitchen to check Irene's thermometer-barometer-humidity gauge combination that was screwed to the wall in the mud room. He had set the pointer on the barometer last evening, and the pressure had moved up a few notches. Rising pressure meant good weather for the flight to Israel.

As he reentered the Cohens appeared, followed by Avi, Russ and Kim.

"Is Michelle up, too?" David said.

"I heard someone in the bathroom." Vera said. "Must be her. Joshua's still asleep."

Because the town had a water tower, they were able to sponge bathe, but to a person their souls longed for a hot shower at home instead of in the communal baths at the YMCA.

"Well. Michael. Sylvia. Avi. How are you folks feeling?" David said. "The big day...here at last."

"I'll tell you, David," Michael said. "We are petrified and excited. Isn't that right Sylvie?"

"I guess," she said. "I'm not so much an adventurer like you folks. I'm more home and family if you know what I mean. But I thank God that you good people have been our family for four years. We'd hardly ever spent much time around gentiles, you know. We were pretty clannish. I can look back and see that now."

"How about you, Avi?" Kim said.

He tried to stifle a smile. "It is a special day for me. I have come to love you people as my own family, but now I am going home. And I think most of you know by now that I had proposed marriage to Michelle. And last evening..." his words slowed for a second. "...she accepted my proposal. We will be married," he said, the smile bursting forth, bound no longer.

Vera walked to give him a big hug and whispered, "God bless you, from one hero to another."

The rest of the group was shaking his hand and hugging him when Michelle walked in, and the room froze and stared at her.

"What?" she said.

"Avi told us," Vera said, and was the first to hug her with the rest of the group lined up for the same. Irene held back to the last, but embracing her with less enthusiasm, not wanting to dampen the moment.

As the crowd buzzed, Kim edged over to Michelle and said, "Maybe we can have a double wedding,"

"It would have to be in Israel."

"Always thought a destination wedding would be nice," Kim said. "Let me check with 'the man'," added, giving Michelle a playful punch on the arm.

"Okay," David said. "Now that we're all here...except for Josh...let's decide what's happening today. We now have a radio signal and actually know what day it is – April 25. It's Tuesday. And the official time is now...7:23 AM. So, synchronize your watches."

As those with watches complied, David added, "I always wanted to say that. 'Synchronize your watches' that is."

"You did it well, sweetie," Vera said.

"You don't call a warrior 'sweetie'," David said, putting an arm around her shoulder. "Now, I have to go to the township building to collect that trunk full of jewelry. I'll let them know I can't be there are all day."

"I'll go with you David," Michael Cohen said. "May be some people there I know. I'd like to say good-bye. And we can pick up our trunks from the house if that's okay."

"Kim and I will try to get back from the landfill in time," Russ said. "No guarantees though, so we'll say our good-byes now just in case."

"Think they'd dock our pay if we left early?" Kim joked.

"It won't be good-bye to you two," Michael said. "We will see you in Israel."

"Avi?" David said.

Avi looked at Michelle, and said, "I would like to spend the day with my future bride if that is acceptable."

"I'd like that," Michelle said. "Unless you need us for something?"

"No. We're good,' Vera said. "Enjoy."

After the group ate and disbursed, Irene, Sylvia and Vera were left in the kitchen, puttering around with the dishes.

"You don't seem pleased with Michelle's decision, Irene," Sylvia said. Vera had been over this ground with her mother-in-law earlier, so she hung back from commenting.

"I'm trying to get used to it. I know, she's a grown woman now and can make her own decisions. It's her life. I just think she'd be happier coming back here to America and settling down with someone from here. Someone with a similar background."

"Christian, you mean?" Sylvia said.

"What? No? Well, maybe. We gentiles are clannish, too. It's all so confusing. My family is drifting away before my eyes. Soon no one will be left," Irene said.

"You have us, Mom" Vera said.

"And, Irene, think about Michael and me. We have no one. Our children and grandchildren are gone forever. We'll *never* see them again. At least you will get to see Michelle and her children and grandchildren."

"Yes, but they're so far away. If they want to get married, why can't they move back here?"

"Because Avi's a chosen one. He will help to rebuild God's nation. He and Michelle will be in the most beautiful place on earth."

"And besides, Mom," Vera added. "You don't know who you will meet and make friends with. If we live hundreds of years, you will meet a lot of new people. Do you think time is going to stop now, like nothing new will happen?"

"Vera's right, dear. You're acting like an old lady stuck in the past. You're actually a very young lady again, with a whole lot of future ahead of you. Think 'adventure'."

"Come on, Mom. Perk up. Don't be grumpy and ruin it for Michelle."

"What do you want to do?" Michelle asked Avi. "Are you all packed."

"All packed. One suitcase."

"I hate to tell you this, but you will be in for a big surprise with my packing." She felt his muscle and said, "You'll have to keep them in shape to lift my suitcases."

"Suitcases? Plural?" he said.

"Plural. A girl needs to look her best for her warrior," she said, slipping an arm around his waist.

He circled her shoulder and said, "Let's go for a long walk."

"Okay," she said. "But I don't know the neighborhood, so let's not get lost. Don't want you to miss the bus...or whatever."

They walked to the end of the driveway, turned left, and headed straight through the maze of damaged house, downed trees, front yards like fields, dangling power lines, and trash strewn about since Kim and Russ had not been able to get a trash truck down their streets yet. At least the bodies were gone.

"Do you exercise?" Avi said. "You look in good shape."

"Is that a compliment?"

"Yes...as well. But, no, really. It is an honest question."

"I used to jog when we were able to run in the open. And I used the treadmills and elliptical machines at the fitness club we belonged to. And at college. And I swim when I can."

"Where did you go to college? And what did you study? And did you graduate?" he said.

"I went to the University of Maryland where my dad taught. We got a tuition break. I was taking communications and had just graduated when the troubles started and I came up to Gran's. You know it from there. Barely got a career started."

"What did you want to do?" he said.

"Be a journalist or investigative reporter. Maybe on TV."

Avi thought for a moment and then said, "I think that, in the Kingdom, careers will be very different. We will work and serve the King, but some jobs will not be needed."

"Like what?" she said.

"I think we will not need military defense forces or policemen, or maybe even doctors."

"Really? Why?"

"Because the King will control nations so that they cannot go to war. And he will have help running the world. I think the Christians who left before the troubles started will help him."

"But they're dead."

"No. Not dead."

"You're right. I know they are alive with Jesus now. But how would they be able to help?"

"I cannot say for sure," Avi said. "I think they will be able to appear and disappear like these angels do. And they will probably help to enforce the laws."

"That sounds weird. 'Bam', they're here. And just like that they're gone. That will take some getting used to."

"Only for us because we've never seen it before. But our children will think it is normal."

She took some time to think that over. "You know, your favorite ditz is still adapting to the idea of being a wife and mother. Be kind to me."

"Forever," he said.

They had to step over a large tree that had fallen across the road. When she climbed up and over, he caught her in his arms as she landed, kissing her forehead, and was slow to release her so they could walk on.

She kept her arm around his waist and said, "So tell me about Israel. What's it like? Where will we live? Will the neighbors like me?"

"I think the neighbors will love you. They will have to fight envy, however."

"Flatterer. But how about the country itself? The pictures I've seem make it look all barren and rocky. And it's not very big, is it?"

"It was that way when I left, but I think it will be changed a lot by the time we get there."

"Like, how?"

"I think it will be flatter. The hills will be leveled out and it will be much larger. Maybe double or triple the size. There will be a lot of people coming there to live."

"Crowded?"

"Not at first. Eventually. And the prophecies tell us that the land will be amazingly beautiful. Plants will grow very quickly. And it will be peaceful. Nothing to fear from crazy Arab neighbors anymore. And no Beast and his people. The King will make sure we will live in peace, and we can sit and watch our children play in the streets. No one will steal from us."

"Sounds wonderful. Do you know where we will live?"

"Ah. Let me check your Bible knowledge. Am I right or left-handed?"

"I don't have much Bible knowledge. But you're left-handed."

"That is a trait from my tribe of Benjamin," Avi said.

"I don't get it."

"The prophecies say that the tribes will have assigned sections of land in the new Israel, as they did in the beginning. Remember I said it would be flatter. Benjamin will have a section of land just south of the new Temple area, which will be the place for the King and the Prince. It will sit on a mountain up above the rest of the land so it will be easy to see."

She squinted and said, "Tell me again. Who's the King? And who's this prince?"

"The King will be Jesus himself, God the Son. And the Prince will be a human ruler who administers things for him. We really don't know yet who he will be. Some think it will be King David coming back to life, but I don't think so. I think he will be someone like David, but not him."

134

"Is it important for me to know that now?" she said.

"No. I do not think so right now. In time we will learn."

"So let me get this straight. We will be right below this mountain where the Temple will be. Can we see it from our kitchen window?"

"Maybe," he said. "I can look for a house that faces that way. Then you and I can stand at the sink and do the dishes together and watch what the King's is doing."

"With the children."

"With the children, yes," Avi said. "Can you see me in the back yard pointing up the mountain to them, letting them know what the King is doing?"

"Oh, very much so. I think you'll be a great father."

His eyes misted over, and he glanced at her and said, "Is this what love it like?"

"Oh, I hope so, Avi. I'm scared and excited and I want to crawl inside you like you said last night. I only hope this judgment gets over with quickly. Do you think we'll be able to keep in touch when you're gone?"

"I cannot say. Maybe these angels will deliver messages if we ask nicely."

Michelle glanced at her watch. "We've been gone an hour. Do you remember how we got here?"

He looked back up the road they had just walked down. "I think so, but now that you are a good navigator, I will depend on you to make sure I am correct if I try to wander off the wrong way. Unlike your American men, I am not too proud to ask for directions."

"Ok, guy, then we'd better start back." They held hands this time, retracing their route quite easily, even to Avi's impromptu bear hug and kiss when she jumped back off the fallen tree.

"We're like a couple of teenagers," she said.

"Is that good or bad?" Avi said.

"Good at this point. I've never actually been in love."

He stayed silent for a minute and then said, "Are you really in love?"

She stopped and swung him around to look at him. "Yes. I really am, I think. I know it takes time for these things to settle in, but I really am."

He pulled her close again and embraced her tightly, swaying softly as if to some silent ballad. "I think so as well. How will I last for a month without you?"

"I guess…if we've waited this long to find each other, another month will fly by. Then we'll have a couple centuries to improve it."

"And to think just a few weeks ago all I could think about was surviving."

"We all were. We're just learning more about life."

"God did say we should 'go forth and multiply' and repopulate the earth," Avi said.

She pulled back and scanned him up and down, and then smiling said, "I've never been good at math, but I think I'm going to very much enjoy learning to multiply with you."

Avi mirrored her gaze and winked. "I will be truly inspired."

They held each other's gaze for a minute and then Michelle said, "Ahem. Before this gets out of hand, I think we should keep walking back."

"Ah. Yes."

"Question," she said. "I sort of have a nickname: 'ditz'. I need one for you."

"You are not a ditz."

"I'm not offended. It's endearing. And most of our neighbors will have no idea what it means. But what can I call you…our special name?"

"You call me 'guy' sometimes."

"Not personal enough," she said.

They each stared at their feet for a minute until she said, "Nothing comes to mind. Let me work on it, and I'll tell you in Israel."

CHAPTER 23

THE DEPARTURE – PART DEUX

"Check this out," Vera said, pointing toward the corner.

It was nearing noon, and David and Michael Cohen had returned with a panel van filled with the Cohens' luggage and the jewelry trunk. They were standing outside sizing up the load, wondering if it would fit in the bus or whatever showed up, when she spied Avi and Michelle wandering up the street, holding hands and laughing.

"My God," Michael said. "I am so happy for them both, but if you would have told me a year ago that Avi Sharon and would act like a love-struck teenager, I'd have said you're crazy. You have the wrong man. Don't get me wrong, Michelle's a lovely girl. Who wouldn't want to be seen with her? But Avi?"

"I didn't see it either, Michael," David said. "And I think this will be a shock for her when she gets to Israel. Will you and Sylvia look after her?"

"Of course. Of course. She's like family. We'll love her as our own."

"It will mean a lot to her," Vera said. "She's in a whirl now, but it will be tough for her in the beginning."

"We'll watch out for her. Don't you worry yourself. It's the least we can do…watch out for your family. To tell you the truth, we're more worried about Irene. She's got no one her age once we leave. Maybe you two can find a nice man for her."

"You want me to be a yenta for my mother-in-law?" Vera said.

"It's a crazy world now, Vera. We're all in this together. And if I understand these angels, *everyone* is Jewish now."

She shrugged and said, "Who knows? It worked with Avi and Michelle."

The couple had reached the van and dropped their hands to their sides.

"Don't stop on our account," Michael said. "We are excited for you two lovebirds."

Michelle blushed and said, "Are we that obvious already?"

"Sure are, and I just had a thought. The two of you come with me," Vera said, and walked them around to the back of the panel van. "David, would you open this jewelry trunk?"

"Why?" he said, following her over.

"Why? Here we have a special engagement and no rings. These dear people are going to Israel along with the jewelry, so let's see what we got to seal the deal."

"You never cease to amaze me," David said, pulling the trunk to the rear of the floor and opening the padlock with the key the township gave him. As they popped the lid up, there was no shortage of jewelry, but it was dumped into a jumble of rings, loose gems, necklaces, broaches, pins, gold and silver dishes and cups and even several tiaras.

"Well, kids, go for it," she said to the couple, gesturing toward the trunk.

Avi and Michelle looked at each other, smiled and started to sort. In about ten minutes Michelle had found a diamond ring that fit perfectly, and Avi found a gold band that suited his style. She slipped hers on and held her hand up to the light to catch the noon sun. "Beautiful, but looks expensive," she said.

"You deserve it," Michael said, standing behind to watch the search.

"I wonder if they found it on a dead person?" Michelle said.

Michael spoke up and said, "Both of you. Give me the rings a minute."

Michelle slid the ring off and handed it to him, and Avi did the same. "Listen to me," Michael said. "We are now children of the great King and are going to live in his land. We are the first generation in the new world. So, it doesn't matter where these rings came from. They represent the past, and that world is gone forever."

Avi and Michelle stared at him, holding hands again.

"I'm the elder in our little family for the moment," Michael continued. "Like our patriarchs of ancient times, I hereby bless these rings and offer them up in honor of the great King. And may you live long and prosper in your lives and have many children. And remember this day always," he said, and handed each the other's ring.

"Now, put them on your love's finger."

They hesitated for a moment, and then did as Michael bid them.

"And you may kiss the bride," Michael added.

"We're not there yet," Michelle said.

"Kiss him anyway. Don't be a fool," he said, smiling.

David closed the lid and locked the jewelry trunk as they all started back toward the house for their lunch break. He looked back, wondering about possible thieves, but trusted the angels to take care of that. There had been no problems since that first day, but they were never certain.

On the way in Vera confided, "The rings weren't a totally romantic idea, you know."

"What do you mean?" David said.

"I want people to see that ring on Michelle's finger."

"Oh. Yeah. She'll get a lot of attention as it is."

"It's a reminder for her. A serious commitment for the first time in her life."

There was nothing to do but wait, peeking at the wall clock every half hour, watching the time inch toward three o'clock. Vera used her digital camera to take several pictures of Avi and Michelle together on the patio, and then printed out several copies with their battery powered photo printer. She gave one each to Avi and Michelle and kept a copy for herself. "To keep your dreams alive while we wait," she said to them both.

By two-thirty they had run out of small talk, and Avi walked his two small suitcases out to the van. While out there, he heard a rumbling noise, and thinking it might be their transportation he was set to alert the folks inside. As it eased up the far corner and stopped, he could see it was a trash truck, and Russ and Kim parked it and walked down to the house.

"You're still here, I see," Kim said, so we haven't missed the bus or whatever. Where is everyone?"

"Inside. They are all getting...what is it you say...rammy?"

"That's it," Russ said.

David had drifted out to meet them, and checking his watch said, "We have a little time left, I think. Might as well give you guys the same opportunity."

"For what?" Russ said.

"Pick out your engagement rings," David said, leading them to the back of the panel van. With that he opened the chest again and said, "Take your pick."

"Wow. I've never seen this much jewelry," Kim said.

"You'll have to be quick," David said. "Once the bus shows up, we'll have to lock it up again."

Russ and Kim took their cue and dove into the pile of jewelry, and within five minutes had selected their rings. David had no sooner relocked the chest when another louder engine noise rose in the distance. In a minute a large bus eased around the corner and started down the street.

"This will be the airport bus for your friends," a voice spoke behind them.

They wheeled around to see the two angels once again. "Jesus," Kim said. "Don't do that. Give us a little warning."

"In the future we will try to so that," Matthew said, "but I must caution you about using your Lord's name as an exclamation."

"Sorry."

"We understand. You should practice with another suitable utterance."

Kim and Russ glanced at each other.

"Are the other travelers inside?" Al said.

"I will go get them," Avi said, and walked back to the house. The group had heard the engine noise, and the air brake whoosh as the bus stopped in front of the house. They could see that their three were not the first passengers. About a third of the seats were already occupied.

The driver stepped out and said, "How much luggage do you have?"

Avi led him to the back of the panel van, opened it and pointed to the contents.

"Okay, not all of this will fit underneath in the luggage compartment. That's why we have that truck back there," he said, pointing to a large box van that they just noticed was following the bus. "Which is the jewelry?"

Avi pointed to the trunk nearest the van door, unconsciously fingering his new engagement ring.

"Let's put on the bus, and the rest will go in the truck. I've got a couple more stops to make yet. Let me pull the bus forward and we'll get the truck up here."

While Kim loaded the jewelry trunk under the bus, David gave the driver the padlock key. "You're in charge of it now."

"Right." And looking at Kim he said, "You let a girl carry that heavy trunk?"

"Oh yeah. They're a team. That's their trash truck at the end of the street."

The driver shook his head and then re boarded the bus, easing it forward and they realized the fateful hour had finally come. When the box van pulled up, two men got out and took the rest of the luggage and loaded it into the truck.

"We got ten minutes," the driver said. "You folks want a moment?"

"Thank you very much Mr....?" Michael Cohen said.

"Williams. Frank Williams."

"Thank you, Mr. Williams. We'll be ready."

The group huddled for the last time, looking at each other, lost for words to encapsulate the four difficult years they had just survived. Whatever astounding future lay before them was masked by the magnitude of this moment. Unbidden, they formed a circle and held hands, and then David led them in a prayer for safety, for a successful judgment, ending in thanksgiving for the vibrant promise of an eternity together.

Once their collective 'Amen' sounded, they took turns hugging each other, weeping softly in the manner of old friends separating for an untimely journey. Avi and Michelle lingered to the end, and as he gave her one last kiss, his hand slid away from hers and he walked away and boarded the bus.

The group listened with trepidation as the driver startled the bus to life, put it in gear and slowly drifted down the street and turned the corner out of sight, its convoy truck in tow.

And then they were gone.

CHAPTER 24

HIATUS

Three weeks passed before their call finally came. This time the angels gave them two days' notice and, with the large number of people traveling, they would go by ship, sailing from the Port of Philadelphia, and that the travel time could be up to twenty days each way. That morning the radio announced it was May 18, so the trip would start on May 20th.

In the interim, since the Jews had left, they continued their adopted tasks. David's crew completed the survey of the township, officially reporting an actual survivor count of only eight percent of the original inhabitants to the best of their records.

Russ and Kim pressed on with their trash collections, and by now had cleaned up almost the entire township. It would be nice to come home to a clean neighborhood. Kim had lifted so many trash bins they winced when she made her playful arm punches.

"Her parents were believers and left before this all started," Russ confided with Irene. "If they could only see her now. On the bright side, she has learned a new utterance."

"Utterance?" Irene said.

"What you say when you're startled. Instead of taking the Lord's name in vain she now says 'rats.'"

"Well, I guess that's an improvement," Irene said, shaking her head. "I just don't understand young people these days."

By networking, Joshua had located three other children his age, in addition to his new friend Angela from the next street. And, he had adopted a stray dog of indeterminate parentage. He was medium sized, tan and shaggy, and very friendly. When they found him, he was scrawny and his fur was matted with mud and briars. It took several baths and a lot of combing and snipping to restore him to respectability.

Dog food was not a problem since it was in low demand. There was an issue of care for him while they would be away, and with some reluctance they conned the angels into feeding him."

"We do have other things to do, you know," Al said.

"It's just for a month," Joshua said. Who could resist a doleful child?

"What is his name?" Al said.

"Phoenix," Joshua said. "Mom says it's like he's back from the dead."

"I see," Al said, and evaporated.

The township had located some capable power line electricians plus some bucket trucks and was on their way to restoring the electrical, telephone and cable lines in the township. Where the poles had been knocked down, they used the nearest tree as a temporary substitute. Once the judgments were over, they would complete the restoration.

In the week before their trip, the electrical power was turned up in their neighborhood, and in celebration they took turns getting hot showers and doing laundry.

As the days lengthened toward June, David and Russ pitched in after supper to keep the grass mowed and fix up the house as much as they could with the materials available. During their infrequent rain storms they didn't notice any new leaks, so they felt the house would hold up in their absence and be a welcome sight on their return.

If they returned, that is. There was that nagging concern.

Apart from their own fate, they were anxious to hear from the Cohens and Avi Sharon. The angels were either not aware of their situation, or wouldn't say, and in the end, it was a message via the township authorities. Rather than broadcast personal news over the regional radio station, a message was sent privately to the township manager, and he passed the news on to David when he came into work.

At supper that evening, he gathered the group together and said, "Before we eat, I have good news. We've heard from Israel, and the Cohens and Avi have passed the judgment. We'll see them in Israel."

"Alright," Russ said. "High fives?"

"Not with Kim," Vera said. "I need my right hand."

"Stop it," Kim said, giving her a playful punch in the arm.

Vera winced and rolled her eyes at David.

"Let me say the blessing," David said, and gave God thanks for the safe acceptance of their friends, and for the food they were about to receive.

They spent the evening before their departure packing for the journey since this time the bus was to pick them up at nine o'clock the following morning. As David started to carry luggage downstairs, he popped his head into Michelle's room and noticed that she was traveling lighter than he would have expected for a permanent move to Israel.

"This all you have?" he said.

"Yeah."

"But you're moving. What about all your clothes in the closet?" he said, pointing to the open door. He knew she was not a light packer.

"If I stay, I can get new things I guess."

He squinted at her. "*If* you stay? Listen, kiddo, sit next to me." He took a seat on the side of her bed and beckoned her to sit next to him.

When she settled in, he put his arm around her and pressed her head into his shoulder, leaning his head in on top of hers so they were connected. "Listen. You're my favorite niece."

"I'm your only niece."

"Not exactly. Your Aunt Kathy's two girls are in paradise or wherever with Jesus. You're my favorite *mortal* niece."

She managed to chuckle.

"So, you're wavering about Avi and the move to Israel."

She didn't answer right away but lifted her left hand and stared at her engagement ring. When she finally spoke, it was almost a whisper. "It's like Avi and I had this three-day spring romance, and then he was gone. I'm really glad to hear the news from Israel, but it seems a long time ago now."

David sensed a wavering spirit, and that this was not the moment for a frontal assault. "Kiddo, I know it was quick, and that was sort of amazing to us as well. But you will settle down and marry someone in this new Kingdom, and I can't imagine anyone better than Avi for you. Not that there won't be other men - you'll get a lot of attention - but I think he's the perfect guy to love you and take care of you. Maybe picked out by God, himself."

"Uncle Dave, I think about that up here a lot," she said, pointing at her head. "It's down here, in my heart. I still have feelings, but I've been having doubts."

"Everyone has doubts when they take a big step," David said. "Vera and I did when we got married. And again, when we decided to move to Boston. It's like your feelings drag along behind your decisions and it takes a while for your heart to catch up. Trust me on this. We've been there. And then one day you look back and wonder why there was ever a problem."

Michelle didn't respond.

"I've seen Chris O'Neill hanging around. Are you thinking about him now?"

"What? No. He's just someone my age."

He took her shoulders in his hands and looked at her square on. "Kiddo, we've been through a lot together. You're a survivor and a pioneer along with the rest of us. You're a lot stronger than you think, and you will become a great woman in Israel."

She avoided his gaze.

"I know you probably can't imagine that right now, but we all have faith in you."

She looked at him and slumped back into his arms. He held her tight as she wept quietly, and then mumbled, "What should I do?"

"Take a step," he said. "Pack another suitcase. Act as if you're staying in Israel and take what you know you'll need."

"You want me to be brave," she said.

"You can do it. I'll take this one suitcase, and you can pack another one."

It was not quite true that *everyone* had faith. Irene shared Michelle's doubts and when she met David at the bottom of the stairs she said, "Are all the bags down?"

"This is Michelle's first one. She's still working on at least one more." He knew better than to feed Irene's doubts. Michelle had enough to deal with.

"I worry about her," Irene said. "I don't have a good feeling about this whole marriage thing and living in Israel. Ari's a nice man, but I just don't see them together."

David added Michelle's suitcase to the accumulating pile in the living room and said, "Come on outside with me, Mom. I need some fresh air."

They wound their way back through the kitchen and out onto the end of the driveway where they could get a good view of the house. It had been Irene's dream home: a half-timbered, Tudor- styled manor house with gables and a slate roof, including the walled-in secret garden and tennis court in the back, hidden away from the hum of the world. Before the troubles it had a canopy of majestic trees and was rimmed by tasteful hedges and flowers, maintained by a lawn and tree service. Her pride in the neighborhood.

"Not like the old days," Irene said, surveying the panorama of the house.

"No, but coming back," David said. "It's still a classy place. My home, too, back in the day. I have a lot of great memories growing up here. Look, the lawn's cut. Russ and Michelle helped me clean up all the branches and we trimmed the bushes a bit. We're not real good at that part. I never worked on a lawn crew."

"The girl is a good worker. She surprises me with that."

"She's had to mature a lot, Mom."

"I know."

They stared in silence, taking in the house and the yard and the collection of borrowed cars in the driveway, and then turned to look at the rest of the houses up and down the street. Except for the O'Neill's, all were uninhabited now.

"What will happen when we get back?" Irene said.

David shrugged. "I don't know, Mom. We'll be the only folks on the block. Did Vera speak with you about our plans?"

"A little."

"We have no reason to go back to Boston, so we'll stay in this area. We could either live with you if you want us here, or pick one of these other houses," he said, gesturing toward the house next door.

The neighboring house had a different design but carried the Tudor theme. "From what we've been discussing at the township, these will all be available after the judgments. The next generation will need places to live."

"The Katz's place. We were friends. I wish I knew if they were safe."

"We'll find out I suppose. Wherever they are, I think the angels would find them if they're still alive. Otherwise, I guess they're gone." He looked over the Katz's place and added, "Looks like a high end, fixer upper."

She smiled at the remark. Perhaps it came with age, but he and Vera felt that she lay awake at night thinking of things to worry about. It was good to see a little contentment.

"What about Russ and Kim?" she said.

"You know, I haven't asked them yet. They have no connections with their old homes anymore. They could go anywhere. They could pick one of these places," he said, gesturing around again. They seem kind of adventurous. Maybe they'd want to travel to some other part of the world."

"I could see that," Irene said.

"I can't see them in Israel, but Kim and Michelle are friends. You never know."

He put an arm around Irene's shoulder, and they took a lingering look at the house. It was still chilly for late May, and she was starting to shiver.

She slipped an arm around her son's waist and said, "You've been my source of strength. All this is so bizarre; I don't know what I'd have done without you. Or what any of us would have done without you."

"I appreciate you saying that Mom, but this was really a team effort. Everybody pitched in at the bunker. Before that, Vera and I were really materialistic. We should have listened to Dad when he told us about the troubles to come and we could have avoided all this. We've all had to grow up real quick."

"You know, I never paid much attention to Daniel's spiritual talks. Seemed too…extreme or something. It didn't fit my church's view of life."

"I wonder if your pastor made it," David said.

She looked at him. "This is sad to say, but he may not have. He always went on about helping the poor and social justice and stopping violence. I know that's all good, but it was all very social. He never once talked about how to make sure you're a believer. In fact, he was very condescending toward people who did that. 'Not our sort' type of attitude."

"Did he live in the township?"

"I believe so. His name is Reverend H. Thomas MacCloud. He used that pretentious first initial."

David thought a minute and said, "I saw the names of all the people still accounted for, and he wasn't on the list. Of course, he may have died in the bombardments, or may be hiding out somewhere else."

"Or perhaps he took the mark," she said. "What an awful thought."

CHAPTER 25

TO THE DOCKS

Sleep was fitful at best, and everyone was up and had gathered in the kitchen by seven o'clock in the morning. The weather was clear and slightly warmer than in the prior week. The morning radio listed the current temperature at 52 degrees, due to rise to 62 in the afternoon.

Russ, David, Kim, and Michelle lugged their baggage out to the end of the driveway and then went back to the kitchen for breakfast. "Our final meal here," Russ said.

"Try to be more upbeat," Kim chided him. "We're just going on a long cruise. We'll be back."

"I hope you're right. This has been dragging out for so long now. I just want to get it over with."

"We all do, dear," Irene said. "And I'm glad we're going through it together."

At eight forty-five, Al and Matthew made their entrance at the kitchen door and announced that the bus would be arriving shortly, and that they should assemble outside. "I should advise you that it will be cold out on the ocean, so be sure to bring warm coats."

"Thanks," David said. "We have them ready."

Before the angels could leave again, Joshua took Al's hand and led him out onto the patio where he showed him a rustic-looking doghouse that David and Russ had cobbled together from scrap wood. Phoenix could stay in there and wander into the yard to relieve himself. The dog food was stored in a trash can with a lid, and they had the water hose trickle into a bowl at the side of the patio near a drain.

"You seem to have thought of everything," Al said.

"He's my friend now. He depends on me. Take good care of him, will you?"

"Of course. Service is what we do."

Vera had followed them out and overhead the conversation. "I was expecting an eyeroll when you told Josh that," she said.

Al looked at her and said, "There is no sarcasm if that is what you mean. We really do exist to serve the saints," he said.

"Um. Sorry. Didn't mean to insult you."

"You cannot insult us. Now, I believe the bus is arriving."

As with the earlier departure, it was a convoy: three buses plus a large box truck trailing along for the luggage. They all pitched in to carry their bags to the back of the truck where two men inside loaded the items toward the front of the container area.

"We have about ten more stops," one of the men said. "No idea how much space we'll need."

The angels spoke with the driver of the first bus and then Al waved the group forward to board. They were not the first. Several of the front rows were already occupied with a mixture of families, couples and two single travelers, including two of the young men who had been with the warlords on their first day home. Both avoided David's stare, and he was not tempted to say anything. God would take care of any consequences from now on. Everyone had the generally bewildered look, and they nodded to each other as they passed by down the aisle to find seats. Michelle sat with Chris O'Neill, and Vera checked to make sure she was wearing the engagement ring. Once they finally settled in, Al spoke to the driver and then stepped off the bus. As the driver started the engine and the bus eased forward, they all looked back at the house, wondering when and if they would see it again.

The process was repeated at nine more stops throughout the township as the convoy picked up more people. At each one Al and Matthew would reappear and give instructions to the driver. In the manner of angels, they were traveling by other means.

When the last set of passengers was collected, Matthew boarded their bus and announced that there would be no more stops until they reached their ship at the docks in Philadelphia. They could relax for the rest of this journey, but he warned them that, if they were familiar with Philadelphia, they would see much destruction along the way.

The driver led the convoy down Broad Street, the main north-south route through the city. He spoke over the loudspeaker periodically, letting them know their progress. "If you know Philly," he said, "there are a couple ways you can get to the docks. Most of them are blocked by collapsed buildings. We'll go down Broad to Market Street and then take Market east to the river. It's a wider road and it's been cleared off."

Someone asked him if he was a regular bus driver, and he said he was a school teacher. "We do what we have to do these days. I'll be on a later ship."

The route down Broad Street passed Temple University and some hospitals, a route that bordered bad neighborhoods before the troubles. Gangs, drugs, shootings; those crimes seemed inconsequential at the moment. They remembered what the angels did to the warlords and wondered if local thugs met the same fate.

City Hall stands at the intersection of Broad and Market Streets, a magnificent old multi-story structure that takes up an entire block, including a courtyard, and topped by a statue of William Penn. Off to the west along Market Street there had been a series of modern glass and steel skyscrapers, conflicting in style with the historical buildings. As they peered out the windows, a series of groans murmured from the passengers. The buildings were all gone; it was a devastated skyline. Even City Hall had not escaped. The traffic pattern was to circle City Hall counterclockwise, which gave them a full view of the destruction. The entire dome on which Penn's statue was mounted had been blasted off, and there were gaping holes in the rest of the building.

Once they snaked around City Hall, they headed east on Market Street. On crossing Sixth Street they could see Independence Hall on the right, a block away. Ironically, it was still standing, seemingly intact, perhaps a sign of brighter days to come. Those who had driven in Philadelphia commented on how quickly the time went with no traffic and no traffic signals. But with the saying came the awful realization of the reason for this ease of travel.

The convoy reached the Delaware River at the foot of Market Street, and they turned right onto Columbus Boulevard and drove south for ten blocks to approach the pier where their ship was docked. David checked his watch: eleven o'clock.

For the first time today, there was traffic congestion. They were obviously not the only convoy travelling; a line of buses waited in queue to drive up to the pier. The driver came on the loudspeaker to let them know they could be in line for several hours before they were close enough to exit the buses and grab their luggage to board the ship.

"In case you didn't notice," he said. "There are no restrooms on this bus. If you need one, you'll see a line of porta-potties off to your left. Feel free to use them now. We'll still be here when you get back."

A smattering of people took up the offer immediately, and gradually everyone took this opportunity. When David went, he met the two young thugs walking back toward the bus.

"Look, mister, we're sorry for what happened back there at your house. We really didn't know what we were getting into," one of them said.

David paused to look at them. "Well, what's done is done. It's between you and God now. You answer to Him, not to me. I hope you're made your peace with him," he said, and walked on.

In the end it was almost one o'clock before their turn came at the pier and they could finally leave the bus and offload their luggage. They had not known what to expect, but to their delight it was a large cruise ship that had been pressed into this service.

There were large carts available, so they piled their luggage on one of them and wheeled them up to the loading area. A woman stood next to the loading conveyer with a manifest and checked off their names.

"I count seven. Traveling as a group?"

"Yes," David said.

She wrote something on a yellow tag and attached it to the luggage cart, tearing off a duplicate section and handing it to David. "Take anything you might need for the afternoon. We plan to sail at six o'clock this evening. Someone will meet you at the top of the passenger ramp for room assignments and other information."

"Thank you," Irene said, and the group started up the ramp. At the top another woman had a clipboard with a copy of the manifest and listing of room assignments. There had been a lot of busses, but the clipboard woman said the ship would only be about two-thirds full since they needed to transport people to Israel on a priority basis. Economic considerations were not important. She finished by taking a meal preference: first or second seating. They opted for first.

Perhaps it was Al and Matthew's intervention because they were all housed close to each other. Michelle and Kim shared a double room, Vera and David and Joshua another, leaving Russ and Irene in individual, smaller rooms. In a half an hour, a man showed up and knocked on David's door, letting him know the luggage was now on deck. "If this was the real thing," he said, "we'd bring it to your room. But we're doing what we can with what we got. You'll have to go and collect your own bags from here," giving him a map of the ship and pointing to the area where the luggage was sitting.

"Thanks," David said, and knocked on the other doors to alert everyone and they went off to collect their belongings. They found the bags in a separate pile in the storage area. David showed a young man his half of the claim check and the man said, "Okay. Be my guest."

"Thanks again. Do you know anything about the schedule? Eating and all that?"

"The captain will make an announcement around four o'clock. You can see the dining area here," he said, pointing it out on the map.

By three o'clock they were unpacked and settled in and reassembled back on deck to scout the layout of the ship and await the captain's announcement. Irene had been the only one in their group to travel by cruise before.

"Does this look familiar, Mom?" David said.

"Somewhat. There is usually a lot more help, and they depend on tips. I doubt we'll see that here. These seem to be people with other careers pressed into service."

They watched the loading process for a while, a steady stream of buses and trucks pulling up along Columbus Boulevard near the bow of the ship. After climbing to a deck where they could make one complete circle of the ship, they returned to the bow and noticed that the flow of buses had dwindled to a trickle of travelers, and soon there were none. Everyone was on board, and it was now four-fifteen.

At four-thirty the captain came on the loudspeaker system and announced that they were on schedule to set sail at six o'clock, and that their estimated travel time to Ashdod in Israel was fifteen days.

"What are we going to do for fifteen days?" Vera said.

David shrugged and said, "It's gotta be easier than four years in the bunker."

The captain continued, noting that the crew was mostly inexperienced (so be patient), that each passenger needed to take care of his or her own rooms (there was no steward service), and that all meals would be served buffet style. And there was no need for tipping if that was your custom.

They all looked at Irene and she nodded in assent.

He finished by saying there would be meetings daily and as needed in the theater area, and that the first dinner seating would be at five-thirty that evening.

"Meetings about what?" Vera said.

"No idea. Guess we'll soon find out," David said.

CHAPTER 26

UNDERWAY

The ship's horn blew at six o'clock while they were eating dinner, and the skyline view began to inch away as the ship backed slowly out into the middle of the Delaware River. David and Russ walked to the window, peering out in time to see the pier shrink as they slid away. There were no friends and relatives waving from the dock. Only a few workers remained; everyone else was on board.

By six thirty the ship had started forward, and the group walked out to the starboard railing to watch the Philadelphia skyline slip by. Or what was left of it. In addition to the skyscraper devastation, the gentrified brick row homes and trendy condominium towers in the Society Hill section along the riverfront had been leveled. Further along, they saw ships partially submerged at their docks, and even some in the river so that their ship had to make evasive turns.

The bridge near the sports complex at the south end of the city had been destroyed, with the two prominent sports stadiums as well. The old Navy Yard area beyond was intact with most of its World War II mothballed ships still in dry dock. Where the city's Schuylkill River merged with the Delaware, the high Interstate 95 bridge over the Schuylkill was demolished, but the international airport further on seemed to be serviceable.

"The Cohens and Avi had to get over the Schuylkill to get to the airport," David said. "Wonder how they did it?"

"Had to use of the smaller iron bridges up stream, I guess." Russ said.

The ship gained speed since there was no other traffic on the river. They had an hour until dusk and stood transfixed as they passed the Chester waterfront and the oil refineries beyond, significant destruction everywhere. There were no lights along the shore, so before they had reached Wilmington, Delaware, it became too dark to see detail.

The night chill was settling in, so by common consent they walked back to their rooms for the evening. Russ took a last look around and said, "Man, I hope he has radar and good charts. I don't even see marker buoys."

"I guess this is where we say we're in God's hands," Kim said. "If he wants us in Israel, he'll have to get us there safely."

Russ put his arm around her and smiled. "Wow. You *have* come a long way."

Each faced a first night onboard with a silent concern that some of their group might never see America again if they did not pass this judgment. To keep a spiritual focus and hope for the future, David suggested they meet for prayer each evening before bedtime, taking turns leading the session. No one objected. The magnitude of the journey swelled as they sailed inexorably toward their fate in Israel.

David kept it simple. "Father...we've had a stressful day. Stressful weeks, really. But you have saved us and preserved us through four years of these troubles. Now keep us safe as we travel to Israel where our fate is in your hands. We're tired and anxious and we need your help. Teach us to trust in you during this time. Thank you...in Jesus's name."

"Amen," they added in unison.

After dispersing to their rooms, they read or chatted or just fell asleep, the weariness of the past twenty-four hours overwhelming them.

Sunrise was at six in the next morning. David was first one up and he slipped out on deck to check on progress. They were out of sight of land now, heading east from Delaware Bay toward Gibraltar and the entrance to the Mediterranean Sea. There was no local radio to give time and temperature, but a steward who stopped by thought it was about thirty-eight degrees. Just the sound of that temperature prompted him to zip up his jacket further and bundle his arms together as he leaned on the railing, staring at the morning sun.

The steward handed him a daily schedule and said, "If you didn't get one of these already, it lets you know what activities are available on the ship."

"Thanks," David said, scanning the bullet points. "It says you have a fitness area."

"Right. Two decks below. Universal units for muscle strength plus aerobic machines – treadmills, ellipticals, bicycles…the usual stuff. And an indoor walking track."

"Great. And it mentions daily talks in the theater area. What are they?"

"I believe it will be more information about what happens in Israel."

"Who does the talking?" David said.

"I think these angels do the talking."

"Are there a lot of them on board?"

The steward paused before answering. "There seems to be a lot of them around, but it's hard to say they're on board. They just appear and disappear. I figure they must go off into some other dimension somewhere, and then they appear when they need to do something."

"Right. I know what you mean. Scares the heck out of you sometimes. My name's David, by the way."

"Tim," the steward said, and they shook hands before he moved on to other passengers.

Everyone was up and about by seven-thirty, so they were able to make the eight o'clock, first breakfast seating. They occupied a large, round table that could accommodate ten people. Eventually their neighbors the O'Neill's would join them, but for that morning they were by themselves, and David reviewed the facilities listing plus the schedule the steward had given him.

"We have fifteen days, so there is really nothing planned out except these mealtimes and maybe the talks at three o'clock," David said.

"Does that mean we just do our own thing in between?" Kim said.

"That's my thought."

"Any idea what these talks are about?" she said.

"Only that the angels will give them, so it sounds like it would be good to attend."

After a morning of exploring the decks, the fitness rooms and the theater area, the group sat for the early lunch and assembled at the theater for the three o'clock talk. The auditorium was large, quarter-round layout with stadium style seating. They wondered if could hold all the passengers, even if the ship wasn't full.

A loudspeaker system played soothing old Christian hymns as background music while they waited. Most of the seats were taken by two-forty-five, and then the music stopped and two men appeared from the wings right on schedule. Neither man was Al or Matthew, at least in the human form that they knew them. The men didn't seem to be wearing microphones, and their voices did not come through the speaker system, and yet everyone could hear them.

"It is good that you have chosen to attend this session," one of the men began. "As you may have understood, my partner and I are both angels and have been sent to accompany this particular ship on its journey to Israel. There are other angels with us as well, but we will be the only speakers at these meetings. You may call me Aaron, and my partner here can be called Nicholas."

"Not Moses?" a voice said behind them. David turned to see a husky, red-faced man with his arms crossed, smirking, and slowly shaking his head from side to side.

"Not Moses," the angel named Nicolas said.

David turned again and the man waved his hand toward the angel.

Nicholas continued, "As your captain stated yesterday, this ship will arrive in Ashdod in Israel in approximately fifteen days. Once docked, you will be taken off and transported to your gathering before the King."

"By King, do you mean Jesus?" a man asked.

"Yes."

"Will we have to wait long once we're there?" another man asked.

"No," Nicholas said. "It will likely be immediately. The King has many people to judge, and they come from all over the earth. He desires the process to be completed as soon as possible so that his Kingdom can begin."

"Should we be doing anything special now?" a woman said.

"You should spend time contemplating what you are about to experience and prepare your mind and heart to come before the King," Aaron said.

"Yeah, right," the grouch said behind them.

David and Vera glanced at each other but didn't turn around. They had a premonition that the man would not pass the judgment, and wondered why he had no concern for his spiritual fate.

"This is a movie theatre here, right?" a young man asked.

"Yes."

"Will there be movies?"

"No," Aaron said.

The blunt demeanor of the angels seemed to stifle any further questions, so Nicholas closed by saying, "This is not a pleasure cruise; it is a journey that will determine your eternal fate. We suggest that you consider that fact and use your time wisely."

"We will meet again each day at this time," Aaron added, and they walked off the stage. On their exit, the music began again.

CHAPTER 27

DAY FOUR

A steady wind with rain squalls had confined the passengers mostly indoors for several days. Passengers milled about the common areas, and even the three o'clock talks had a high attendance. In their group Kim and Russ seemed most affected since they had relished the great outdoors on their trash routes. With the outdoor decks inaccessible, they haunted the fitness room and indoor walking track, dragging the rest of the group in with them for company at times. Even Irene took up walking to pass the time.

At dawn on day four the sun finally emerged and the wind swept the decks dry enough to venture outside to take the air. Irene made one circuit of the deck with Vera and then took her book and settled into a deck chair against a wall as a wind break, content to enjoy the relaxing motion of the ship.

She alternately read and stared out to sea for half an hour when a man about her age approached and asked if he might take the seat next to her. She looked around and saw there were other seats available but saw no reason to refuse him. It's difficult to judge height while sitting, but he seemed to be about David's height, thin with a full head of grey hair and matching beard. He was casually dressed in jeans and deck shoes and a fleece-lined blue denim jacket over a cream-colored wool turtleneck sweater. He seemed...unthreatening.

"My name's Walter...Walter Petersen," he said as he settled into the chair next to her. He retrieved a paperback novel from one jacket pocket, and then a pair of silver-rimmed eyeglasses from another.

"Irene Owens," she said, nodding slightly.

"I believe true confession is the order of the day," he said. "This isn't a random visit. I've seen you at various parts of the ship with a group of younger people and a small boy."

"My family and some friends," she said. "Are you one of the angels?"

He looked startled. "Goodness no. Pure mortal."

"Well, you said you were watching, and that's what they do."

"Ah. I see. True. However, watching for a different reason."

"Which is?" she said.

"I guess to see if I could strike up a friendship. I'm traveling on my own, and everyone seems so preoccupied with this judgment process to come. After a while you just want to sit down and talk with someone, especially an attractive lady."

She slipped in a bookmark, closed her book, and placed it on her lap. "Thank you for the compliment, but aren't you preoccupied with the judgment?" she said.

"Yes and no. It's inevitable and sounds...overwhelming if you know what I mean. But in the end, my fate is in God's hands. There's nothing I can do about it now."

"Have you been going to the talks in the afternoon?"

"Yes, I have. I sit in the front row. When you sit back further others make comments or movements and it's distracting."

"I know. We've been sitting around some hecklers, which seems amazing under the circumstances," she said.

"Exactly. If your eternal fate is on the line, you would think they would pay more attention."

They fell silent for a minute, both staring out to sea. Several pods of walkers and joggers passed by, enjoying the early sun and the breeze.

"Do you mind if I call you Irene?" he said.

"No, why?"

"It struck me that I've been awfully forward, barging into your space like this. I don't usually act that way. Then again, I don't usually travel to Israel for an audience before the King of the universe either."

She thought for a moment and then said, "He *is* the King of the universe, isn't he?"

"And we get to see him."

Irene studied his face as he looked out to sea again, and then stared at one of the power walkers who sped by with a peculiar gait. Walter was pleasant looking. Comfortable, like one of the average men she used to see in television commercials.

As he broke out of his vacant stare and started to look her way again, she said, "Where did you come from in the Philly area, and how did you survive the troubles?"

"Ah. That. Actually, I am not from Philadelphia. I was in the Reading area, and this is the ship that a number folks from our area were assigned to. Some had gone on an earlier ship."

"Did you stay in Reading?"

"No. I was northwest of there at a cabin up in the mountains. It started out with two of us."

"Your wife?"

"No. I'm a widow. This was with a buddy...Fred. We hunted and fished together, and we had recently bought the cabin."

"And your friend isn't here on the ship?"

"No. Fred was killed in one of those bombardments."

His gaze dropped toward the deck, and he remained silent for half a minute. "That was hard. Fred and I had been friends for almost fifty years."

"I'm sorry. That sounds awful." She waited a moment and then said, "How about the rest of your family?"

"That's another sad tale. I have two daughters, and they and their families all took that damnable mark on them in order to get along with this Beast fellow. I warned them not to, but they wouldn't listen. They kept pressuring me to join them, and even had some block organizers talk to me to try to enlist me. I started to get nervous around all of them. It just didn't feel right. It was creepy in fact."

"So, you told them you were leaving?" she said.

"I didn't tell them anything. I got together with Fred, and we just disappeared. We left no trail."

"They didn't know where the cabin was?"

"No. Fred and I hadn't owned it very long, and none of them had ever been there. It was going to be a retirement getaway place. And, really, they had no idea where I went."

"So how did you become a believer, then?"

Walter collected his thoughts and then said, "I mentioned we started out just the two of us. On the way to the cabin, we picked him up a hitchhiker, and it turned out he was a Jewish kid, right from Israel."

"This sounds familiar," she said.

"What do you mean?"

"Finish your story, and then I'll tell you about our experience."

Walter looked at her for a few seconds and then said, "Well, Eben... that was his name...told us he was a witness sent from Israel to tell people about this kingdom that was coming. That it would be centered in Jerusalem or somewhere and the king would be Jesus himself. And he said he was having a rough time of it. People mocked him. Even got beat up once."

"How did you respond to that?" she said.

"Neither Fred nor I knew what to make of it at first, but we could see he needed help and some place to stay, so we took him along. And he thanked us, of course, and said he really didn't have money or food or anything, but he did have the good news of salvation in this kingdom."

"So did you believe him?"

"Not at first. But then we heard those voices in the sky talking about the same thing, and Eben told us it meant some really bad things would to start happen, and that the King would come soon and that we should be prepared and believe in him."

"Did you do that?"

"Yes. We both did. It wasn't like one of those old evangelical church services with people raising their hands and walking down front. We were just standing on the cabin porch when we looked at each other and it just sort of sank in. Eben was right. We had to do that."

A cloud blocked the sun for a few minutes, leaving a chill where they sat. Irene pulled her collar tighter and crossed her arms for warmth.

"So how did you exist?" she said. "What did you eat?"

"Well, we didn't know how long we'd be there, but we bought up a lot of survivalist food items and beans and tuna fish and crackers. And there was a stream running by the cabin, so we had fresh water. No electricity, though. Strictly cold, all year round."

"Could you build a fire?"

"We didn't want to make any smoke."

"Yes. Of course. Did you have any visitors? Thugs looking for people who wouldn't follow the Beast?"

"No, come to think of it. We had hidden our car deeper in the woods. And we knew about these small surveillance drones, but we were so deep in the woods they couldn't fly there. Probably out of their control range anyway."

"Your friend was killed in a bombardment, you said?"

"Yes. He wanted real fish and took his pole with him. We'd risk a small cookfire. But one of those bombardments started up and he couldn't get back in time. He was hit by one of those big hail stones. Must have died instantly."

"They were awful."

"Yes. Eben and I buried him and covered the spot. Then it was just the two of us until those angels showed up and told us the troubles were over, and to go back home and wait for further instructions."

"Did you have a home to go to?" she said.

"It was damaged but standing. It's a wooden house so it was more flexible than all those brick places that crumbled in the earthquakes. And I didn't have any big trees around to fall on the house like a lot of places did."

"Did you find your family?"

He looked away for a moment and spoke without turning back toward her. "Yes. I did. They were lying in my older daughter's house. Must have been dead a year or more. All dried up. Sores all over their skin."

"I'm so sorry."

"It was awful," he whispered, shaking his head from side to side. "What might have been..."

To be polite, she stared out to sea for a few minutes. Finally, Walter composed himself and said, "I'm sorry. That's the first time I've related those events, and it all came back."

"It's horrible. I know."

"Well, Eben and I stayed around the neighborhood, helping out with the cleanup where we could while we waited for this trip. And of course, Eben took off first, so I've been on my own for three weeks."

Irene counted back and wondered if this Eben was on the same flight to Israel with their Avi Sharon.

Irene set her book on the deck next to her chair and joined Walter in staring out at the horizon again. Walter shifted in his chair to make himself more comfortable, and then said, "So may I ask how you and your family survived?"

"It's a long story," she said.

"We've got nothing but time for a couple weeks. But I won't be intrusive if you don't want to talk."

She looked at him and said, "No. It's not that. It's just that I've been in an intense situation for seven years, and the people around me all know the story. I haven't really tried to explain it to someone else."

"I'm an easy listener," he said.

She thought for a moment and then said, "Alright. But can we get up and move around? I'm tired of sitting now."

"Sure," he said, and they both stood up and strolled across the deck. They leaned on the railing and stared out for a few minutes and then she started her tale.

"I think I have to go back before these troubles started…the tribulation or whatever it's called." She paused again to collect her thoughts. "I was married and had three children: two girls and a boy. The two girls were also married and had children, and my son David – he's here on the ship with us – is married but had no children when the troubles started."

"He does now?" Walter said.

"Yes. He and his wife Vera have a son, Joshua, who was born a year into the troubles. He's six now."

"I've seen him with you. A nice-looking young child."

"Yes, he is. But I'm biased of course. Anyway, David's next oldest sister, Katherine had been divorced and then remarried to a man named Steve. She had three children from her first marriage, and one with Steve. Steve was the owner of a business in New Hope, and the young couple you see with us worked for him."

Irene looked up at him, and he said, "I follow you so far."

"Good. Since Katherine and Steve and their children were believers, they all disappeared. My husband, Daniel, was also a believer, and of course he disappeared as well…along with his brother Dennis. So, in one moment, eight of my family members just disappeared."

"That had to be traumatic," Walter said.

"Extremely. David and my eldest daughter Abigail were in shock. Afterward we found out that thousands of people had disappeared, and nobody knew where they went. And then the government came up with a lot of conspiracy theories, blaming those who disappeared for causing trouble."

"No one wanted to admit that they were wrong, and the believers were right. I know how that went," he said.

"My daughter Abigail and her husband lived near Washington DC and believed the stories, and when this Beast person came to power, they decided to go along with him and took the mark. Their two boys joined them, but their daughter Michelle sensed something wrong and came and stayed with me. She's the pretty blonde girl you may have seen with us."

"Er...yes." He smiled and said, "I think a lot of the young men have seen her."

"Well, there's more to the story with her, but I'll come back to that."

They turned around to lean back on the railing, their gaze following walkers while they passed by.

"So, at this point, Katherine and her family are gone, and Abigail and her family are joining up with this Beast person...except for Michelle that I mentioned. And that left David and his wife Vera, and me. They were living in Boston at the time. He wasn't a believer, obviously, or he would have disappeared. And Vera is Jewish."

"If she's Jewish, why is she here now? Wouldn't she have gone on one of the earlier trips to Israel?" he said.

"I'm guessing you saw some angels as well."

"Yes."

"Our angels gave her the option of staying with her family or going ahead. She chose to stay."

"That makes sense. That first wave of Jews was for people who want to resettle in Israel after this judgment. I gather she and your son didn't want to do that."

"No. They will live with me. Or perhaps next door. We have plenty of empty houses in our neighborhood."

"So did David come down to Pennsylvania?" Walter said.

"Yes. He is pretty quick on the uptake with news events, and he knew something was very wrong. We knew Katherine and Steve and Daniel, and they were serious believers, not the evil people that the government was making them out to be. And this is the key point: my husband Daniel had a premonition or something about this and wrote out a five-page letter predicting events. From the Bible prophecies, he said."

"Had he given it to you earlier?"

"No. He warned us that things would be getting bad, but we brushed it off. He left it in with his final papers...his will and so forth...'to be opened if and when I disappear' it said on the envelope."

"So, you opened it and read it, and what did it say? And what did you do?"

"Actually, David read it first, and the letter had a lot of Bible verses listed along with the description of what would be happening. And in the end Daniel concluded that it would be best if we all got away before these troubles really started to get bad."

"Which you did, I gather." Walter said.

"Yes. The question was where could we go? And when? The details take too long, but a friend of a friend had an automobile junkyard on a country road in northeastern Pennsylvania. It had a large cinderblock office with a wooden second floor. It was built into the side of a hill. The owner was leaving as well, but he was going to Montana with his daughter's family and said we could use the place."

"You stayed in an office? For how long?"

"It ended up being four years. We disappeared like you, but before things really got dangerous. And besides David's family and Michelle, my granddaughter, we invited the young couple that worked in Steven's office to come along."

"That was your daughter's husband, right?"

"Yes. Katherine. The one that disappeared. And the young couple,

Russ and Kim, helped David fix the place into an apartment for twelve people. They started a few months before we moved in and built rooms and insulated the ceiling so no heat would leak out. Besides keeping the place warm in the winter, David's a tekkie and was afraid of satellite images that would detect heat."

"Ingenious idea," Walter said.

"He's clever that way. And there was running water from a spring in the hillside. And he stocked up on bags and bags of dried foods like lentils and powdered milk. It was a pretty monotonous diet, but we made it."

"Did you actually have twelve people?"

"No. In the end it was only ten. The seven of us that you've seen, plus a Jewish couple, the Cohens, that my husband Daniel knew, and another one of those Jewish witnesses or evangelists from Israel. His name is Avi Sharon."

"And they went off on a flight to Israel."

"Yes. Perhaps on the same plane as your friend Eben."

Walter turned around to look out to sea again, and Irene did the same.

"However, and this was a shocker for me, before Avi left, he proposed marriage to my granddaughter Michelle, and she accepted. So, he is to meet her when we get to Israel."

"Was it that sudden?" Walter said.

"Well of course they had known each other for four years while we lived in the bunker. That's what we called the junk yard building. But the marriage subject had not come up at all. And he's a few years older than her."

"I gather you were not so enthusiastic?"

"No, actually. But it's her life. And as folks have told me, who knows what life will be like in this kingdom? And if they live hundreds of years like these angels say, I guess a few years won't mean much."

"That's certainly true," Walter said, and then staring in silence at the water rushing by the side of the ship below them. He glanced at his watch and said, "It's getting on toward lunch time. Are you in the first seating?"

"Yes."

"I've really enjoyed talking with you and hope I haven't bored you at all. Perhaps we can continue this later?" he said.

"I'd like that," she said, walking with him toward the cabins.

CHAPTER 28

WEDDING PLANS

Kim and Michelle had just rounded a corner and were heading along the deck toward the stern of the ship when they spotted Irene walking ahead of them.

"Who's that with your grand mom?" Kim said.

"No idea. Think we should catch up?"

"Yeah. Let's."

They sped up and, in a minute, had reached the older couple, and Kim said, "On your left."

Irene and Walter slowed and drifted right, not recognizing the voice at first. When Irene recognized then, she said, "Well, hello. Where did you girls come from?"

"We were just putting on a sprint for the cabins and lunch and saw you ahead of us," Kim said, her eyes drifting toward Irene's companion.

"We were as well. I'd like you to meet Walter..."

"Petersen," he said, extending his hand to Michelle and then Kim. "That's quite the grip you have young lady."

"You have to watch her," Michelle said. "Don't let her sock you in the arm."

"Stop it," Kim said, giving Michelle a playful punch.

Irene stopped the banter by saying, "Walter and I were chatting for an hour or so. We shared war stories: how we handled the troubles. Very interesting how we all made it through that time."

"Do you have family with you?" Michelle said.

"No. They're all gone I'm afraid. And as I told Irene, my best friend was killed in one of the bombardments. At this point I'm on my own."

"Ooh. Sorry. Then why don't you join us for lunch?" Kim said. "They're usually some empty seats at the table."

"Oh, I don't know."

"Do, Walter," Irene said. "Meet some other people."

"Why thank you. That's very gracious of you."

After lunch, Kim and Michelle returned to their cabin to change into something warmer and decided to sit out on the deck themselves. They wound their way to the bow of the ship on one of the higher decks and found some lounge chairs where they could face ahead.

"Think about it. Before this trouble, people spent money on cruises like this, loafing around on the decks," Kim said. "And here we are getting it for free and it's too cold for bathing suits and a tan."

"Not the right atmosphere for bikinis," Michelle said.

"Yeah. You're right. You mind the wind?"

"No. It feels good. And it's funny...Avi asked me that when we were driving to Maryland. He wanted to roll down the car window. The weather was still cold then."

"What'd you tell him?"

"That the breeze felt good. I wasn't trying to be polite or anything."

The sky roiled with dramatic cloud formations, greys and whites boiling up in fantastic mounds. They were content to stare at the morphing shapes for a few minutes, lost in their own thoughts.

"Have you thought any more about a double wedding in Israel?" Kim said, still staring at the clouds.

Michelle was slow to respond, as if she hadn't heard the question. Kim was about to repeat the questions when Michelle said, "No. I haven't."

"Is there a problem?"

"I don't know. Just a lot to think about."

"You're in luck; we have plenty of time to think at the moment," Kim said.

"I know. Maybe too much time."

Michelle didn't elaborate, so they lapsed into silence for a few minutes.

"Are you having second thoughts about marrying Avi?" Kim asked.

"What? No. Or I guess maybe I'm not sure," Michelle said.

Kim hiked herself up on one elbow and turned toward Michelle. "Really? What are you going to tell Avi when you see him in Israel?"

"*If* I see him. We still have this judgment thing."

"You're dodging the question. Let's assume you make it through. What then?"

Michelle didn't reply. She took a deep breath and fell silent, staring at the clouds again. Kim reached out and gave Michelle's arm a soft squeeze and then lay back in her chair, content to watch the clouds herself.

"Sorry," Kim murmured. "I don't mean to push you. Just saying...it would be nice,"

Michelle looked over at her and smiled. "I know."

"Russ and I talk about it, but we don't even know who will do weddings. All very confusing," Kim said.

"Really. How long have you known each other?"

Kim had to think for a minute, recalling their time working for Michelle's uncle-in-law, Steve Engel, and the time in the bunker. "I think about fifteen years. We were sort of amazed ourselves that we hadn't thought about marriage earlier. We hung out a lot when we worked for Steve but were like most people in our crowd. Didn't take life seriously enough to think of marriage."

"These troubles force us to make decisions, don't they?" Michelle said. "It seemed so much easier just to be able to drift along. Just...live, I guess."

"I think maybe those days are gone forever."

A small commotion broke into their reverie as a pod of two young men and three girls about the same age wandered past them to the railing at the bow, complaining about something. The pod hadn't noticed Kim and Michelle sitting there at first, and they only overheard bits of the conversation over the sound of the wind and the waves running by the ship. It seemed to be about the lack of anything to do on board, and no entertainment except for the afternoon meetings with the angels.

"...can't even get a beer," they heard one of the men say.

"What're we gonna do for another two weeks of this...?" one of the girls added.

"...three years hiding out and now this," they heard another girl say.

The pod finally noticed Kim and Michelle and one of the young men shouted over. "Hey. Didn't see you there. You girls bring any booze or drugs with you?"

"Nope," Kim said.

"Whaddya do for entertainment?" he said.

"Exercise, read, watch clouds," she said, pointing at the sky.

They followed her pointing for a second, and then he said, "Seriously. Whaddya do?"

"I am serious. We're here with family," she said.

The pod huddled for a few seconds, and finally one of the girls wandered over and looked at them and said, "Look, We're on our own here. We don't have a family. Do you know what's going on? These guys make a joke of everything." She nodded back toward the pod.

"Come on, Jen. They're not gonna be any fun," the loudmouth said from behind her.

"Shut up Kevin," she said over her shoulder. Jen stared at Kim and shook her head slowly from side to side, as if at a loss about how to absorb all this. "This is scary stuff, and those two guys are out of it. Are you two scared?"

Michelle and Kim looked at each other, and then Michelle spoke up.

"Yeah. Kind of. This is all new for us, too. We've just decided our fate is in God's hands. All we can do is wait to see what happens."

Kim glanced at Michelle as she spoke, nodding in agreement with her response.

"I wish I had your attitude," Jen said.

"Nothing stopping you," Kim said. "Do you go to the afternoon meetings?"

"No. Kevin and Herbie don't want to."

"Why?"

"It's not cool for them."

"What's stopping you...and the other girls?" Kim said, looking past her at the pod that was now watching Jen's back.

"What're you two talking about?" Kevin yelled.

"None of your business," Jen yelled back, rolling her eyes. "See what I mean?" she said, looking at Kim.

"Do the other girls think like you do?" Kim said.

"No. I'm kinda the odd one out."

Kim thought for a moment, and then said, "That's a tough one. But listen if you want to break away and hang with us...any time. We'll be around, and we'd love to have you. We usually walk the next lower deck or go to the fitness center. And we go to the afternoon talks. Anytime. Just show up."

Jen stared at Kim, as if sizing up her sincerity. "Thanks. I might do that," she said, and wandered back to the pod. Kevin looked annoyed and looked back and Kim and Michelle as he asked her questions. He grabbed her arm and Jen pushed him away. The boy looked overly aggressive, so Kim got up from her seat and walked over to him. He was thin, covered with tattoos and only slightly taller than her.

"You're name Kevin?" she said.

"Yeah. What of it?"

"Here's what of it. If I see you push Jen again, I'll deck you."

Kevin stood back and scanned her head to foot and said, "Look girl. I don't know who you think you are, but you're no match for me."

Kim stared him down and said, "Try me."

The rest of the pod began to twitter, and finally Kevin said, "I don't fight with girls. Let's get out of here," and they stared at Kim as they wandered off again. Jen was the last to go and she looked back at Kim and mouthed, "Thanks."

When Kim walked back to sit down, Michelle said, "Would you really have hit him?"

"Oh yeah. Guys like that really piss me off." And after a few seconds she added, "Should I be saying that now?"

CHAPTER 29

DAY SEVEN

As they neared the half-way point on their cruise, the weather remained unpredictable. Some days were clear and cold, and others peppered with rain squalls that forced all but the hardy indoors. Adding to the mood, a growing apprehension began to infect almost everyone on board and people seemed more introspective. Conversations were mechanical, covering only the basic concerns of life: food quality in the dining area and the weather. No one was digging deeper into their thoughts, at least in public.

Jen broke away from the pod and began to hang with Kim and Michelle and some other girls. Her pod mates didn't like that, but when the troll named Kevin became aggressive, one of the angels stepped in and instilled fear into his life. There were no more incidents after that, and they arranged for her to change rooms to bunk in with another girl who was more serious about her fate.

The ship was not child friendly. It had been strictly an adult cruise liner in its former life, so the children on board were left to entertain themselves as best they could. It was fortunate that they all had spent some years in hiding where they were not used to video games and television and movies. Creative self-entertainment was the only option.

Joshua and his neighbor Angela hung with a group of six other children that were about their same ages. They took over an unused lounge area on one of the decks and invented games and worked on crafts as much as their parents and the crew were able to give them supplies. No one worried about their safety; there was no place to go, and the angels watched over them as well.

On one visit, the angel named Al appeared to ask Joshua how he was doing.

"Fine," he said. "How is Phoenix?"

Al said, "Let me check," and disappeared for a few seconds. On his return, Al said, "He's doing well. Sniffing around in the yard at the moment."

"Whoa. Will I be able to travel like that?" Joshua said.

"Someday," Al said, and dematerialized again.

David and Vera were glad there were children his age on board for playmates. Not that they minded watching him, but Josh had been cooped up with nine adults for so long it was good for him to socialize with kids his own age.

"Does everyone play well?" Vera asked him that evening.

"Yeah. That part's okay I guess," he said.

"Is something not okay?"

"It's Angela."

"Do you have a problem with her?" Vera said.

"No. It's her mom and dad. They fight a lot. She's afraid of them. She just wants to keep away from them, and we never go near her room. Me or the other kids."

Vera hugged him and thought over his description. She hadn't heard the arguments herself but knew the whole judgment process was stressful for everyone. Maybe Angela's parents weren't emotionally equipped to handle the tension.

"Did any of the other parents talk to them?" she said.

"I think Scott's parents did. They have the room next to Angela."

"But nothing's changed?"

"No. They still yell at each other."

This did not bode well for Angela, or for the other kids on the rest of the trip. But there didn't seem to be anything she could do. Maybe pray for them or something.

"Well then, Josh, it's good you told me. It sounds like Angela really needs friends right now. Can you and your buddies help her out? Try to make her happy...for a while at least each day."

"That's what we're doing. We have our own club. It has a secret name."

"What's the name?" Vera said.

"I can't tell you. Then it wouldn't be a secret."

Vera squeezed his shoulder. "You're right. I shouldn't have asked."

"That's okay Mom. When do we eat?"

The time wore heavily on Michelle as each day brought her closer to Israel, and doubts plagued her spirit like impending doom. She grew increasingly introspective, sensitive to any hint of a question about her mental state and a decision about Avi. Solo walks hadn't provided any answer yet, but at least she didn't have to talk about her doubts with anyone.

She had slipped away from Kim and worked her way up to a bow deck where she and Kim had met Jen a few days ago. The wind was still strong, and the storms had left choppy whitecaps and the bow lunged into the waves, spraying water onto the lower decks.

She was leaning on the railing, enjoying the wind, when a male voice intruded from behind her. "Michelle?"

She stood erect and turned around to see a young man her age smiling at her. "It is Michelle, isn't it?"

"Yes. Do I know you?"

"Ron. Ron Mercer. We had some classes together at U Maryland. And you were at some of our frat parties."

It took a few seconds to scan her memories and then she smiled back and said, "Ron. Yes. I remember now. Sorry. It's been almost ten years. So how are you doing?"

"Okay now, seeing you. You're the only person I've met on this ship that I actually know."

Ron stood beside her and leaned on the rail, staring at her. "Still gorgeous, I see."

"Was I gorgeous back then?" she said.

"Oh yeah. All the frat brothers had a thing for you. You were dating one of them, right?"

"Yeah. Tim Collins. We broke up and I lost touch with him. You know anything about him?"

"Not once we graduated. I think he got married and moved out west somewhere. Oregon, maybe. So where have you been? Made it through these troubles so far, I see."

Michelle turned to face out to sea again, letting the wind stir her spirit. Ron turned to face outward alongside her, brushing up against her. She edged away slightly, and he stayed put.

"I was still living at home and had just graduated when these troubles started to get really serious. We lived in College Park near the college. My dad taught there."

"I think I remember that," Ron said. "Don't think I had him for any classes."

"Me either. Funny. But when that Beast guy came to power, my whole family sided with him and decided to get that mark. They trusted him to restore some order or something."

"And you didn't."

"I was uncertain and was up in Pennsylvania with my family up there when we decided to go into hiding. And then I never heard from my family again. A friend and I went to look for them a month ago. The house was there but there was no sign of them. They left me a note saying things were really bad and they were going away, but if they took the mark, I'm guessing they're all dead. I don't even know where they might have gone."

"I'm sorry."

"Thanks. But the more I tell people about this whole thing, it seems to get more impersonal. Like it's someone else's story now. Not mine anymore."

"So now that you've survived this far, what've you been doing?" he said, staring at her face.

"Mostly just waiting around for this trip. Helping clean up around my grandmother's house...where we've been living. Helping the neighbors clean up." And to deflect the interest, she said, "How about you? How did you survive, and what have you been doing?"

Ron looked around out to sea as if collecting his thoughts, and when he looked away, she slipped the ring off her finger and put it in her pocket.

"Where have I been? My folks lived in Frederick, and when I graduated, I got a job with a brokerage firm in Baltimore. Commuted at first from home, and then got an apartment in Towson and commuted into town from there. One of the guys I worked with had a rich uncle or something and they had a chateau-like place back in the hills in western Virginia. When things started to get really bad, four of us went there to hide out."

"What did you do for food and all that?"

"His uncle had it pretty well stocked. Including booze. We could have lived there another year, I think. He had a lot of freeze-dried stuff. And a portable generator and a big tank of fuel. We made out okay."

"Didn't anyone come looking for you?"

"The scouts or whatever you call them? The Beast's people?"

"Yes," she said.

"Once or twice. We told them we were doing the same thing as them. Like, we were a remote outpost."

"You lied to them?"

"Had to. They were pretty dumb; they believed us. Whoever picked them didn't get the brightest lights."

Michelle thought over what he said and not everything added up. "So how did you get on *this* ship? I mean, you would have to be in Philadelphia."

"South Jersey, actually. I had a girlfriend in Vineland, New Jersey, and I was wondering what happened to her. I took a car and worked my way up to your area. It was hard to get over your river there. All the bridges were knocked out. I ended up taking a ferry from Philly to Camden, across the river, and then one of those town watch people let me use another car. I told them I was looking for my sister."

"Your sister?"

"Well, if I said it was a girlfriend, they could have said it was non-essential and told me to go away," he said.

"So did you find her?"

"No. Never did. I found her house, but no one was there, and the one neighbor I spoke with didn't know anything about her family. So, I drove back to Camden and was there when one of those angels caught up with me and said it was time to catch the ship for Israel."

"What about your family?"

"My parents? I'm an only child, and they took the mark like your folks did. I knew they were gone. It would have been pointless to look for them."

As he said this, Ron looked out to sea again and Michelle watched his expression for a few seconds, trying to fathom his emotions. He delivered his story in such a matter-of-fact manner that she couldn't tell if it were just well rehearsed or he had no real feelings about the whole matter.

In a minute she heard Kim's voice behind her and turned around.

"There you are," Kim said, looking at Ron as she spoke. "Wanted to make sure you were okay."

"I'm fine. Kim, this is Ron Mercer. We were at U Maryland together."

Ron reached out a hand and Kim introduced herself and shook it in greeting. "Nice to meet you. You live in the Philly area now?"

"Not exactly. I'm not exactly living anywhere right now. Michelle can fill you in. I just happened to be near Philly when this ship was sailing."

"I see...I guess," Kim said.

"Well, listen, good to see you again," Ron said. "Let's talk some more later. Okay?" he said to Michelle.

"Sure. Later."

Kim watched Ron walk off and then said, "Nice looking guy. Did you date him or something?"

"No. I dated one of his frat brothers for a while. I used to go to their parties. Listen, do you have a tissue?"

"Yeah. Here," Kim said, fumbling in her coat pocket and handing it to Michelle. When she used her left hand to blow her nose, Kim noticed her ring was missing and asked if she'd forgotten it.

Michelle stared at her hand for a few seconds and then said, "Oh. I must have left it in the room."

CHAPTER 30

DAY NINE

The captain announced on the loudspeaker that they were approaching the Strait of Gibraltar, only a day or so away now. Nearing the Mediterranean Sea, the weather began to warm up and seas were calmer. Hurricanes back home normally formed south of their course off the coast of Africa, and as they approached June it would have been the start of the traditional hurricane season. But so much had changed during the troubles, no one seemed to know. Did God have tighter control on the weather now?

Walter Petersen had become a fixture in family life, joining them for meals and spending a lot of time with Irene meandering around the decks, chatting and laughing and staring aimlessly out to sea.

"Is it weird for you seeing your mom sort of dating?" Vera said to David.

David thought about the question for a moment, and then said, "Yeah. A little. I like Walter a lot. Seems to be a really nice guy, and I know Mom needs to be around people her age. It was good to be with the Cohens, but they'll never be back in the States."

"You don't sound so sure."

"I think it's too early yet. For my whole life it was Mom with Dad. Even after he disappeared, I still always thought of him as Mom's husband. Not her *deceased* husband."

"Well, we never really knew if he died, did we?" she said. "I mean, even his life insurance wouldn't pay off at first because Mom couldn't produce a death certificate. All those companies got richer hanging onto the life insurance money from everybody that disappeared."

"It was a good thing that Dad had the foresight to squirrel away enough money for Mom to survive for a few years. He seemed to anticipate that situation."

"He was quite the guy," Vera said.

"Dad would be a hard act for anyone to follow. I don't envy Walter."

"Could you see them getting married?"

"Hmm. Don't know. Maybe. But like I said, it's way too early."

Ron Mercer found ways to run into Michelle during her daily excursions in the lounges or on deck when she wasn't hanging with Kim or Jen or some of the other young women. Although she was initially wary of Ron, with each passing day she became more comfortable in his company. He was a throwback to more carefree times, when responsibilities and expectations were casual, when decisions didn't seem to have eternal significance.

With each meeting she would conveniently forget to wear her ring, or slip it off, and the subject of her engagement to Avi Sharon never came up until Kim saw them one morning and invited him to have lunch with the family.

"We usually have a couple empty chairs at the table," Kim said.

"Oh, I don't know if Ron really wants to be around a bunch of strangers," Michelle said.

"I'd love to," Ron said. "And they won't be strangers once I get to know them. I've seen you with them, and they seem like nice people."

"It's settled then," Kim said, and she hooked Ron's arm and led him off toward the dining area. Michelle straggled along behind them, staring at the deck and rubbing her empty ring finger.

They had selected their food from the buffet line and were settled around the table. Ron had started to tuck into his meal when David stopped his progress by offering to say the blessing. Ron set down his utensils and looked to the others for directions, and when they bowed their heads, he was the last.

Once the 'amen' sounded, they began to eat in earnest. Everyone had heard of Ron Mercer by now, but few knew any life details.

"So, Michelle tells us that you were in college her," Vera said.

"Yeah." He smiled at Michelle and then looked back at Vera. "We had a few classes together and met at a few parties. Usual college stuff."

"And you're from Maryland?" David said.

"Right. Frederick. West of Baltimore."

"I'm familiar with it. So how did you survive the troubles?" David said.

Ron finished chewing what was on his fork, nodded his head and then said, "A couple buddies from work and one of my frat brothers holed up at his uncle's chalet. It's out in western Virginia...up in the hills."

"Was it a big place?"

"Yeah. Pretty big. Would hold, maybe, ten or twelve people if they were on vacation. Like one of those big family rental places they have down along the Carolina coast. Or used to have, anyway. May not be there anymore," Ron said.

"Did you take anybody with you?" David said.

"Just the people I mentioned. Why?"

David looked at him and shrugged. "No reason, I guess. I was just wondering if there were people around your neighborhood that needed a place to go to hide out. Sounds like you had extra room."

Ron thought a bit and then cocked his head. "There may have been. I was working and living in Baltimore, and once things started to really go to hell there, we just wanted to get out. So, we took off. End of story," he said, and went back to eating.

The family glanced at each other as Ron ate. They had heard enough survival stories from other passengers to know that variety was the common denominator. Everyone's description was a bit different, but Ron's experience seemed a bit shallow. Michelle stared at him rather than join in their gaze, trying to make the best of it, smiling at Ron's head as he ate rather than sharing in their stares.

When the meal ended, Ron said he was glad to have met them and looked forward to more time together and excused himself to join some other fellows he had met on the ship.

After he walked off, Vera took Michelle aside and said, "Let me see your left hand."

Michelle was slow to respond, but Vera reached for the hand and said, "Girl, where's the ring?"

"I must have left it in my room."

Vera eyed her and then said, "Does this Ron Mercer know you're engaged?"

Michelle looked away for a few seconds and then muttered, "No."

"And why not?"

Michelle didn't answer. She shrugged and looked away, avoiding Vera's gaze.

"Come with me," Vera said, and gripped her arm to steer her out onto the nearest deck, away from anyone who might overhear their conversation. When they reached the railing, Vera leaned on it at stared at Michelle.

"Look, girl, your life is your own," Vera said. "If you make out okay in this judgment, you'll have hundreds of years to make choices and screw things up if you want to. We won't stop you. And everybody but your grandmother thinks the world of Avi and that he's a great match for you. And even she's coming around. Maybe Walter's a good influence on her."

Michelle didn't respond. She leaned on the railing and stared down at the waves rushing by the side of the ship.

"What I'm saying is this. I don't know what you're thinking now. Like, is this Ron guy an emotional fling? Or an escape from reality? No matter what, you owe it to Avi to keep that ring on and let Ron know your situation. Then see how he reacts."

"What do you mean?" Michelle said.

"If you tell him you're engaged, and he congratulates you and wishes you well, my opinion of him will be higher than it is now."

"You don't like him?"

"He's a frat brother that never matured. And that's not what you need. You're having trouble holding your life together, and he's an empty suit."

"That's kinda cold," Michelle said.

"Yes. It is. You can test him. If you tell him you're engaged, and he tries to talk you out of it, you'll know the truth. He's unworthy. You deserve better...and you have better waiting for you."

Michelle continued to stare out at the horizon. When it became apparent that she didn't want to talk anymore, Vera put an arm around her shoulder and gave her a hug and whispered in her ear. "Remember. We love you, and you belong to the greatest family in the whole new world. That includes Avi...and the Cohens."

With that, Vera gave her back a final stroke and walked off.

CHAPTER 31

DAY TEN

As they passed through the Straits of Gibraltar, spectators who had not seen land for a week and a half lined the deck railings. Michelle, Kim, and Russ watched the Rock slip by on the port side of the ship, while those on starboard caught sight of Morocco. For the thoughtful, the significance was palpable; they were on the last leg of the journey that would seal their eternal fate.

Ron Mercer had tracked down Michelle again and squeezed onto the railing next to her. A couple of the friends he had been hanging with strayed off and found a place next to some girls further along the railing. As the Rock shrank from view, Kim and Russ wandered off to go to the fitness center, and Ron stayed, leaning against Michelle. She didn't edge away this time, but just gave him a weak smile and looked back out to sea.

When she finally mustered enough courage, she said, "Ron, I hadn't mentioned this before, but you need to know something."

"What's that?" Ron said, turning toward her.

Michelle held up her left hand to display the engagement ring. He stared at it for a few seconds and then said, "What's that? You're married?"

"Engaged."

"You're engaged?" He stood erect and looked around and said, "So where's your finance?"

"He's in Israel. I'm meeting him there."

Ron was at a loss for words for the moment. Finally, he stood erect, crossed his arms and squinted at her. "So…why is he in Israel? What's going on here?"

"He's from Israel. He was one of the chosen ones. He stayed with us in our bunker during the troubles."

"He's Jewish?"

"Well, yeah. He's from Israel."

Ron put his hands on his hips and stared at the deck for a few seconds and then said, "Look. I thought we had something going on here. Like, I figured we could get together after all this is over when we get back home."

She stared at him but didn't respond.

"Why didn't you tell me this before?"

Michelle shrugged and said, "Look. Ron. I love my family and friends here. We've been through a lot together. And besides Avi, I have some other friends in Israel."

"Who's Avi?"

"My fiancée. So anyway, when you showed up, it was really glad to meet someone from my past. And the subject of the engagement and what we're going to do in the future didn't come up. Right? I mean, I don't know what you're going to do either."

Ron just stared at her. The lack of a response was unnerving, so she said, "Do you have any plans?"

"Yeah, I have plans," he said. "One word: success."

"What do you mean? Success at what?" she said.

"At whatever comes along. When opportunity knocks, I go for it."

"But you don't even know what things will be like if you get back there."

He cocked his head, and said," *If* I get back there?"

"We all have to go through this judgment you know."

"You think I'm worried about that?"

"Aren't you?" she said.

"No. Why should I be worried? I survived so far, and I handle myself well with people. They trust me. That's why I've done well in sales, and why I'm gonna be great when I get back. No competition."

"Do you think you're handling yourself well with me?" she said.

"Look, babe. You've been hanging out with me these past few days because we're great together. I know it, and you know it. Why would you want to waste your life in a backwater place like Israel when you could be with me. The country is starting over, and we'd be there at the beginning. Opportunity. Think about it."

Michelle just stared at him, not knowing how to take his response. Without replying, she turned to stare out to sea again.

"Look. You know I'm right about this. Think about it," he said, and tried to give her a hug. Her body stiffened at his touch, so he backed off. Before he wandered off, he said, "I'll talk with you later."

CHAPTER 32

DAY THIRTEEN

Once into the Mediterranean the Captain steered their ship through a series of obstacles: half-sunken vessels and other floating debris. They would periodically catch a glimpse of land on the horizon, Africa or Europe. The angels continued their daily briefings and mentioned casually that, if anyone had been on a cruise in this area before, the topography would now be different. Certain islands like Malta and Crete were now gone altogether, and Sicily had been reduced in size as parts of the coastline had crumbled into the sea during the earthquakes.

In a series of final, mandatory briefings, the angels assembled everyone on board to describe the events that would happen once they docked at Ashdod the following day. They noted that there were a number of ships assembled at the port, and depending on their schedule, they might have to queue up to dock the ship.

"Where do we stay once we get there?" a woman asked.

"You will stay on the ship until it is time to travel to the Valley."

"What valley?" a man asked.

"The Valley of Jehoshaphat where you will be judged."

"Where's that?" he said.

"Near Jerusalem, if you are familiar with the landscape."

"How do we get there?" another man said.

"There will be a convoy of busses."

"Will we stay in Jerusalem afterwards?" a woman asked.

"No. You will either come back to the ship, or you will be sorted out."

"Sorted out?" she said.

"You will not return to the ship," the angel said, without elaboration. The attendees looked around at each other, pondering the implication of that statement.

"Does that mean what I think it means?" a young woman said.

"You mean get exterminated or something? I hope not," her friend said.

The angels lingered for a few more minutes, and asked if there were any other questions. The group was subdued, but an older man asked, "What should we do now?"

"You should consider your spiritual life," the angel said, and then the two of them walked off the stage.

Walter joined them as David gathered the group together in a remote area of their deck and asked them how they felt about what they had just heard.

"I don't know what to think," Russ said. "I mean what more can we do at this point?"

"Have you all placed your faith in Jesus, or the King, or whatever he's called now?" David said.

They each stared at the deck for a moment, and eventually all of them mumbled words to the effect that they thought so. None of them had been church goers in the past, at least with any regularity or with any seriousness about their spiritual lives. They didn't know any gospel jargon or how to make a profession of faith and weren't even sure what faith meant for that matter.

"David," Irene said. "You've been our leader in this journey, and I think you're right to remind us about our spiritual life. But at this point, I can only remember something in the Gospels that I think Jesus said. I didn't read the Bible much. Anyway, I think he suggested that people come to him as little children. Like Josh here," she said, wrapping an arm around his shoulder. "If he's now our King, let's respect him that way."

Josh looked up at her, and then at his parents.

"Good thought," Vera said. "Anybody have any better ideas?"

The group looked around, shaking their heads 'no', and then David said, "Okay. We've come this far. It's been a very long journey, and we've survived. I'd say that, as much as is in us, we're probably okay. So, let's have a word of prayer."

They formed a circle, held hands, and bowed their heads and David said, "Dear God. This is all very mysterious for us. We don't know what to think, or what to expect. But you have preserved us so far, and we would like to continue on in your Kingdom or whatever happens next. Help us to be…courageous through all of this. You know we're weak and imperfect, but if you can accept us, use us as you see fit. And thanks for everything. Amen."

"Amen," they added, in chorus.

Ron Mercer had been watching from a distance, and once the group disbursed, he took Michelle aside and asked her if she had made any decision about what they would do after this time in Israel was over. They had met off and on since she mentioned her engagement, and she had been evasive about promising anything.

As she listened to Ron, there was a profound disconnect between her prayer time with the group and his question, and something seemed to click in her emotions. She crossed her arms and looked at Ron and said, "Were you in one of those sessions today?"

"I was there, but I didn't really pay attention. Why? Did I miss something?"

She continued to stare at him, digesting his response while she fumbled with her engagement ring, twirling it around her finger. She glanced at the ring for a few seconds and then said, "Ron. It's been nice seeing you again, but I'm afraid this is good-bye." And with that, she turned and walked back to her room.

"Where've you been?" Kim said when Michelle came in.

"I think I just had a reality check."

"Something with Ron?"

"Yes."

"Good or bad?"

"Good for me, I think. I'm not sure about Ron. Vera called him an immature frat boy."

Kim shrugged and said, "I could see that. I wasn't into frat and sorority stuff in college. The sorority girls I met seemed a bit...shallow."

"Like me?"

"Awk-ward," Kim said. "Let's say, like you *used* to be, before we lived in a bunker for four years and ate lentil soup every day and had all kinds of things fall out of the sky on us and survived earthquakes and God knows what else."

"Does that mean I'm the new Michelle now?" she said, smiling for the first time in a while.

Kim looked at her and said, "Yeah, girl, I think you are."

"Thanks. And please no punches to congratulate me."

"You know me, eh? Well, maybe it's the new Kim as well. And the new Kim may never eat lentil soup again."

As the day lengthened toward dusk, David and Vera walked out on deck, catching one last sunset before their fateful arrival the next morning in Israel. As they made occasional comments about the trip and the group, another couple settled in beside them.

"Big day tomorrow," the man said.

"Yeah," David said.

"You anxious?"

"A little. But we are what we are at this point."

"That's the way we feel. I'm Mark, by the way, and this is Wendy," he said, standing back to bring his wife forward.

"David, and my wife Vera," he said, and they took turns shaking hands.

They all turned back to look over the railing again, and David commented that he hadn't seen any fish at all on this trip. No whales, no dolphins, nothing.

"I noticed that as well, so I asked one of the angels after a briefing," Wendy said, "and he said they're all gone. They were killed off at the end of the troubles."

"Really?" Vera said. "No fish at all?"

"Apparently not. Seems weird: huge ocean, but no fish. At least for the moment. They may come back."

"Which may eliminate one future career," Mark said.

After they pondered that fact for a few moments, David added, "The other odd thing is that I've not been able to find some of the constellations I was used to seeing at night. The few cloudless nights we've had, I mean."

"We asked about that as well," Wendy said. "A number of them just disappeared at the end. And did you notice it's been darker during the day?"

"Yeah, now you mention it. But where can a star go?" Vera said. "You can't just make it disappear, can you?"

"Looks like God can," Mark said.

Vera thought that over for a few seconds. "Wow. Islands sinking. Stars disappearing. What next I wonder?"

They lingered on the deck with Mark and Wendy until dusk blended into darkness. Josh had wandered out to join them, wedging himself between the two couples. There was just a sliver of a moon, and they had grown accustomed to pitch darkness except for lights from their own ship. There was no shoreline they would pass that offered any signs of life. But for the first time they did see a light on the horizon: behind them.

Another ship seemed to be trailing along their same route. And as they lingered, another ship passed, this time going in the opposite direction.

"Must be busy at the port in Israel," Mark said.

"Our turn tomorrow, I guess," Wendy said.

The other couple took their leave and David and Vera and Josh lapsed into silence again, content to savor the warm Mediterranean breeze and the sound of the sea rushing by the side of the ship.

"I know we should turn in," David said, "but I can't get it out of my mind that this is the last night of the world as we know it. And for better or for worse, I just want to remember what it feels like."

"Sounds like a line from a sci-fi movie," Vera said.

"It does, doesn't it? But isn't this whole experience like the plot of a sci-fi movie?"

"In a way, but I don't think the angels would like to hear you say that."

"Do you mean us?" a voice spoke up from behind. It was Al.

"Oh my God. "Don't do that," Vera said.

"Our apologies. We just wanted to see how you are doing, and to suggest that you get some rest for tomorrow," Matthew said.

"Do you have any questions?" Al said.

"How's Phoenix?" Joshua said.

"Still doing well."

"Thanks," Josh said, and patted the angel on the arm.

"I have a question," David said. "Will our friends be able to meet us at the dock? I mean the people who were in the bunker with us when you found us."

"We know who you mean," Al said. "You will not be able to meet anyone until the judgment time is over. After that, we will arrange a meeting if necessary."

"Ok. Thanks. You guys have been an encouragement," David said.

Al and Matthew looked at each other in the dark. Guys?

"I think we'll take your advice and head off to bed now," David said.

CHAPTER 33

LANDFALL

By dawn on day fourteen, the ship's engines had gone silent, and when David emerged on deck, he could see that they had finally reached their destination. Israel was several miles away yet, but as far as he could see to the side of the ship a brown shoreline stretched toward the horizon. He crossed through the hallways to the other side of the ship and the view was the same.

To get a better view he climbed up several decks until he could walk to the bow of the ship and get a view straight ahead. A number of passengers had already clustered along the railing, and when he found an open spot, he asked the man next to him if he knew what was going on.

"One of the angels was up here a little while ago. He said we're next in line to land, once that dock clears," he said, pointing to a spot on shore to the left of their direction. "Maybe in two or three hours."

"Wow. Finally here."

"Amazing," the man said. "I guess when we've waited this long, a couple more hours won't mean that much."

David watched for another ten minutes, trying to see what was happening on shore, but it was too far away yet to make out any detail. After a while he said good-bye to his neighbor and walked back to the cabin.

At breakfast, David informed them that land was in sight and that it would not be too much longer before they docked, repeating the information he had been told on deck. By nine o'clock the group had finished breakfast and started to head upstairs to the forward deck to watch the proceedings. As they walked up, they felt the ship's engines start up again and knew they were under way.

The forward deck was packed with curious passengers who seemed to arrive and depart in shifts. When a space for a few people opened up, David and Russ slid in as placeholders, and they rotated time at the railing. An outward-bound ship passed them, and they assumed it had just vacated the space they would be using.

The ship's speed dropped to a crawl as they neared the docking area, and finally the captain stopped the propellers and they felt a jolt as the propellers reversed to slow the ship down as it inched into the port. Deckhands appeared with thick ropes while dock workers stood waiting for them to come to a complete stop. Once done, the ropes were tossed on shore and the ship made fast to the bollards.

They were in Israel at last.

They had assembled in David and Vera's room when the captain came on the loudspeaker to announce their arrival for anyone who had not witnessed the process. "You will exit the ship within the hour, once the gangway is in place, and do not bring anything with you," he said. "Your personal effects will be safe on board in your absence.

"Once on land, you will be directed to a series of buses that will take you to the judgment area. It is about a fifty-mile trip, and the roads are only recently patched up. I believe the trip will take a little over an hour. If you have other questions, there will be guides on the buses who can help you." Then he thanked them for their patience with any inconveniences on the trip, wished them Godspeed and signed off.

The group members glanced at each other, and David said, "You want to wait on deck?"

There was a general murmur of agreement, and they took a last look around the cabin and started to leave.

"Should we leave our purses?" Irene said.

"Sounds like it," David said. "Like he said, it'll be safe here."

"And nothing to buy," Kim said.

Once back on deck, the day was cloudless, sunny, and warm with no humidity, comfortable enough for the moment. Irene asked if anyone had sunscreen, to which the reply was no, and that it likely didn't matter at this point anyway.

The gangway was in place within a half hour and they could see passengers from the lower decks making their way down to the dock and then walk along the ship toward a queue of buses that were waiting for them. As they waited for instructions from someone on when and where they were to go, the buses first in line moved forward to allow the next series to load.

In another half an hour a steward appeared to say that it was time for them to make their way down to the gangway deck and walk to the buses. They looked around, took a deep breath and Russ spoke for them all when he said, "Well. This is it."

Back on land, they glanced up at their floating hotel as they walked toward the buses, home for the past two weeks. Not a huge cruise ship, but large enough with room for a small town. It was remarkable that they all fit with room to spare considering they came from an area with millions of people back in the Delaware Valley. How many people survived the troubles?

There was no time to ponder the past since the passengers were herded onto one bus after another until a convoy of thirty-five buses formed. The group stayed together, including Walter and Angela and her parents, and David saw that Mark and Wendy from last evening were also on their bus.

Thankfully the buses had working air conditioning, and after another half hour's wait the driver announced that they would begin their journey now. A young woman dressed in a long, white robe with a sash around her waist had boarded last and stood in front holding a clip board. She scanned the passengers and then found a seat behind the driver.

"Is this the new dress code?" Vera whispered to David.

He raised his eyebrows and shrugged.

As the buses wound away from the port, they headed through city streets in Ashdod where they could see damage reminiscent of the devastation they had seen in Philadelphia. Once free from the city limits, they headed into flat, open countryside. There was destruction here as well, mostly ruined military vehicles that were clustered around what must have been civilian homes and businesses and orchards, all of which appeared to have been burned in some sort of fire.

Their acquaintance from last evening, Mark, was peering out the window at the scenery and chatting energetically with his wife. He looked over and saw David watching him and said, "I was telling Wendy that this is all different. I was here a long time ago on this package tour with my daughter, and as recall we should be climbing up a mountain by now. I mean, Jerusalem sits up on some mountains. It's not flat like this."

The clip board woman saw them chatting and made her way back to ask if they had any questions. When Mark mentioned his concern, she advised him that he was correct. It used to be a climb up into the mountains to Jerusalem, but that the land had been changed. The whole nation was now quite flat, and the only high ground would be a plateau in the middle where the new Temple would be erected.

"Where are we going now?" David said.

"To the judgment area in the Valley of Jehoshaphat. It is just east of the city of Jerusalem."

"Why there?" Mark said.

"That is where the King chose to meet with all the gentiles. It is near the site where he was crucified," she said.

"Ironic," Mark said.

"Exactly," she said, and made her way back to the front of the bus.

"Who do you think she is?" Vera said, nodding toward the woman.

"I don't know. Not one of those people like Avi. They were all male," David said.

"She's strange though. Kind of cosmic looking."

David glanced up at her again. "Yeah. I know what you mean."

The destruction scenes dwindled as they drew closer to their destination. It was still a flat plain, but it appeared to be newly excavated landscape where their highway had been recently installed, probably for this very purpose. To the left of the bus a mesa appeared, rising several hundred feet above the plain. Mark caught the clipboard woman's attention and signaled her back again to ask what it was.

"It will be the site of the King's Temple. Construction will begin shortly," she said.

He and David glanced at each other and nodded as she walked back to the front of the bus.

In an hour the bus started to slow and eventually stopped, and the driver announced that they were almost there. They could not see anything different from their window viewpoints. "It's probably straight ahead but we can't see for the buses ahead of us," David said to Vera.

After a few minutes the driver moved on again into a wide bus parking area, and with a whoosh from the air brakes the bus stopped, and he opened the door in front. Then he turned to announce they had reached their destination and stated that their guide would direct them from this point on.

With that the clipboard woman stood up and said, "Would everyone please exit the bus now and form a line behind me outside. I will direct you to the staging area once we are outside."

With some last glances around inside, the passengers got up from their seats and filed out onto the asphalt and lined up behind the woman.

When the last person had exited, she walked toward the crowd of people who had arrived in the buses in front of them and who were halted in front of two large archways such as you might see at a sports stadium back home.

"Stay together," the woman said. "We will remain as a group until the sorting."

Russ was holding Kim's hand and looked at her and said, "The sorting?"

Kim looked at him and said, "I know. One more weird thing."

Eventually the woman stopped their group and said, "We will wait here until our turn at the gates."

Their group looked around at each other, puzzled at the terminology.

As they drew closer to their turn, they could see that there were two large archways, and that the people ahead of them were being split into two groups, some going through the right arch and some to the left.

Finally, their turn came, and the woman announced to the group that they should speak to her in turn and state their names and addresses. One by one they did so, and with each response she consulted her clipboard list and directed them either to the right or left-hand arch. Eventually the seven of them spoke to her in turn, and she directed each of them toward the arch on the left.

David and Vera had gone first and waited for the rest of the group to catch up. As they did so, there was a slight commotion behind them and saw that Angela's parents had been directed through the other arch and she was by herself, looking afraid. Kim saw what had happened and walked back to speak with her.

"Why can't I go with Mommy and Daddy?" Angela said.

Kim looked over and saw her parents looking in her direction from the other side of a chain link fence and trying to mouth some encouragement perhaps. Kim couldn't hear what they were saying. She took the little girl's hand and said, "You can come with us and meet your parents later. You'll be with Josh and us. Okay?"

Angela didn't look convinced, but the line was bunching up behind her. She looked up at Kim and then again at her parents who were waving at her and gesturing for her to stay with Kim, and then she walked with Kim to catch up with her group.

Michelle had been staring around with the rest of the group, scanning the crowds for familiar faces on both sides of the fence. She caught sight of Ron Mercer at one point on the other side of the fence, and then he melted into the crowd and disappeared from view.

========== o҉n҉n҉o ==========

BEFORE THE KING

It was mid-day, and the bright Middle Eastern sun beat down on the crowds as they crept forward. The paths between the two groups gradually diverged and they moved apart, and in front of them the area over the heads of the leading crowds began to glow. David looked up toward the sun again and realized the glow could not be from that, unless somehow it was being reflected off some surface toward which they were heading.

As they drew closer the source of the glow became apparent. A high platform had been erected in the space between the separate crowds, reminiscent of the stages for rock concerts he had attended. But there was no lighting or musicians or prancing personalities. Instead, a golden throne had been placed in the center, and on the throne a man sat wearing a brilliant white robe similar to the one their bus guide wore. He had silver hair and a beard, but it was his face that was most remarkable: it glowed like the sun, reflecting off everyone who faced him.

"My God. Is that...Jesus?" Vera said to David.

"Must be."

Several other of the guide-type beings in white robes were in attendance on either side of the man on the throne, standing motionless, their hands at their sides, scanning the crowds.

As they reached their designated gathering areas, each crowd spread out into a large pool in front of the stage. There were no seats, and when the last of the groups had arrived, a voice sounded out saying, "Please kneel before your King."

None of them had ever experienced a king before, so there was no precedent for the protocol. But slowly, one-by-one, people began to kneel until everyone held that posture and instinctively bowed their heads. It seemed the thing to do.

After a few minutes of silence in which the group each tried to digest the wonder of this all, the King began to speak, and they all looked up.

"As prophesied by my servant Joel several millennia ago, we have brought you here to reveal your worthiness to enter my Kingdom. You have been divided into two groups for a reason that will become apparent."

The King paused for a few seconds and then directed his attention to the crowd on his right where David and Vera's group were kneeling. He spoke and said, "Come, you blessed of my Father, inherit the kingdom prepared for you from the foundation of the world: for I was hungry and you gave me food; I was thirsty and you gave me drink; I was a stranger and you took me in; I was naked and you clothed me; I was sick and you visited me; I was in prison and you came to me."

Their group looked around at each other, wondering what he was talking about, and then a voice in front yelled out, "When did we see you hungry and feed you, or thirsty and give you drink? When did we see you as a stranger and take you in or naked and clothe you? Or when did we see you sick, or in prison, and come to you?"

To this question the King said, "Assuredly, I say to you, inasmuch as you did it to one of the least of these my brethren, you did it to me."

"His brethren?" Vera whispered to David.

"Avi and the Cohens?" David said.

"I guess."

The King then turned his attention to the other crowd, kneeling on his left. He spoke and said to them, "Depart from me, you cursed, into the everlasting fire prepared for the devil and his angels: for I was hungry and you gave me no food; I was thirsty and you gave me no drink; I was a stranger and you did not take me in, naked and you did not clothe me, sick and in prison and you did not visit me.'

A muffled yell arose from that side as well, and someone said, "When did we see you hungry or thirsty or a stranger or naked or sick or in prison, and didn't minister to you?"

The King did not hesitate in his response. He was just as direct and replied saying, "Assuredly, I say to you, inasmuch as you did not do it to one of the least of these, you did not do it to me."

Michelle's thoughts drifted to Ron Mercer, seizing the 'opportunity' when he and his frat buddies took off without offering to help anyone. And to Kevin and Herbie and the other trolls in their posse that were so callous about their fate.

The King was still speaking and ended his judgment of those on his left by saying, "…and these will go away into everlasting punishment, but the righteous into eternal life."

As quickly as it began, the judgment was over. The King addressed those on the right again and said, "Your guides will give you direction from here," and then arose, stepped down from the golden throne and disappeared toward the back of the stage.

They were stunned. Seven years of the troubles, the beginnings of reconstruction back home, a two-week sea voyage to Israel, and now this: a ten minute ceremony that had determined their fate for the next one thousand years and beyond. The group had struggled to their feet, looking at each other, tears welling in their eyes, a mixture of joy and relief.

The same could not be said for the crowd that sat to the left of the King's stage. A low moan began, rising to a loud wail within a few minutes as the crowd was seen moving off in the distance away from them. Some charged the fence separating the groups, attempting to join them, but to no avail. They were drawn back by men in blue robes, angels perhaps. It signaled the misery that was to be their eternal fate, and the group stared at the ground in silence, aware that they would never forget that sound.

"What will happen to them do you think?" Russ said to Kim.

"I don't want to know," she said above the din, and then remembered that Angela's parents were numbered among them. Seeing the bewilderment on the little girl's face, and the tears streaming down her cheeks, she knelt down again and hugged Angela for all she was worth, covering her ears as best she could. Russ and Michelle and Joshua joined her, holding the little girl in a group hug until the wailing diminished and silence returned.

CHAPTER 35

WHAT NOW?

The crowd had begun to disburse, walking back toward the buses. Walter and Angela moved with them as they aimed for their bus number twelve. Mark and Wendy were near as well, and smiled at them, the relief evident on their faces as well. Irene caught sight of her neighbors, the O'Neill's, but their son Chris was not with them. Was he among the condemned?

The other crowd's path was empty as it merged near theirs, a reminder of their awful fate and that none of them would return to the ship. Kim and Joshua held Angela's hands, and as the little girl stared at the blank trail she looked up at Kim and said, "Mommy and Daddy aren't coming back with us, are they?"

Kim sensed there was no way to soften the blow on this and said, "I'm afraid not, Angela. But we'll take care of you. We're your family now. And it's like you now have a brother: Joshua."

Josh smiled at her and squeezed her hand.

None of their crowd had clearly understood the gospel message of the gift of salvation through Jesus Christ or else they would not have been in this judgment. But enough had attended church to remember some of the old hymns. In the distance a lone voice began a mournful solo of the first verse of Amazing Grace, and within a minute the entire group joined in a joyous rendition at full volume. They would recall the moment, the first spontaneous worship of the King, a phenomenon that would become commonplace in the years to come.

As the singing died down, Michelle walked between David and Vera, staring at the ground. Finally, she said, "Well. One crisis over."

"There's another?" Vera said.

"Avi. What do I do now?"

"What do you want to do?" Vera said.

Michelle put her arm around Vera's shoulder and would have leaned her head on it except she was much taller. David resolved the issue by circling her shoulder as they walked, pulling her head gently onto his shoulder. "What are you thinking?" he said.

Michelle sighed and said, "I feel drained. Really whacked. You know, on the trip over I was wavering about the engagement. Even had feelings for Ron Mercer. Just like my old life. I mean, how can I face Avi knowing I'm such a ditz?"

"What does Avi know about all this?" Vera said.

"Nothing, why?"

"Then that's your answer. If you want to honor your promise to him, don't even bring up the subject. If you get bored someday, like five hundred years from now, you can mention it then. We're certainly not going to say anything."

"But *I* know," Michelle said.

"Kiddo," David said. "Think about what we just went through. We've been accepted to live in this new kingdom, and what did we do to earn it?"

Michelle thought for a minute and then said, "I don't know. Did we do anything?"

"We helped out Avi and the Cohens. And we helped out others in the neighborhood. But I don't think that's why the King accepted us. I think it's just because we trusted him."

Irene and Walter were straggling behind them, and David smiled when he turned around to see Walter pointing up at the plateau to their right, north of this valley. Probably talking about the Temple.

David looked back at Michelle and said, "Look. I'm no preacher. But think about it. How much does God...and now this King...Jesus...know about you?"

"Everything I guess, Uncle Dave."

"And yet he said to Michelle Sandahl: 'Come on in.'"

She considered that for a moment and then said, "So you're saying I was invited because the King wanted me, not because I'm a good person."

"Yes. I mean, personally I think you're a great person, but then I'm prejudiced. And the envy of every girl on the ship," he said, squeezing her shoulder again."

Vera was listening and added, "I think what Dave is saying, if the King likes you, and he knows everything, you think Avi is going to complain? You're the daughter of a King now."

Michelle smiled at the irony. "So, I'm a princess, and Avi would be marrying royalty?"

"That might be overstating it, but that's the general idea," Vera said.

Michelle stopped their pod and gave David and Vera each a generous hug and then said, "Thanks. I need to walk and think some more."

"Okay, but don't overthink. Follow your heart," David said.

As Michelle walked off ahead of them, Vera looked at David and said, "Are you getting poetic all of a sudden?"

David shrugged and said, "Hey. Must be the new world."

"Well, if she doesn't decide this thing soon, I'm going to have grey hair," Vera said. "Let's hope they can cure *that* in the new world."

As they arrived back at bus number twelve, their guide met them to address any concerns they might have. A few people asked her questions and then boarded the bus. When their turn came, the group bunched around the guide and David spoke for the group and said, "Do you have a name?"

"Yes. It is Rose."

"Well, Rose, here's our situation. We had hoped to meet some Jewish friends who had come to Israel before us, and we have no idea how to contact them. Can you help us with that?"

"And who can perform a marriage now?" Kim said, her arm around Russ's waist.

Rose studied the group for a few seconds and then smiled. She asked for the names of the Jewish friends, wrote them on her clipboard, and said she would send word ahead to the dock. And as for the marriage, she was not sure but would find out. The question had not come up before.

"You should board now," Rose said. "Other buses will be arriving for the next judgments and we need to make room for them."

Within twenty minutes the buses had been reloaded. They noticed a number of empty seats. In addition to Angela's parents, it appeared that eight or ten other passengers were not returning. Being practical, Walter commented that it might have been more efficient to condense the passengers into fewer buses, but the guide reminded them that all the busses had to return to the port in Ashdod to meet future ships.

They were not long away from the staging area when another convoy of buses passed them heading toward the judgment valley. How many of them might never see this highway again? From brief glimpses of passengers, they seemed to be of another race – mostly Asian. This really was a worldwide judgment.

In a little over an hour, they were back at Ashdod, winding their way through the city streets and finally stopping at the port. One by one the buses unloaded and pulled away, and when they stepped off number twelve a voice shouted from behind a barricade.

"Over here," he yelled, waving his arm in the air over his head. It was Michael Cohen with his wife Sylvia.

At his call, the group rushed over and hugged and shook hands and cried once again. Michelle was the last to arrive, looking around for Avi

Sharon, nowhere to be seen. When her turn came to hug the Cohens, Michael whispered in her ear, "Beautiful as ever dear."

"Is Avi here?" she said.

The answer was a hand on her shoulder, and she turned around to see him standing in front of her, tears streaming down his face. She shot a glance at Vera and David, who nodded, and then she grabbed him and hung on for dear life, sobbing quietly on his shoulder for the next few minutes. He held on just as tightly and they swayed in an invisible breeze. The group drifted back away from them, leaving space for the enormity of the moment to play out.

Rose walked over next to David and said, "A special reunion?"

David smiled and put an arm around her shoulder to hug her and said, "Yes. You could say that. They're the future of this country."

Rose looked at David's hand on her shoulder and then up at him. He glanced at her and said, "I'm sorry. Didn't mean to offend you."

"I am not offended at all. It has been some time since I have been hugged by a mortal."

"What?" he said.

"You do not know? We are not mortal anymore. We are those who left before your tribulation started. I am a resurrected human."

"What's wrong?" Vera said when David walked back over to her. "You look like you've seen a ghost."

"I have," he said, and beckoned the group over to explain with the guide just told them. As he spoke, they glanced her way, but she was helping other passengers.

"Man. This really is a new world," Russ said.

CHAPTER 36

THE WEDDINGS

It was midafternoon and the sun was heading west into the cloudless sky. While it was a dry climate, the temperature on the dock approached ninety degrees and everyone was anxious to get back onboard and into some shade. Various guides had circulated through the groups milling on the dock, advising them that the ship would be sailing that evening around nine o'clock. From David's watch it was now three o'clock, allowing about six hours to get caught up and find out about the wedding options.

They could not board immediately, which gave time to introduce Walter and Angela to Avi and the Cohens. That done, they watched while dock workers used a crane to load food and other supplies on the ship, and tanker trucks refilled the fuel and water tanks. Further along they watched deck hands and dock workers join to carry items down the gangway: suitcases, trunks, loose clothing, purses and other personal effects, the residue of those who would not be returning. David cornered one of the guides and mentioned that Angela would be traveling back with them, and hoped they hadn't removed her items as well.

"We have allowed for that situation. Her belongings will be in her room."

How could they know that? On reconsideration, the question was silly. They were now dealing with the supernatural.

As they waited, Rose reappeared with another young man, also in a white robe, and announced that he was one of the judges and that he could answer their questions about the weddings.

"Is he...?" David said, gesturing at the man with his thumb.

"One of us? Yes," Rose said. "He has a different function in the kingdom. You will meet more of them as you travel home."

"My name is Peter," the judge said, and I will need to speak separately with the two couples who asked about marriage. Would you follow me over here," he said, and walked off to the side.

When the two couples joined him, he paused for a moment before beginning. "As you have probably learned, I was a mortal like you and was taken away before the troubles began. It is a longer story than you need to know right now as to why I am performing this function as a judge. It will be explained later.

"For the moment, it is sufficient to say that you two couples present an unusual situation. The reason for that is that now you are in the Kingdom, and there is no longer a distinction between secular and religious activities. The King decrees that all men will now have the common worship pattern, and that includes such events as marriage ceremonies."

Avi stopped him for a moment and said, "Will we use the traditional Jewish ceremonies?"

"Yes...for the most part. There will be some changes, but to put the matter squarely, every survivor of the judgment is now Jewish."

"Or a proselyte?" Avi said.

"That is more precise. Thank you. Now is this your bride?" he said, indicating Michelle.

"Yes."

He looked at Avi and said, "And you are Jewish?"

"Yes. I am one of the chosen ones from the start of the troubles. I was a witness in her nation and lived with her family and friends for four years during the troubles."

"But your bride is not?"

"No."

"I see. And the other couple - were you part of the group that stayed with this man? And neither of you are Jewish?"

"No, we're not Jewish...or weren't as you just said. But we're like family now," Russ said.

"And where will you be living?"

"Back in the United States I guess."

"And you?" Peter said, looking at Avi.

"We will live here in Israel."

Peter looked thoughtful for a minute, then said to Michelle, "May I speak privately with you for a few moments?"

She looked at Avi and he nodded his assent, and they walked a few yards off. When they stopped, Peter said, "I must ask you something very personal. Are you a virgin?"

Michelle stared at him, startled at the question. "Er, no. Back when I was in college..."

Peter raised a hand to silence her. "The details are not important. Does your fiancée know this?"

"No. The subject never came up. Avi proposed to me, and we had, like, a four-day engagement before he flew over here."

"I see," Peter said, pondering her response.

"Is that a problem?" Michelle said.

"It could be. Again, it would take too long to explain Jewish marriage rules at this point, especially when your ship is leaving this evening. And keep in mind that I was not Jewish either before I was taken away."

"What does this mean then? What happens in this case?"

Peter looked at her and said, "The first generation will have some unusual situations. That is not expected. But I need to consult with someone about this. In the meanwhile, here is what I want you to do. Take your fiancée aside and explain to him what you just told me. He needs to know that in order to comply with Jewish tradition. Can you do that?"

"Sure," she said, and watched as he evaporated in the same manner as the angels had done. She shuddered at the sight, and once she regained composure wandered back to Avi, Russ, and Kim.

"What did he say?" Kim said.

"He said that Avi and I have to talk, and then he disappeared to go to talk with somebody. I mean literally disappeared. Did you see that?"

"Er, no. We were trying to be discreet," Kim said.

"So, what do we need to discuss?" Avi said once he and Michelle had walked off by themselves.

She stood in front of him, took both of his hands in hers and said, "I have to tell you something. That I am not a virgin."

"What?" he said and just stared at her.

She was trying to read the emotions in his silence. "It was a pretty common thing back in the States to have sex when I was in college. Almost everyone did, and it didn't matter later on when you got married. And then you proposed and left for Israel so quickly that the subject didn't come up. I didn't even think that it mattered."

He looked crestfallen, and anxiety began to well up inside her. She started to say something, but he held up his hand for her to be silent and wandered a few paces off.

Michelle looked back and Kim and Russ, and they held their hands up to gesture 'what?' She shrugged in response and then wandered off herself to relieve the tension.

Without paying particular attention she wandered about a hundred yards to the end of the pier, running through scenarios. Maybe Irene was right after all, and this was a bad idea. Maybe Ron was right. Maybe she would *never* get married in this Kingdom thing because she was now a tainted woman. She gave a great sigh, placed her arms on her hips and stared down at the water. There was too much stress for one day. Maybe the best course was to just get back on board, travel home and see what developed. After all, she'd have hundreds of years to work on the project.

Terrific.

A hand rested on her shoulder and Avi turned her around to face him so he could hold both her hands. His eyes were red, and a few tears still lingered on his cheeks.

"I do not know how to tell you about all my feelings," he said. "Too many are coming at one time. But I will try."

He stared at her for a few seconds and stroked her cheek. "Such a beautiful face. Such a beautiful soul: kind, gentle, helpful, courageous... what more could a man want?"

He paused again, taking a deep breath and exhaling before continuing.

"I was chosen to be one of the hundred and forty-four thousand, in part, because I am a virgin. So, this is all new for me. How would you say this? Before I met you, I had a vision of marrying another virgin and helping to build the new Kingdom. We would start out in all purity before our great King. We would be his servants."

"I understand," Michelle said. "It's your country, and you've served your King well already. And if it's important to you to be with someone more suitable, I'll understand. You were our hero, and you deserve the best."

Avi looked at her, tears streaming down again. Then he pulled her near and held her tight to his body and said, "I am being unclear. Once the King approves you and takes you into the Kingdom, you are pure in his eyes. There are special requirements if you are a Temple servant like one of the Levites, but not for someone like me."

This was getting confusing. "What are you saying?"

He stepped back and held her shoulders at arms' length, staring at her face. "What I am saying is that I am...happy and satisfied that you told me about your past, and if you can forgive a very confused man who is now very much in love with you and would like you to be my wife, do you still want to marry me?"

The emotional roller coaster was on the way up again. In an instant, as she looked at her gentle hero, a herd of images fled by: the only Nordic-looking wife on the block, old world traditions she didn't understand (would Avi be weird with them?), a new religion, living in the King's back yard...and all this for hundreds of years.

Then again, it was all new to everyone in this new Kingdom, and she wouldn't be facing them alone. In one of those momentous decisions, she edged toward him and reached up to stroke his chest and said. "Big guy. I think we are two thoroughly confused people. And this doesn't really make sense to me, but yes, I'd like to marry you."

He stared at her for another few seconds and then held her so the King himself could not separate them. "Thank you my dearest, and may our King bless us always."

She smiled over his shoulder and looked up to see that Peter had reappeared, speaking with Kim and Russ. "It's show time," she said.

"What?"

"Never mind," she said, and after giving him a long kiss, took his hand as they walked back to the judge.

CHAPTER 37

THE VERDICT

Peter watched them walk towards them, and Kim said, "Looks like they worked it out, whatever it was."

"That would be my conclusion," Peter said.

Kim looked at him and said, "Will we talk funny one day like you?"

Peter squinted at her.

"I'm trying to see if you have any sense of humor. If we're going to be living together for the next thousand years, I need to know my boundaries."

Peter still just stared, and so Russ apologized and told the judge Kim was suffering from post-traumatic stress syndrome.

"We will have more time to talk later. I am new in this responsibility," he said.

Once Avi and Michelle had arrived, Peter delivered the verdict. "I spoke with my superior and have this to tell you. You should keep in mind that the traditional marriage process here would normally take up to a year. That includes the betrothal process and counseling. Even the wedding ceremony and celebration can take seven days."

"That's right," Avi said, nodding to the other three.

"And we only have five hours," Peter said.

"What does that mean for us?" Russ said. "Can we do this now?"

"Under the circumstances, meaning your desire to have a joint ceremony, and the unlikely prospect that you two will be back in Israel any time soon, I have been authorized to perform the ceremony. You will be my first."

"We learn together," Avi said, slapping the guide on the back.

"I have a ceremony written out here, plus an official document to sign in front of witnesses," Peter said.

"We'll have plenty of witnesses," Kim said, pointing over toward the rest of their group.

"Excellent. Shall we go then?" Peter said and nudged them toward the rest of the group. He held Michelle back and said, "You spoke with Avi?"

"Yes."

"And he accepts you?"

"Yes. You were right. It was hard on him, but he decided that we should still marry."

"Very good. That would have been a serious problem for you under the law if you got married and he did not know about your situation."

"Why? What would happen then?"

"You could have been stoned to death."

It was now four-thirty, and most of the passengers had re-boarded the ship once the gangway was cleared. Their group had walked up but waited at the top for the two couples and the judge to return. The Cohens were familiar with the guides and judges by now, and filled the rest of the group in on what they knew.

"It's a whole new world, Irene," Sylvia said. "You wouldn't believe all the activity. Clean up, construction, houses, and offices I guess, and most of all the work they're starting on the Temple. We're told it will be magnificent. Greatest of them all."

"Even better than Solomon's Temple," Michael Cohen said.

"Where are you living now?" Irene said.

"We're in temporary housing with Avi until the land is cleared enough and we can build our own house. It's not like back home yet, but it'll be beautiful. You'll have to come visit, Irene," Sylvia said.

"Is it close to here?" Vera said.

"Not far from where you went through that judgment. Just south of there. We're from the same tribe background as Avi, so we'll be next in order, just south of the Temple area," Michael said, fumbling in his pocket and unfolding a map of the tribes in the new Kingdom.

"How do you know what tribe you're from?" Vera said. "I thought that was all lost."

"We did, too, but the guides seem to know these things," Michael Cohen said.

"God knows all things. He can figure these out," Sylvia said.

"Look. Here they come up the ramp," Vera said, and they shifted over to the top to greet the two couples.

"Well?" Vera said when they reached the top and settled on the deck.

Peter took the lead and said, "I have been given approval to conduct two marriage ceremonies, and we have two willing couples," he said, gesturing to the couples. We do need some witnesses, however. Any volunteers?"

Seven hands shot in the air, including Walter and Angela.

"Now, we would normally have a canopy and some other ceremonial events, but due to the shortness of time we will have to improvise," Peter said.

"That archway over there," Michael Cohen said, pointing to the entrance to one of the hallways. "That will have to do."

Peter looked over and nodded in agreement. "You have been through this ceremony yourself, is that not correct?"

"Many years ago," Michael Cohen said. "Sylvie and I were wed in a full ceremony by our rabbi. We had the canopy, and the glass to break at the end. The whole bit."

"This will pale by comparison," Peter said.

"Oh no," Silvia said. "We always said, 'Next year in Jerusalem' and looked forward to this time. And now it's here, and these dear young people are here...in Israel... fulfilling the prophecies. How could we be disappointed in that?"

"Forgive me, you are correct," Peter said.

"Does he talk funny?" Vera whispered to Kim.

Kim smiled and nodded.

'Very well, then, shall we proceed?" Peter said.

In response, the two couples huddled in the doorway cum canopy with the rest of the group arrayed around them. Curious onlookers stopped to view the proceedings, their first official ceremony in this new world.

Peter looked at his notes and before he began, he asked if they had rings to exchange. Both couples displayed their hands with the rings selected back in Pennsylvania. "Great. If the brides will remove them and give them to the grooms for the moment, we'll shall proceed."

He read through the marriage ceremony that they would all hear many times over in the centuries to come, but none as special as this first one on the day of their acceptance in the presence of friends and family who, alone, could appreciate the trials they had undergone. At the conclusion, the grooms placed the rings on their brides' index fingers of their right hand, and Peter instructed them to kiss their brides. That done, Peter turned to the gathering crowd and announced that these two couples were now married in the presence of the great King in the new Kingdom.

The onlookers roared in applause and good cheers, wishing them well and great prosperity, and taking turns in kissing the brides...especially Michelle.

"I don't remember that part in our ceremony about Michael now kissing his bride," Sylvia said to Peter.

"I added that. I was not Jewish, remember."

"Did you speak English before?" Vera asked him.

"No. I was from Moldova. Peter is not my real name, actually. But Peter is much easier to pronounce for English speakers."

"Well, you're doing very well," Sylvia said.

"I should let you know that language will not be a concern when the Kingdom officially begins," Peter said. "You all will speak the same language then."

"What language?" Vera asked.

"I do not know. The King knows. It will be explained later. And now, I must go. I have some other duties to perform. But the guides will still be with you to help you."

"Are the angels gone then?" Vera said.

"No. They will still be with you. They will maintain order as needed."

Having seen the angels at work, no further explanation was necessary.

CHAPTER 38

GOOD-BY FOR NOW

As the onlookers drifted away, the wedding party wound their way up three flights of stairs to where their rooms were located. The first item of business was to remove Michelle's luggage and transport it to the dock. She had been sharing a room with Kim, and when Russ and Avi entered, they couldn't tell who belonged to what, so the girls shooed them out into the hallway until they could repack.

Figuring that this could take a while, Avi and Russ wandered out onto the deck and leaned on the railing, watching the slow movement of passengers and dock workers as they prepared the ship to leave. The fuel and water trucks had gone, and there were no other vehicles in sight that might be bringing items to the ship.

"Think of it, Avi. In one day, we stood before Jesus, the King, and were approved by him to enter this Kingdom. And on the same day we got married," Russ said.

Avi looked at the ring on his finger and then at Russ and said, "Amazing."

"If you don't mind me asking, what was that all about on the dock, when you and Michelle wandered off? Peter looked a little concerned."

"Ah. I am afraid that will have to remain a secret my friend. It was something special between Michelle and me."

"Not a problem." Then he reached an arm around Avi's shoulder and said, "We've been through so much together, and I've learned a lot about courage and dedication just being with you. And now we share this wedding date, I guess for the rest of this whole Kingdom thing."

"Even beyond," Avi said.

"Yeah. You're right." And as an afterthought Russ said, "So will you and Michelle go back to your place tonight? Or do you have some place here you can stay?"

"We will go back. The Cohens drove down with me, and I need to return them to their apartment. We live in the same apartment building for the moment, until we can build a house."

"Hey. Great. Do you know where you want to live?"

"Yes. I am from the tribe of Benjamin, and there is a section of land set aside just for us, just south of the Temple area. My dream is to have a house next to the Temple Mountain so we can see where the King lives. I have asked for a piece of property to build on, and I should know shortly if it is approved. And when it is, you and Kim must come and visit us."

"Wow. Love to. Sound like Camelot."

"Camelot?"

"Ah, sorry. It's a famous English musical play where they sing, 'I wonder what the king is doing tonight?'" From the blank stare, Russ could see this was going nowhere, so he said, "Forget about it. Or ask Michelle sometime."

Avi looked at him and said, "Okay. I will do that."

They had bought enough time at the railing for Michelle to complete her packing and join them on deck. "The stuff's ready now," she said to Avi. He nodded to Russ, and the two of them went back to the room.

"From what you said, I thought you might have a lot more luggage than this," Avi said.

She had said that didn't she? Michelle covered by mumbling she didn't know how much they would be allowed to bring onboard, and that she could probably get whatever she needed here in Israel. It was true as far as it went; any sin was in the omission. When they were married five hundred years, she could tell him then…if it even mattered any more.

"Okay, then," Russ said, and he and Avi hauled the suitcases down three decks and down the gangway onto the pier. From there they borrowed a cart and wheeled them over to Avi's van and loaded them into the back.

"You gonna lock it?" Russ said as they started back.

"No. We are in the Kingdom now. It would not be a good day to be a thief."

When they returned to the ship, Kim and Michelle met them at the top of the gangway. "We're meeting in the dining room," Kim said. "Dinner isn't ready yet, but we have a table to ourselves, and you can get something to drink."

The rest of the group was chatting when the two men returned; each got a bottle of water and took the seats saved for them next to their brides at the round table. Avi stared around at his friends and said, "Do you know what this reminds me of?"

"What?" Vera said.

"Our first outdoor picnic at the bunker. When the two angels told us we could come out."

"That's right," David said. "We were freed then, and now we're freed again."

"I'm sorry I don't have any wine this time," Michael Cohen said.

"Doesn't matter," David said. "I propose a toast with whatever you're drinking." Holding up his plastic water bottle, he said, "To our newlyweds, Avi and Michelle and Russ and Kim."

"Hear, hear," the group replied.

"And to the great King," Avi said, holding up his bottle.

The group was somber in their response, but echoed his toast and said, 'To the great King'.

The enormity of their situation welled up again. But for the King's grace, they could have been on the other side of that fence earlier today, their voices joining in the horrific wail that would haunt their memories for centuries.

"You know," Kim said, "I think what I really learned today was that God really takes all this stuff seriously. I'm probably not saying this right, and you guys know I can be a little crude when I talk. But I'm thinking that everyone on the other side of that fence today had the same chances we had to listen to God and put our trust in the King."

"But they didn't," David said.

"No," Vera said. "They were stubborn. And I was the worst. When I think back to that time in the bunker, I thank God for David and all of you folks for being so firm and insisting we all commit ourselves to God."

"You weren't the worst, dear," Irene said. "We were all totally bewildered, grasping for help to understand things."

"And for that we had Avi to explain what was going on," Michelle said, looking up at him and squeezing his hand.

"Hear, hear to that," Michael Cohen said. "He saved Sylvie and me. We were more stubborn than all of you put together."

Avi smiled and looked around at the group. "I received more in return with my new family. The King was gracious to use me that way." Looking at Michelle he said, "And I ended with the greatest prize of all," he added, tears welling up again.

Walter hadn't spoken before, and he addressed the Cohens and said, "Michael, tell us, how did your judgment go? Was it the same place we were today?"

"No. We flew to Ovda airport in the Negev, and they put us up in a hotel overnight. It had a lot of damage but was livable. Better than the bunker. And then they drove us to a place in the Sinai desert they called Mount Horeb for the judgment. It's south of here. And they sorted us into two groups, just like they did with you from the way Irene explained it."

"It was sad for some...the Jews that wouldn't believe in their King.

They were taken away, with that wailing that Irene talked about," Sylvia said.

Michael added that, "After we passed, they bussed us to this apartment complex, just below the new Temple area, where the people from Benjamin will live. And Avi's in the same complex, and we've been picking out land to build on. Who knew?"

"Our dream home for the next thousand years maybe," Sylvia said. "We'll be sure to have nice guest rooms for when you dear people visit."

"I'd like that," Irene said. "And you're always welcome back with us as well. Do you want us to do anything with your house back home?"

Michael and Sylvia looked at each other, and then she said, "No. This is our home now. Whatever happens to it is not our concern now."

The dining room crew had been setting up dinner while they talked, setting out the usual array of buffet items. Delicious aromas had begun to waft their way, reminding them that they had not eaten all day.

"Can you stay for dinner?" Irene said to the Cohens and Avi and Michelle.

The Cohen's looked at each other and then said, "We'd love to, if Avi's okay with it. He's driving."

Avi looked at Michelle and she nodded.

The dinner stewards were not standing on formality, and when the last food tray was set in place, people were lined up right behind them. Their group queued up quickly, and once they had loaded their plates and resettled at the table, David gave his usual thanksgiving for the food and now their new life in the Kingdom, and they all tucked in.

During one of the pauses in the conversation, Kim said, "So how are we gonna keep in touch? Do you folks have addresses here in Israel?"

"We have the apartment address for the moment," Avi said. "I think you can use that. I will write it down for you if someone has paper and pen."

"And we know your address back in Pennsylvania," Sylvia said.

"Write Michelle's cell phone number on there as well, and if you have more paper I'll give her my number," Kim said.

Walter and Angela were the odd ones out in the conversation, not having shared in the trials and triumphs of the group. For Angela's sake, they didn't want to dwell on the fate of the condemned. Kim sat next to her, an arm around her, stroking her back and squeezing her shoulder constantly.

"How do we contact you, Walter?" Sylvia said.

He shrugged and said, "I don't know where I'll be staying when I get back."

"You can stay with us," Irene said. "We'll pass messages along."

CHAPTER 39

THE PARTING

David checked his watch: six o'clock.

They had eaten well, seconds even for the men and Kim, and the conversation had begun to lag. The weariness of the day's events had run its course through everyone's emotions. It was time to settle down and prepare for the return voyage and all that lay before them.

Avi watched David's action and drew the same conclusion. With a knowing glance at Michelle he said, "I think we should take the Cohens and drive back to our apartment. You will all want to get settled in and get ready for the trip home."

They all knew this moment would come, and Vera looked around at the group and spoke the sentiments of everyone when she said, "I guess there's really no way to hold onto this moment. I think I'll focus on that tonight. It will be burned into my memory for however long. Centuries?"

"Centuries it is," Sylvia said. "We'll tell our grandchildren."

"We don't have children, Sylvie," Michael said.

"Oh. Right. Well, if we did have children, we'd tell the grandchildren."

They arose, returned their dirty plates and silverware, and walked slowly out to the top of the gangway. "Don't bother walking down," Michael Cohen said. "We'll say our good-byes here."

"It's not good-bye, Michael. Just for a while anyway," Sylvia said.

They joined for one last circle prayer, holding hands, as David once again led them in thanksgiving for their acceptance, and asked God for safety and wisdom, and for all the blessings that would come their way in this new Kingdom. As he finished, and the chorus of 'amens' sounded, they took turns hugging one another, soft tears again flowing from every eye.

Kim held Michelle in a long embrace and whispered in her ear. "Keep in touch, girlfriend. We still need that spa date, remember. And it's our wedding night."

Michelle mumbled in response. "Spa here or spa back in the States?"

"Let's do both and then rate them,"

"Good idea," Michelle said as they released and backed up to stare at each other, smiling and nodding. "Really. Our wedding nights. Not at all what I expected when I was growing up."

"You're doing great," Kim said. "Enjoy the ride. Avi's a great guy."

"Take good care of Michelle," Irene said to Sylvia.

"She'll be kosher before you know it. I've not been a Jewish mother for a while now, but I think it will come back quickly."

With a lingering glance the two couples started slowly down the gangway and turned right at the pier toward the van. Avi and Michelle ambled behind the Cohens, holding hands, staring at the ground or up at the side of the ship to wave, and then at each other. Just before they disappeared from view, they saw the newlyweds kiss and put their arms around each other, her head on his shoulder.

"Speaking of newlyweds, you better move your stuff into Kim's room," Vera said to Russ.

"Already done," Russ said.

"And I moved into Russ's room," Walter said.

"Wow. You guys don't waste any time."

Which left Angela, now all alone. Irene took charge and said she could stay in her room for the trip home if she would like that.

"I guess," Angela said, tearing up again.

Kim knelt down to hug her again and said, "Can I call you Angie?"

"Yeah."

"Okay, Angie, we're gonna stick to you like glue. We're not your parents, but we'll be the best family you ever have."

Angela looked at her, lower lip puckered out. "Can I stay with you?"

Kim looked up at Russ and he nodded 'yes', then back at her. "Tell you what. Our room only had two single beds, but I think there are some bigger rooms we can move into. We'll find one tomorrow. How about you stay with Irene tonight, and you can move in tomorrow."

Angela studied Kim's expression and then said, "Okay. I'd like that."

Irene gave them a knowing smile and put an arm around Angela's shoulder to lead her away. "Where is your room, dear, and we'll go get your things."

David and Vera trailed Irene to help with the move, mindful that the room would be empty except for the little girl's things. "Maybe we should just go in and get things, so she doesn't have another reminder about her parents. I guess their stuff is all gone now."

David puffed out an exhale and said, "Yeah. I think you're right."

Kim and Russ lingered on deck for a few minutes, leaning on the rail to catch the orange glow of the evening sunset glancing off the Ashdod shoreline.

"What a day," Russ said.

"Almost too much to take in," Kim said.

"You really like Angela, don't you?"

"Yeah. I do. Or maybe it's just the situation. I mean, you gotta feel for her, losing her parents just like that. I think I'd want someone with me that I can depend on to get through everything."

"What about when we get back home?"

Kim thought for a minute and said, "I guess we can see if she has any relatives. Probably not. Or ask one of these guide people...if they're really people. I know there won't be any child services anymore."

"There doesn't seem to be much of *any* services anymore. We're starting from scratch," Russ said.

"Which could leave us...as a group. Maybe we should talk it over with David and Vera. See what they think."

"One thing I am thankful for now," Russ said.

"What's that?"

"That we have our wedding night alone," he said, smiling and giving Kim a kiss.

"Right. It's not like this is our first time though."

"It's our first *official* time. We're starting the Kingdom off right," he said, squeezing her close.

She studied his face, smiled, and said, "We should probably wait until later...just in case we want to spend some time on deck when the ship takes off.

"Good point. Then I'm going to shower."

"Me, too. Maybe I'll join you," she said, and pecked him on the cheek as they walked up the three decks to their room.

CHAPTER 40

AVI AND MICHELLE

As the Cohens settled into the back seat of the van, Michelle slipped into the passenger side next to Avi and he cranked the engine to life. Since it was still daylight, it was easy to follow the road that the bus convoy had taken that morning to wind through Ashdod and out into open countryside. With a series of new drivers enlisted for the convoys, every few miles the route was marked by 'To Valley of Jehoshaphat' signs in several languages.

Michael and Sylvia chatted in the back seat, pointing out the ruins and debris and the flat topography of the land, and this newly created valley that had appeared when the King returned in triumph not that long ago. They had never been to Israel before, but friends who had visited commented on the hilly terrain.

Michelle was quiet, transfixed on the road ahead of them, only occasionally looking around. Finally, Avi said, "What are you thinking about?"

She paused a second to absorb the question, and then said, "It's really strange. This morning I was on this same road and didn't know whether I'd ever see it again. Or whether I'd see you, or Michael and Sylvia. It was like a...bad cloud or something hanging over me. Over all of us I guess. And that little girl Angela was with us with her parents, and they never came back."

She paused for a minute, looking over at Avi, and then reached out to stroke his arm. He was focused on the road ahead as a bus convoy approached, returning to the port.

"And, what, six hours later I'm on the same road with my husband and friends and going to a new home in a new country. A country with God as King. It's a lot to take in."

"Trust me, dear, it's a lot for all of us to take in," Sylvia said.

"And you're not alone," Michael said. "We're all family now. And you're like the daughter we never had."

"But we did have a daughter," Silvia said.

"Yes. But we never had one like Michelle," Michael said.

Sylvia thought for a second and then said, "That's true. Who would believe a tall, blond Norwegian?"

Avi and Michelle glanced at each other. They smiled and he reached over and squeezed her hand.

They didn't drive as far as the judgment area. After forty minutes, Avi turned off to the right and took a side road, heading off into a more deserted area. The roadbed was bumpy, pockmarked with asphalt patches, and the landscape was still littered with burned military vehicles and crumbled buildings.

"It is a little improved from when we first arrived," Avi said. "When we came none of these holes were filled in. We had to drive very slowly."

"Is this your van?" Michelle said.

"Ah. It is like back in Pennsylvania. We took it over; the original owner was killed in the fighting."

"Why do all these army vehicles look burned?"

"They are from the armies that had surrounded Jerusalem to attack the city. When the King returned, he was up there," Avi said, pointing skyward. "The people who were here then witnessed it. They said he cast fire down on top of them and burned them all up."

"Were there bodies all around."

"Yes. But there were cleanup crews, just like back in your home area."

"So where is Jerusalem?" Michelle said.

"It is north of where we are now," he said, pointing off to their left. "Not that far. This is a small country compared to America. Actually, the whole country was smaller than your grandmother's state of Pennsylvania."

"*Was* smaller?"

"Yes. When the King returned, there were big changes. No more mountains… only the mountain where the Temple will be located. And now the country will go all the way to the Euphrates River."

"I have no idea where that is. You can show me on a map later," she said, and stared out the window again.

"Of course. It is very interesting, these changes," Avi said.

"I do have one question, though. How did you know we would be on that ship today?"

"Ah. One of the guides had been keeping us informed about the ships, so we had the van ready. And then this afternoon a guide came and told us you would be at Ashdod."

She looked at him and said, "Do you understand this is really weird?"

He smiled and squeezed her hand again. "Of course. It is strange for me as well."

In another twenty minutes they approached the outskirts of a small settlement. Avi slowed the van and drove through what appeared to be the main street. Michelle saw a few buildings with storefront windows, with signs in multiple languages saying they were for groceries and clothing and furniture.

"Is this our town?" she said.

"Yes," Avi said.

"Does it have a name?"

"Settlement Number 28," Michael Cohen said from the back seat. "Not too picturesque. We call it New Hope, like back home. There may be a better name later."

"But it is only temporary anyway. The name does not matter," Avi said.

When the van reached one of the side streets, Avi made a left turn and drove a few blocks and turned right into the parking lot of a multi-story, concrete apartment building. Here the settlement ended. Open space lay beyond the parking lot, littered with burned military vehicles. In the space between and around the vehicles, hardy bushes of some description were springing up, some with yellow or blue flowers.

"We're home," he said, pointing up at the building.

Michelle stepped down from the van and wandered out to look at the field, and then back at the building. It looked like all the Middle Eastern architecture she had ever seen on television: rectangular lines, drab brown concrete, dusty. Compared to the rich greens and building variety back home, it was a shock.

Avi walked up beside her, circled her waist, and hugged her to himself. "I have seen where you live, and I can tell this is a surprise for you. But remember that this is temporary. In the Kingdom this country will be filled with color such as you have never seen before."

She leaned her head on his shoulder and said, "I really hope so."

"Wait and see. I like color myself. I very much loved your country. Even when I could not see much from the bunker, I could still see the flowers in the spring. They cheered my soul."

She looked up at him and said, "Okay, Big Guy. I'll take your word for it. So can I see the apartment?"

"Of course. Of course. Let me get your bags."

Avi retrieved her bags from the van, and since two would be a struggle for one man to carry, Michelle carried the lighter one herself. "Pioneer woman," she said.

The Cohens had waited for them, and Michael held the door open when they entered a stairwell. "We are fortunate enough to have a working elevator," Michael said, pressing the button for Floor Three.

When it arrived, there was just enough space for all of them and her luggage and in quick order they were on the third floor.

"We are right down here at Number 303," Avi said. "The Cohens are at the end of the hall at Number 312."

"We'll leave you newlyweds alone, now. And welcome to Israel, Michelle," Sylvia said, giving her a last peck on the cheek before ambling down to their room.

It was definitely a man's apartment. Once they carried the bags in, she stood in the middle of the living room and surveyed the scene. Plain beige walls with no pictures. Basic furniture: a couch and two stuffed chairs in an ugly brown and purple striped pattern, end tables with lamps, and a large area rug spread over grey linoleum flooring. There was a wooden entertainment center with a television sitting on top.

"Do you get television reception?"

"Not yet. We are hopeful."

"What are the other rooms?" she said.

"There are two bedrooms on the right here," he said, pointing in that direction. "One of them has a shower and toilet in it, and the other only a small toilet. And the kitchen is there on the left."

She ducked into the kitchen and took a quick look around while Avi watched. Then she reversed direction and smiled at him as she walked past him to scout the bedrooms. Both had plain linoleum floors and double beds, but one seemed to be mostly an office. The furthest room with the shower seemed to be the sleeping space. There were no built-in closets, only two wardrobes and two bureaus, one with a large mirror mounted on top. The rooms were not large by American standards, so the floor space was limited.

Avi watched her return and said, "Well, what do you think?"

She smiled at him again and said, "It's comfortable looking. What a home should be like. And as you say, it's temporary."

"When we build our own place, you can design it any way you like. I want it to be your dream home. We will be there a very long time."

She studied his face, fascinated with the simplicity and trust this courageous man displayed with his very own ditz. "I'll make you proud."

She looked at a set of double glass doors and said, "What's out there?"

"Ah. Come and see our balcony."

Avi led her out onto a concrete deck that overlooked the parking lot and the open fields beyond. It was dusk now, but from this height she could still see more of the battle debris. There were sidewalls for privacy, two folding deck chairs, and four five-gallon plastic buckets, two on each side, with an assortment of white, red, yellow, violet and blue flowers.

She smiled and said, "I like your planters."

"They are not very fancy, but I think color is important in this drab scenery. I had hoped for better planters, but we make do. We cannot really see the sunset because west is that way, behind the wall," he said, pointing off to the left. "Still, I enjoy sitting out here in the evening. I am sorry we do not have air conditioning. Only fans. But this is a desert area, and it can get very cool in the evening."

She slipped an arm around his waist as they stared out into the field, and he put his arm around her shoulder and turned her to face him. "My beautiful bride."

"In the middle of nowhere in Israel," Michelle said. He started to say something, but she put a finger on his lips. When she dropped her hand, she circled his back and pulled him toward her and kissed him, holding the embrace for a minute, releasing it only to lean her head on his shoulder and whisper in his ear. "It's been a very long day, my prince, and I could really use a shower and then just relax."

"Of course. Of course. Let me show you how the shower works and where the towels are," he said, taking her hand and leading her to the main bedroom. After a quick lesson on the quirky in-line water heater for the shower, he closed the door behind him and wandered back out to the balcony to stretch out on one of the simple lounge chairs and catch the last glimpses of daylight before night took charge.

He took off his shoes and socks, and had been sitting for about half an hour, dozing off at times, when he sensed soft footsteps pad up behind him and a hand stroked his shoulder.

"Like my wedding night outfit?" Michelle said.

To get the full effect, Avi rose to his feet and faced his bride, who was wearing a plain cotton bathrobe. As he tried to think of a compliment for such a mundane outfit, she slowly opened it to reveal a very short red negligee of the type you only saw in upscale women's catalogues back home. She was breathtakingly beautiful, and he was overwhelmed with a desire he had no idea even existed.

"Oh...my.

When he became speechless, she waited for a moment and said, "Are you offended?"

"What? No. I am...how would you say...overwhelmed. The most beautiful woman in Israel is standing before me. I am at a loss for words."

"We don't need to talk," she said. "I think we do what comes naturally."

Avi woke at dawn staring at her face, savoring her sweet breath as she slumbered next to him. He reached up and shifted a few blonde strands back over her ear, mesmerized once again with his princess. His heart ached with joy, and he thanked God again for this great gift. As softly as he could, he draped an arm over her, snuggled his face up against Michelle's and fell back to sleep.

CHAPTER 41

SETTING SAIL

Dusk had settled on Ashdod, and the group made a slow climb up several decks to where they could watch events as the ship left port. There were few onlookers this time and they bunched up along the railing. City lights were beginning to emerge, a sight they would be unlikely to see again until they returned to the Delaware River. Dock workers drove forklifts and other machines around the pier, going nowhere obvious. Down below, deck hands were lingering around, ready to retrieve the hawsers when they were cast loose.

"Just think," David said. "We've only been here twenty-four hours and we're already heading home. Pretty quick turn around."

"I don't guess everyone came here came by ship. I would think if you came from the east or north or south, you probably drove," Walter said. "The King can probably conduct these judgments around the clock. He's not going to get tired, and those guides won't either."

"I wonder how they picked up the jungle Indians...like from the Amazon. They probably never even heard of the Beast and that mark. Do you think they would have responded to the King's message about his kingdom?" Vera said.

"Probably people like Avi went to see them. God seems to work all that sort of thing out," Irene said.

"We'll find out soon enough. Since we'll have these guides on the ship, we can ask them," Walter said.

The deck crew retrieved the gangway, and soon they could hear the great engines churning to life, their sound echoing off the nearby warehouse buildings. It was completely dark now, but they were able to make out the dock workers as they moved through pools of light on the pier. They watched them uncoil the hawsers from the bollards on the pier and cast them into the water. The ship's crew then hauled them up and coiled them on the deck.

At ten to nine the horn blew, and the ship began reversing into open water. It took another half hour to slow to a stop and ease forward to clear the harbor. By ten o'clock they were up to full speed, heading home into a dark sea.

By dawn they returned to the monotony of endless seas, no land visible except for occasional glimpses of North Africa as the ship once again wove around major debris in the water and skirted the coastline. Occasionally ships passed them in the opposite direction. The smell of dead fish lingered but was much less noticeable under steam.

During breakfast the captain announced there would be a mandatory meeting in the ship's auditorium at ten o'clock, which gave Russ and Kim just enough time to corner one of the stewards to commandeer a larger room so they could lodge Angela. The steward was very helpful, especially when he found out about her parents. There was an empty room a few doors away on the same floor, and they were able to move their entire luggage and other belongings before this meeting started. And once done they had a few minutes on deck to catch the morning air before heading inside.

When the group arrived, the auditorium was already quite full, and they had to find seats near the front. They looked around for people they might know but saw only strangers.

"Have you seen your neighbor, the O'Neill's?" Vera asked Irene.

"No. And that's odd. I'll try to find them after this."

Soon two of the white-robed guides appeared on the stage, surveyed the audience, and then said, "We will begin and five minutes."

Both guides were male, one tall with blond hair, the other a bit shorter with dark hair and a beard. They glanced at each other, and then the dark-haired guide began to speak. Even without amplification his voice carried well throughout the auditorium. He explained that this would be the first of a series of daily meetings to be held during their return journey to Philadelphia. The purpose was to explain what was expected of them as they began life anew in the Kingdom. They would provide an opportunity for questions, which could be answered either in the meeting or individually if they thought of something afterwards.

There were no hecklers. People coughed or cleared their throats or shifted in their seats to find more comfortable positions, but their attention didn't waver from the guides.

The guides took turns speaking, varying slightly in their presentation styles, but both were very direct, no-nonsense presenters. They projected an attitude that this was not an elective course.

"It may help to close your eyes and think of the world you left behind when you came to Israel," the shorter guide said. "Think of your neighborhoods, your government, your careers, your worship preferences. Much of this will change."

After a suitable pause, the pair began their description of life in the Kingdom, or at least the initial, noticeable changes. They would contribute and help to build this new world, so what they were explaining were merely the basics.

Many in the crowd had already heard of promised long life, and also sketchy information on new careers. Addressing this point, the guides added that once they had returned home, they or the judges would pursue this topic in more detail. They said that local and national governments would be subordinate to the King back in Israel. It would neither be like the impotent United Nations of pre-tribulation days, nor like the malevolent dictatorship of the Beast. This would be a benevolent King who, while strict, would insure peace and justice on a worldwide basis.

Walter and Irene looked at each other, nodding in approval.

The topic of worship came next, and the guides noted that, by default, everyone in the world would conform to a modified version of the Mosaic Law. In essence, then, they were now all Jewish. As a consequence, there would be some practices they would adopt that would be difficult for them at first but would be accepted by all subsequent generations. This included the traditional Sabbath evening worship pattern, and the Sabbath as a rest day. It also meant they would adopt the lunar calendar instead of the solar calendar that had been in use for centuries.

"Why would we use the lunar calendar?" a man in the back said.

"Because the feast days and special ceremonies are based on the lunar calendar dates," the taller guide said. "As we noted earlier, this will be difficult for you at first, but will become familiar with time."

"And you will have centuries to adapt," the other guide added.

"Will we all have a rabbi now?" a woman said.

"There will be teachers who will instruct you in the knowledge of the King and the expectations of your spiritual life in the Kingdom. There may not be rabbis in the same sense as your Jewish friends used to have. This will develop with time. The important point is that everyone should get the same teaching."

Irene's thoughts drifted to the various synagogues and churches she had visited in her lifetime, the design of the buildings and the order of their services. She resolved to discuss this with Walter later, and that reminded her that she was beginning to rely more and more on his companionship and insight.

The guides then described the Feast of Tabernacles, an annual celebration that would link each nation to the King for the duration of the Kingdom. It would require that representatives from every nation make an annual visit to Israel for a one-week minimum ceremony and celebration. This would be mandatory. Failure to comply would result in disciplinary action by the King.

The crowd murmured a bit with this statement. "What sort of disciplinary action?" a man said.

"Among other things, the King will withhold rain so their crops will fail," the taller guide said. "However, rather than focus on what can go wrong, focus instead on worshipping your King and this will not be an issue."

David looked at Vera and said, "Hey. I'll volunteer to go every year. Get to see Michelle and Avi."

The subject of crops led into a discussion on diet. The guides advised them that they need not be vegetarians in the Kingdom, but that more abundant crops would be available.

"It will seem strange to you, but carnivorous animals would now be vegetarian and would be harmless to humans," the taller guide said.

"You mean like a lion? How can that be?" a woman said. "How could a lion grow big just on leaves and grass?"

"Consider the rather large animals you have now, like an elephant or a buffalo. They are vegetarian already. The King will provide for them," the shorter guide said.

The taller guide then ended the session by saying, "This is a lot of information to comprehend in one session, so we will review these points in more detail in subsequent meetings. However, I believe there are two more important points to consider.

"First, your great spiritual enemy, Lucifer – you know of him as Satan or the Devil – is confined until the ending of the Kingdom. And that includes his minions as well. Their nefarious work, instigating strife and warfare and temptation, was perhaps transparent to many of you. But you will notice much less tension and temptation. If it is there, it will be of your own making. It cannot be attributed to Lucifer."

"The second point," the shorter guide said, "is that there will be a common language that all humans will speak once the Kingdom begins. You will no longer need an interpreter, which will be useful when you travel and when you meet humans from other nations."

"What language will that be? Hebrew? And will we have to study it?" a man said.

"It will be the King's language. And no, you will not have to study. It will come naturally when the time comes," the guide said.

CHAPTER 42

QUESTIONS

The meeting ended just in time for lunch, and as the group settled in at their round table, David gave the blessing and they began in silence, mired in their own thoughts.

"*That* is really a lot to take in," Kim said, speaking for them all. "How are we going to absorb all those changes?"

"I think it may not be as difficult as you might imagine," Walter said.

"Whaddya mean?" Kim said.

Walter was deliberate in answering, measuring his words. "Well, it's not like we have careers to go back to that would occupy all our time. I expect that when we are involved in the rebuilding work back home, we will have plenty of time to think. And these guides and judges will be available to teach us."

"I could see that. I think of our trips to the lake in Maine. If you went for a week or more, you really started to slow down and absorb things better. You weren't so distracted," David said.

Irene looked at David and said, "I know this is a bit off the subject, dear, but do you think our cottages are still there at the lake?"

"Hmm. Hadn't much thought about them. We can put them on the list of things to check out."

"I can see Walter's point, too," Russ said. "Kim and I were able to chill out and adapt just by driving that garbage truck for a couple weeks. And we'll have months."

"Years," Kim said.

"Centuries," Vera said.

"Wow. How much stuff will we know in a century? Two centuries? Think we'll be able to remember everything?"

"Supposedly the human brain is never used to its capacity," Walter said. "So maybe that's why God made us that way."

"What? Over design?" David said.

"Sure. I believe we were meant for greater things than what we have seen. We've probably been too lazy to develop our potential," Walter said.

"Or too evil," Irene said.

"How long is a century?" Joshua said.

David looked at him and Angela and said, "I'm sorry. We've been ignoring you both in this discussion. We're all just sort of…mystified."

"A century is one hundred years, Josh," Vera said. "That means in one century you and Angela will each be one hundred and six years old."

The children looked at her, then at each other, and then snickered at the thought. "That's older than grand mom." Josh said.

"And just think how old I'll be then Joshua," Irene said. "You will never catch up to me."

The children glanced at each other again and shrugged. That might be important. They didn't know.

They lapsed into silence again, fumbling with their silverware and probing at the last few items on their plates. The men returned to the buffet table for desserts and more coffee, and then settled back in their places.

"What do you think will be the biggest challenge in all this?" David said to no one in particular, tossing out the question.

Kim looked at Russ, seated next to her, and stroked his back. "I'm a new bride, and I want to cook for my man here. I barely cook as it is, and now it's trending toward vegetarian cuisine. We'll have to find some cookbooks or something."

"I might have some," Irene said. "We'll check when we get back."

"The lunar calendar?" Russ said.

"That will be weird," Vera said. "Maybe they'll have a conversion table. I'm a little familiar with it since I'm Jewish, but you gentiles are gonna have a hard time figuring out Christmas."

"If there will even be a Christmas," David said. "Maybe the Christian holidays are gone now."

"Who would know?" Irene said.

"Tell you what," Walter said. "I'll take notes. Then we'll ask these guides or judges."

"This government thing is strange, with the King and all. I mean, what do we know about a king?" Russ said.

"You mean because we fought a Revolutionary War to get *rid* of a king, and now we have one back?" David said.

"And the Mosaic Law again?" Vera said. "We weren't very observant Jews in my family. But from what I remember reading in the Torah, it was really strange. How can that come back? It didn't work back then. Why would it work now?"

The group stared at Walter, and when he looked up, he said, "Er, don't look at me. I'm no biblical scholar. I'm taking notes. I would suggest that you keep giving me questions we don't have answers for, and then I'll write them down and we'll corner one of these guides and ask them."

"That should work," David said, and they spent the next fifteen minutes brainstorming questions, with Walter writing shorthand notes to try to keep up. When their curiosity had finally petered out, they disbursed for the afternoon and headed their separate ways.

One of the questions centered on Angela and her future, and Russ and Kim stumbled upon Peter, the judge who married them, on one of their strolls around the deck.

When they described the issue, Peter said, "A curious situation. I believe we may encounter more of them."

"We know that much already," Kim said. "So do you have a solution?"

"I believe so. As I had explained earlier, we will be the law, as you call it, in your country. By that I mean that we will handle most of the functions that mortals performed before."

"Like police and courts, right," Russ said.

"And what about social services?" Kim said.

Peter squinted at her and said, "What are social services?"

"They're local government departments that were supposed to help people in need. Like if they didn't have enough money. Or the husband was beating up his wife and kids and they needed to get away. Or finding foster care for children if their parents couldn't take care of them. Make sense?"

"Foster care?"

"Temporary care for a child until they could find a permanent home for him."

"Ah. I see. Well, as you describe it, there will be no need for such services. There will not be poor people in need of help. And we will not tolerate family violence. The King will deal with that."

"Will you handle that?" Kim said.

"No. The angels will enforce the King's rules."

"Probably don't want to mess with them," Russ said.

"No. Excellent conclusion," Peter said. "Now as for your child question, the obvious answer would be for one of you adults to adopt this girl, unless she has relative back home that might take her. The King loves children, and desires that they should all be well cared for."

"Would there be some paperwork or something?" Russ said.

"No. No paperwork. Just your commitment," Peter said. "However, I would suggest that it would be good to have a ceremony to mark the adoption. In that manner you will commemorate the event and you will be accountable to your friends and relatives. Are you two considering this?"

They looked at each other and then Russ said, "Considering. We've obviously no experience, but we like Angela and really feel for her situation."

"Feel for?"

"It means we have sympathy. Empathy is maybe a better word," Kim said.

Russ looked at Kim and said, "Wow. Beauty *and* brains. I've married a scholar."

He instantly regretted that statement as she gave him a punch in the arm.

CHAPTER 43

WALTER AND IRENE

Walter and Irene now spent most of their waking hours together, reliving their histories and pondering the future. Toward dusk on the fifth day, they were on the bow deck as they crossed through the Straits of Gibraltar again, heading into the sun and the open Atlantic.

"Plus Ultra," Walter murmured.

"What?" Irene said.

"Plus Ultra. That was Columbus' motto in Latin as he went past this landmark, the Pillars of Hercules as they were known then," he said, pointing to the Rock on their right. "It means 'more beyond'. He was heading out into unchartered seas, and he was hopeful about what he would find. Pretty courageous when you think about it. Their ships were tiny compared to this cruise liner."

"You seem to know a lot about history," Irene said.

"Ah. More of a hobby, really. I've always enjoyed memorizing facts. Connecting the dots as they used to call it. And I had quite a library at home."

"Did it get destroyed?"

"Mostly. Or stolen while I was in hiding. Couldn't take the books with us, of course. Like I said, I didn't want to tip my hand. I just disappeared."

"Have you decided what you will do when you get back? Do you want to go back up to Reading?"

"I don't think so. My family is gone, and probably all the friends I had there. It's wide open at this point. Which is certainly an interesting situation, don't you think? I mean, how often in life can you quite literally just start over, no questions asked?"

Irene pondered the question and then said, "Hardly ever, especially as you get older. Maybe when you're a young person and decide to move west or overseas."

"Or you're in the witness protection program," Walter said.

Irene stared at him. "You actually do have a sense of humor...sort of."

Walter flinched and looked at her. "Do I really seem humorless?"

"My impression is that you are a very serious man. And that's probably called for right now," she said, patting his hand. "I think we should all be very serious about what's going to happen now."

Walter went quiet for a minute, staring straight ahead. Great piles of white clouds were piling up on the horizon.

"Have I offended you?" Irene said.

"What? No, of course not. You made an honest statement...if that's the way people see me. What I was just thinking about was whether God has a sense of humor. And if he does, then am I being too...confining or something."

"Do you think God does? Have a sense of humor, that is?" she said.

"I suppose we could ask one of the guides. But if we work backwards from the end result to the designer, you have to think that a giraffe and a loon indicate a sense of humor."

"Loons? We had them at the lake in Maine. When they would make that crazy call and splash around in the water. It was like they just took a fit or something."

A seagull trailed along beside the ship on their right, then veered across the bow and hovered on the opposite side, looking around in expectation of finding food. With none apparent, after a few minutes it made a reverse turn and headed back toward the African coast.

"Tell me about this lake in Maine," Walter said.

"Yes. Maine. Well, it has two family cottages, small houses really, on Heron Lake, which is a small lake near Moosehead Lake if you know where that is."

"I do."

"Daniel's father built those years ago, and we used to go up there for family vacations each summer. There was enough sleeping space for everyone between the two houses, and as I think about it, it was one of the last times that the whole family had got together. It wasn't too long after that when the troubles started, and we never did go up again."

"It would have been a long drive."

"It was. About fifteen hours for Daniel and me. David and Vera lived near Boston, so they could make more frequent trips up there. And of course, they didn't have Joshua then, so they were more flexible. They didn't have to worry about school schedules."

"Was it a special place for you?"

She frowned and cocked her head. "I think it was more special to Daniel and the children; not so much for me. I did like it, mind you, but it was a long distance away and primitive by my usual standards."

"Worse than your bunker experience?" Walter said.

"No. Of course not. And that's the irony of all this. Daniel and Katherine and her family - and his brother Dennis - all loved the primitive life up there. And then they disappeared, to be with Jesus as I understand it. In Paradise. And here am I, the one who appreciates the luxuries of life, and I spend four years in the bunker."

Walter waited to see if she would say more. "You seem to have endured the trial quite well if you don't mind me saying so. And your family seems very supportive."

"Thank you. I believe I surprised myself through that experience. It certainly was humbling."

"By the way, did you ever find your neighbors? I've forgotten their names."

"The O'Neill's. Yes, I did run into them, and it's as I feared. Their son Chris was one of the condemned people. They're inconsolable at the moment, so I've been keeping my distance. We'll do what we can for them when we get home."

Walter reached an arm around and gave her a hug. "You went through that as well."

"That's true, but I wasn't there when he perished or whatever happened," Irene said. "And the odd thing was that Chris was taking an interest in Michelle. They were hanging around the house. Imagine if they became serious and then were split up at the judgment."

Walter studied her face as she leaned on the railing and stared ahead. No words were necessary. As Kim had said on their first day out, it was a lot to take in.

"Can I ask you something?" Walter said.

"Of course."

"Would you mind if I stayed with you folks when we get back. At least until I get some idea of what my plans will be."

She looked up at him and smiled. "Walter, you can stay as long as you like. It's not like any of us have great plans for the future. You fit very well into our little family. Remember that Kim and Russ are not relatives... neither were the Cohens or Avi. We all just survived together and became a family of sorts. And you seem to fit right in."

"Thank you. I appreciate that."

"Do you like the rest of the family?"

"Oh yeah. I must admit I'm a bit envious of your camaraderie – the way you endured in your bunker for four years."

"I'm sure we will remember that for many years. *Many* years. And if you feel cramped, you can pick out another house in the neighborhood. Lord knows there are enough empty ones now. It's a nice area but needs a lot of work to clean up and repair the damage. There will be plenty to do if you're willing to work."

"I'm more than willing," he said.

She slipped an arm around his waist, and they stared ahead in contented silence.

CHAPTER 44

ANGELA

Whether it was God's doing, they couldn't say, but the weather continued calm and sunny, with none of the squall days they had experienced on their outbound voyage to Israel. Joshua and Angela had located the other children who were playmates on the way over, and now there was even more empty space for them to haunt and make up games. The children were less affected by the monotony of the days at sea with nothing to do except attend the guide meetings, eat, roam the decks, and ponder the future.

The children's only plans for the future were to be with their adults in whatever adventures might come their way. There would be no formal public schools when they returned; all those details would have to be worked out.

Their adults. The lingering question for the group was: who would be Angela's adults?

By Day Ten of the voyage, Kim and Russ had grown to enjoy this little girl who ate with them and strolled with them and talked with them and slept in their room. True, it was a small sample of time, difficult to predict how things would work out in the long haul. They spoke with the group and related their conversation with Peter, the judge, and his suggestion that one of them should adopt her. Realistically that could only be one of the two younger couples.

The group had settled into a daily discussion time after lunch, following the guide meetings, and after the kids asked to be excused to go play, Kim brought up the subject of Angela's future. "Angela would have a built-in brother if she stayed with David and Vera," she said. "How important would that be?"

"I don't know," Vera said. "The other side of the coin is that Josh has been an only child for so long that it might be a shock for him to share the attention. Especially if Angela is needy emotionally."

"How would you two feel about having a child in your life so soon after you're married?" David said to Kim and Russ.

"We've been wondering that ourselves," Russ said. "Like, when you had Josh, you were there from the start of his life. You've made him into the boy he is today. We'd be inheriting a life with maybe a lot of baggage."

The dining crew were clanging the chafing dishes and wiping the serving tables, giving them a few minutes to think through the situation.

"If I can interject something," Walter said. "If we're learning anything from these sessions with the guides, it's that the rest of our lives are meant for enjoyment...of each other and the King that is...and in service to others."

The group watched him as he paused to compose his thoughts. "What I'm getting at is that perhaps we're looking at this from the wrong angle. It's not so much how Angela would affect *our* lives. It's how we would affect hers."

Irene looked at him and said, "Are you saying we should disregard our needs in this matter, and that we dedicate ourselves to her?"

Walter thought about that phrasing and then said, "That may be putting it too strongly, but in essence that's the idea. If we're going to be helping others in this new spirit of serving the King, then she would be an obvious choice of someone we would dedicate ourselves to helping out."

"And no matter what, she would inherit an extended family. I think all of us would pitch in to help her through this time. She can come to any of us," David said.

Kim and Russ looked at each other, and he nodded. "There is one... wrinkle," Russ said. "We hadn't mentioned this earlier, but Kim and I have been considering moving away. It's certainly nothing to do with all of you. You're family, and always will be. But if this is a brand-new Kingdom, and we're told to go out and resettle and repopulate it, then we could be adventurous and go anywhere."

Kim added, "We mean, you are related to each other. We're *super* grateful that you invited us to stay with you in the bunker, but you will always have each other. And Michelle. I wonder how's she doing, by the way? And while we're like family with you, too, we're thinking this might be the perfect time to explore."

The group didn't respond right away, and Kim said, "Does that offend you?"

David looked around at the others and said, "No. Not at all. And as you explain it, it kind of makes sense. Your families are gone, and except for us, you have no ties to the Philly area."

"Did you have someplace in mind?" Walter said.

"We talked about a couple places. Maybe South America. Most likely the Pacific Northwest. We'd been up there on vacations and liked the area," Russ said.

"Do you think this would affect whether or not you adopted Angela?" Irene said.

"Sure. Because not only would she be missing her parents, she'd be missing her friends in the neighborhood. Everything familiar would be gone," Kim said.

"Now, I'm impartial in all this since I don't know your neighborhood, and very little about Angela or her parents," Walter said. "But this could actually be a good thing for the girl."

"What are you thinking, Walter?" Irene said.

"I'm thinking that the negative side of being in her old neighborhood would be the memories of what life was like before. She had two parents, and now life is without them. They would be constant reminders. Of course, that would probably fade with time, but early on it could be more difficult."

"So, you're thinking that a cold turkey adventure into a whole other area might be better?" David said.

"Could be. I'm only offering the suggestion."

"Hmm. This is getting interesting," David said.

The dining crew had cleaned up all the other tables and were closing in on theirs. They knew they should vacate the space quickly, and before leaving Irene had a suggestion.

"The one thing we are not discussing here is what Angela would like to do. Who would she like to live with?" Irene said.

"And if it's us, then what would she think about moving away?" Kim said.

The logic was there, but it was as far as they could go at the moment. Before disbursing for the afternoon, David said, "Here's my thought. Why not have Kim and Vera take her aside and talk with her. See what she thinks. Just tell her that we want what's best for her, and there's no pressure to decide. But it will give her something to think about on the rest of the way home."

Kim and Vera looked at each other and Vera said, "Sounds like a plan."

CHAPTER 45

THE TALK

On Day Eleven, intermittent rain squalls had returned, and the sea tossed with deeper swells. The ship glided rhythmically in the troughs and peaks between swells, and only those hardy souls who could avoid seasickness ventured out onto the decks to take the air. From the forward viewing deck they watched waves break over the bow and flood across the lower decks.

The captain announced that a tropical storm was developing in the Caribbean to the south and, depending on its course, might intersect with them as they approached the mid-Atlantic coast. With each stroll outside, passengers kept a wary eye on the cloud formations off to port, watching for signs of the impending storm.

In the morning session, someone asked the guides about their safety, and to reassure the audience, they said that, if the King had chosen and preserved them, they would all be quite safe – even if their stomachs were queasy.

The guides' discussion for the day focused on options for their government once they returned. The King's emphasis will be on morality, they said, not on efficiency or opportunity or acquiring wealth or power in the hands of a few. "For those of you who wished for peace and justice, this will be the fulfillment of that desire," the tall guide said. "The King will guarantee it."

"Will we need to elect a king?" a woman asked.

"No. You can choose any type of government as long as its intent and operation conforms to the will of the King. You can even rearrange your traditional state and national boundaries if you like. This need not be finalized immediately. We would advise you to take time to consider your options carefully since you will live with it for a very long time."

In their lunchtime discussion, the group tossed out their impressions and conclusions from the morning session.

Walter began and said, "It's ironic. The conventional wisdom was always that you cannot legislate morality. We laid great stress on separating church and state. And I suppose that made sense when you had a lot of conflicting religions."

"But in the end, it was the people with no religion, or at least with no spiritual considerations, who took over, and look at the result: the Beast," David said.

"Well, we don't have conflicting religions now," Vera said. "I guess that's why there's no problem *combining* church and state."

"Exactly," Walter said. "You know, I've been reading some of those books David lent me…the theology books you got from somewhere. There doesn't seem to be a lot of specific information on this Kingdom we're now a part of. Some ideas, but it seems mostly left to the imagination."

"Like we're filling in the blanks by experience," David said.

"Right. And it is supposed to last for a thousand years, and then there's a great rebellion at the end…once Satan is let loose again for a short while. They all march on Israel or something."

"Avi and Michelle would be in the middle of it then?" Kim said.

"I guess," Walter said. "But they'd be pretty old by then of course. Anyway, what struck me is that this whole Kingdom is like one great test."

"What do you mean?" Irene said.

"Well, when you think about it, we'll have a near perfect environment: no wars, no crime, no sickness, and plenty to live on. If people experience centuries of that, and they *still* rebel at the end of that time, it would be almost unbelievable."

The group stared at him, each considering that thought. If he was correct, what did that say about human nature? *Their* nature, for that matter.

"It's good to be saved by God's grace," David said. "If the King didn't judge us worthy, we might be included."

Kim added, "Here's a thought. If we know about this rebellion in advance, and we're still around when it happens, will we speak up and try to stop it? To warn people?"

"I certainly hope so," Irene said. "Like those guides said, we'll be the only generation to remember what it was like before the troubles, what led up to this Kingdom when Jesus returned. Everyone else will only know it from history."

"If there's a bright side, then, it's that we have a thousand years to work on the presentation," Russ said.

"And I wonder if we'll think back to this day and the discussion we had." David said. "I'd mark the date, but it will be in the lunar calendar by then and I have no idea what that is."

When Joshua and Angela asked to be excused to join their friends, they held Angela back and told Josh she would join them a little later. The children looked at each other, and then Josh shrugged and wandered off.

Kim took Angela back to their room and found her warmest jacket. As she zipped her up, she said, "We're going out on deck with Aunt Vera, and it might be a bit chilly in the wind."

"What are we gonna do?" Angela said.

"We're going to talk with you. Nothing bad," Kim said as she put on her own jacket and led Angela outside. Vera was waiting for them and headed for some deck chairs that were out of the wind. It was still cloudy, and the ship tossed in the waves, but it was bearable, and Angela didn't seem to get seasick.

They seated Angela in between them and then Vera began. "Angela, we want to talk about who you will live with when we get back home. We know this has been an awful time for you, and like Kim says, we'll stick to you like glue to help you through it. Isn't that right?" she said to Kim.

Angela turned to look at Kim, who said, "That's right. Always and forever," reaching out to stroke her hair. "But tell me, do you have any relatives back home? Aunts or uncles? Cousins?"

The little girl pursed her lips and shook her head 'no'. "I had an Aunt Julie, but she didn't go with us when we went away to hide."

"Do you know where your aunt lives?" Vera said.

"No."

Vera and Kim glanced at each other. Children had little sense of location at the best of times.

"Do you like Aunt Julie?" Vera said.

"She's okay."

"Does she have children?"

"I don't remember."

"Okay, then. We'll assume Aunt Julie is out of the picture," Vera said. "So, here's what we want to ask you, sweetie. When we get back, you can come and live with Uncle David and Josh and me, or you can live with Kim and Russ. We want you to think about it. We probably have four or five days before we get back, and maybe you'll make up your mind by then."

Angela looked back and forth between the two women, and then stretched her legs out straight and stared at her feet for a minute. Taking their cues, the women leaned back and stared out to sea.

"I like you both," Angela said.

"We both love you as well," Kim said.

"Will you still like me if I pick just one of you?"

"Oh, sweetie, we'll never stop loving you," Vera said. "It's just that we are not all going to be living in the same place, like we are on this ship. We'll be in different houses when we get back home. So just because you pick one of us, it doesn't mean you won't be friends with everybody else."

The little girl thought some more, and then said, "Would I still have Joshua as a friend?"

"Of course," Vera said.

"Then I'd like to stay with Aunt Kim and Uncle Russ. Is that okay?"

"That's fine, Angela," Kim said. "Now, there's one other thing. And this will be a little tougher." She paused for a moment, and then said, "What if we moved somewhere else, so we wouldn't be in the same neighborhood as Joshua? You would still be with Russ and me, but you would be making new friends."

Angela looked up at her, then at Vera, and then back at her feet.

"I can tell, sweetie, that you seem to make friends easily," Vera said. "We've only been on this ship for less than a month, and you've already made friends with four other children. Think of how many new friends you could make when you have years to make them."

"In a century?" Angela said.

They were surprised that she remembered the number. "*Especially* in a century," Kim said.

"Can I go play now?" Angela said.

"That's fine," Kim said. "Like we said, we wanted to give you some time to think about this. And whatever you decide will be fine with us. You'll still be family with all of us."

"Okay," she said, and stood up and walked back inside.

"What do you think?" Kim said.

Vera took a deep breath, and then said, "If I had to guess, I'd say she'll go with you and Russ. We just need to give her time to think about it. Maybe she'll come to the same conclusion we did, that it might be better not to live in that neighborhood any more now that her parents are gone."

"You okay either way?"

"Sure."

"Fist bump then to seal the deal," Kim said, reaching across Angela's chair.

CHAPTER 46

CONGUS

HEADING HOME

The tropical storm had veered northeast and passed behind them, and apart from a few squalls, they were fortunate, and the rest of the voyage was uneventful. By dawn on Day Fourteen, land was once again in sight as they approached the flat Delaware coastline and turned northwest into Delaware Bay, skirting past Cape May to starboard.

Land became visible on both sides of the ship now between Delaware and New Jersey, a relief after two weeks of vast emptiness. Their future might be a mystery, but at least they would be home on solid ground.

The Delaware River narrowed as they drew near Wilmington and then north to Philadelphia once again. Little devastation had been repaired in their month's absence. The oil refineries below Chester on both sides of the river, the city of Chester itself, and finally into Philadelphia, all looked the same. Anyone who could work on reconstruction was either going to, or just returning from, Israel. Rebuilding would not begin in earnest until all survivors returned.

As they neared the port of Philadelphia, the ship slowed to a crawl, and this time a tugboat met them and eased them into their pier. It took almost an hour to maneuver the ship into place. David watched the proceedings, recalling their departure from Ashdod, the coiled hawsers thrown onto the pier now serving their purpose for the last time on their voyage.

As the deck crew extended the gangway, the stewards circulated through the crowd of onlookers instructing them to retrieve their luggage and prepare to disembark. There were no forklifts or other motorized vehicles in view, but there were luggage carts they could use.

Once on the ground, the group felt the early summer heat and humidity, a drastic change from the chill winds onboard. They grabbed a luggage cart while David tracked down someone who might know about transportation back to their homes. The O'Neill's joined them while they waited and stared around and up at the ship, their home for a month for the adventure of their eternal lives.

"I wonder if we'll take cruises in this Kingdom." Kim said.

"Who knows what transportation might be like," Walter said. "Take some talent and imagination, and a couple hundred years to work on the project, and we might defy gravity or something like that."

"Now *that* would be cool," Russ said.

As they chatted, David walked back to say he had located the bus that would take them back home. It was the same driver, and he would retrace their route through Philadelphia and back out into the suburbs, stopping along the way. And with that they turned away and headed for the bus.

It was still a caravan, but with fewer buses and a smaller box van that followed to carry luggage. Once the bags were stowed in the truck, they boarded the bus and noted more empty seats, Angela's parents and Chris O'Neill among the missing.

After much thought, Angela had decided she would like to stay with Russ and Kim, even if it meant moving away. Affection and the promise of adventure overcame the lure of the familiar, and the unhappy memories of her old neighborhood. She sat by the window with Kim's arm draped around her shoulder, and Kim pointed out such landmarks as she knew. After all, she was a Jersey girl, from central New Jersey at that time.

They retraced their route west on Market Street to the ruins of City Hall, then turned north on Broad Street to the edge of the city where the bus driver began to wind through suburban neighborhoods, depositing passengers along way. When they arrived at Pendragon Way. Irene pointed out the house and the driver slowed to a stop in front. Here, too, nothing had changed; the driveway still looked like a used car lot.

As Russ and David retrieved their luggage, Walter stared in amazement at the half-timbered, Tudor-style house, much larger than he had imagined. And when he looked around, the street was lined with a number of them with a similar motif.

"Impressed?" Irene said.

"Very."

David spoke with the driver, thanking him for his service and asked if there would be more trips to Israel.

"I think everybody's gone by now. We're only making return trips. I've been at this steady for over a month."

"Have you been?" David said.

"Yes. I actually had a chance to fly over and back. Nothing special about me. I think they just needed drivers, and they wanted to get a supply of us judged and ready to go. How did your trip go?"

"Fine," David said. "Everyone passed the judgment from our group, but my niece stayed in Israel. But the little girl's parents didn't make it," he said, pointing to Angela.

"What's she gonna do now?" the driver said.

"We'll adopt her. Have you met the guides and judges yet?"

"Yeah. In Israel. Is that weird or what?"

David patted him on the shoulder and said, "What a strange new world. Well, we'll probably see you around. Thanks for everything."

"My pleasure. And I guess 'Praise the Lord' is the word to say now, right?"

"Right."

A rising wail rose from the back of the house, and suddenly Phoenix rounded the corner, leaping and squirming and squealing in joy, jumping up at everyone in the group to be stroked and soothed.

"Your dog I take it?" Walter said as he fended off the more aggressive lunges.

"He's a stray that Joshua has been taking care of, and he talked one of the angels into watching him while we were gone," Irene said.

"Really? Like the police motto: to protect and to serve."

"I guess."

David and Russ helped the O'Neill's take their luggage up the street to their house, and when they returned the group was gathered around Irene, sorting out the sleeping arrangements. She was saying, "Michelle's room is empty now, but we've gained Walter and Angela. I think I'll put Walter in her room, and we'll give Angela a choice. She could stay with Kim and Russ again, but that room is small. Are you okay sleeping in a room by yourself?" she asked the girl.

"I think so. I did at home."

"You'll be near us," Kim said.

"Okay."

That settled, the group collected their luggage and wound their way inside and upstairs to the second floor. As Irene settled Walter in Michelle's room, he scanned the room: simple beige wall paint with a few tasteful pictures, built in closets, a bureau and mirror, and an alcove with a small desk set into one of the dormers.

"This was my daughter Katherine's room when she was growing up. She wasn't a great student in high school, so the desk has plenty of use left in it," Irene said.

"Your sense of humor?" Walter said.

"More like irony. In the end she was smarter than us. She became a believer and avoided all that we went through. She was married young and then had three children before her husband deserted her. Then she went to nursing school and met Steve Engel – Russ and Kim's boss – and they got married and she had another son. And then they were all gone..."

Walter put an arm around her shoulder and stared at some pictures. "Is that her?" he said, pointing to one on the wall: at a pretty brunette who appeared to be high school or college age.

"Yes. Her high school graduation photo. She never liked it, but I thought it caught her well. You can see she was very attractive, but she was rebellious and more of a tomboy. She liked sports; was a jogger all her life."

There was a group photo next to it, and he moved closer. "That's a family picture after she married Steve. She's holding their son. The oldest girl, Jenny, was in college by then."

He peered at Jenny in the picture. "Very pretty redhead. Who had red hair?"

"Her first husband, Scott."

"Was he a believer?"

"He was a scoundrel. I doubt we'll see him again."

He stepped back and looked around the room again. "Irene. Thank you again for your hospitality, and for sharing some of your life. It makes me feel like I'm among good company here in this room. I wish I could have met these folks."

"That would have been nice. But we can't relive history. Take your time and settle in. Oh, the bathroom's just across the hall. Sorry there's not one in each room."

"I'll be fine."

"Good. And I'll see what we can find to eat."

CHAPTER 47

DAWN

Walter awoke at first light and checked his watch: five-thirty. They'd all lost track of the date, but the local news radio would later tell them it was June 29. Almost the Fourth of July if they still recognized that holiday.

He dressed and wandered outside to catch the morning mood. The temperature was seasonable for mid-summer: 78 degrees. He slipped on a windbreaker and took along his binoculars. The front lawn now had a month's head start on the mowers, and he could see it would be a challenge to get it back in order. Irrepressible peony, daylily and hosta shoots were sprouting in the flower beds along the house walls; like them, survivors. Birds flitted about, and when David wandered out to join him, he was peering through the binoculars at the top of one of the larger trees.

"What're you looking at?" David said.

"I think it's an oriole," Walter said. "They're a common species, but you rarely get to see them. Here, take a look."

Walter handed David the binoculars and pointed to a higher branch. David adjusted the lenses and followed his direction, scanning around until he spotted a striking black and orange bird. "Wow. Neat looking."

David handed the binoculars back to him and said, "You a naturalist type?"

"Strictly amateur, for my own enjoyment. It's like hunting without shooting anything."

"You ever hunt?"

"I have, sure. Usually in deer season."

"Never have myself," David said. "Not really interested, and my dad wasn't a hunter."

"It does tend to run in the family. Not to change the subject, but this is quite the house you grew up in."

"Yeah. It was Mom's dream home. She loves British things...Welsh actually...and was much more into status stuff than my dad. Not that he didn't like it. It's a nice area. He made friends. Was on the school board. Played golf. Met people...like Michael Cohen."

"What did your dad do?"

"He owned his own manufacturing company. Then sold it and retired."

"I take it he was religious," Walter said.

"I don't know if he'd have put it that way. He attended church with Mom, but whenever he spoke with us, he referred to it as a relationship with Jesus rather than a particular religion."

"Was your sister Katherine the same way? Your mom showed me her family picture up in room I'm staying in."

"Yeah, I'd say so. And my Uncle Denny. Dad's brother. And Kathy's husband Steve. They were all a breed apart. We had nothing against them, but we didn't want to hear about that religious stuff."

"And now they're gone and we're here."

"Yeah. Funny. Or not so funny..."

The pair ambled around the property toward the patio in the back. David swung his foot through the grass, estimating whether he could cut it with just the mower. When they neared one of Irene's planters, a startled bird shot out and found a nest with four tiny cream-colored eggs tucked under the flowers.

"What was that?" David said.

"House finch. You can tell by the purple head and chest," he said, pointing to the agitated bird, chirping at them from a nearby branch. "We're in her territory now."

"Good to see signs of normal life again. At this point I can even appreciate squirrels and dandelions."

"So, what were you all doing before you left for Israel?" Walter said.

"Working around the neighborhood. Early on we mostly cleaned bodies out and then later we did surveys to see who might not have returned so we can tell which houses are unoccupied now. Kim and Russ drove a garbage truck."

"Is that how Kim gets her physical nature?"

"You mean plonking people in the arm? Yeah. She was right there with Russ tossing the garbage cans. And I think she took karate or something when she was younger."

"A good couple. I like them both."

"Yeah. Michael Cohen used to say they were both real mensch's, whatever that meant. And Angela takes to them. I think they'll make good parents."

They wandered to the end of the patio and Walter turned around to look at the house. "I take it this was totally walled in before the troubles started?"

"It was. I think it must have been those giant hail balls that then melted. We didn't find any rocks."

As Walter peered around at the broken wall sections, David said, "Maybe you told us, but what did you do before all this? I mean, what was your career?"

"I was a civil engineer. Worked on bridges and road construction."

"Really? I bet the township guys would like to meet you then. They're scrounging around for talent for rebuilding the place."

Walter looked over at him and said, "I was retired, but I'll do what I can."

"I don't think anyone is retired anymore."

Once everyone was up and had eaten something, the group held their first terrestrial planning session in the new world, deciding who would do what. David took Walter, Russ and Kim and drove to the township building to ask about rebuilding plans now that almost everyone was back who would be returning.

The three mortals from before were there, but they were now joined by an immortal guide and a judge, and so the township officials deferred to the judge for any plans for the future.

"You all make it?" the lead official said.

"Mostly," David said, recounting the situation with the Cohens, Avi and Michelle, and the loss of Chris O'Neill and Angela's parents.

The judge, who called himself Ezra, asked about Angela's welfare, and Kim and Russ said they would adopt her, following the advice of another judge named Peter.

"Very good," Ezra said. "And my congratulations to you all on passing through the judgment successfully. I know it must have seemed highly unusual to travel all the way to Israel to do that, but it was necessary to fulfill the King's prophecy."

The four glanced at each other and shrugged, each with the same reaction. At this point, nothing was really unusual anymore.

The guide was a woman named Elena, and she advised them that they were waiting until all the ships returned before beginning the state and national reconstruction, but that all the local folk had returned by now so that they could begin in their neighborhoods. "One of our first tasks will be to conduct a skills inventory," she said, "so we can assign labor for the reconstruction."

"If you don't mind my asking, who is in charge of the country now?" Walter said.

"We are, on behalf of the King," Ezra said. "We will assist you in forming governments, but we will ensure that your government conforms to the will of the King."

"That sounds like a dictatorship," Russ said.

"It is a benevolent dictatorship and will certainly seem strange to your generation since you were raised in a republic. But I believe you will find it most agreeable once you experience it."

Kim leaned into Russ and whispered, "They're talking funny again."

Elena added, "If I may amplify what Ezra said, you will not be concerned with favoritism. We guides and judges have been purified by the King, God the Son, so we are incorruptible. We only serve the King, and his desire is that you would experience the joy of his Kingdom."

"And those joys will far outweigh any concerns you might have about serving a King," Ezra said.

"Has this Kingdom already started?" Walter said.

Ezra and Elena looked at each other, and then she said, "No. It will not start until everyone has been judged, and all the condemned have been removed. We do not know the exact timing, but we believe it may be a few weeks yet."

"How will we know when it starts?" David said.

"It will be obvious," Ezra said.

Before heading home, the four filled out a skills inventory survey, adding extra surveys for Irene and Vera, and left their addresses to be contacted. The township men said that they had logged in most of the survivors so far and would be working on a reconstruction plan with Ezra and Elena.

Since only eight percent of the inhabitants had survived, David asked about the procedure for occupying the abandoned homes. There was no formal process yet, but with Ezra's blessing they checked off two neighboring houses on the township map, writing in David's name on one and Russ and Kim's name on the other.

"Any update on phone service?" David asked.

"You should have cellular service within the week," Elena said.

"How about food and gasoline?" Russ asked.

"We are replenishing food stocks from more remote areas. There should be plenty for this area. And most electricity and water and sewer service has been restored," she said.

"Will there be a money economy again, or is this just a barter system or something like that?" Walter said.

"We do not know about money at this time," Ezra said. "For the moment you are the servants of the King, and he will provide all your needs. You will receive what you need as you need it."

"Okay, I guess," Kim said. "And I hope you guys are not offended if we say this is all really strange."

"Not at all," Ezra said as the foursome turned to leave. As they left the room, he turned to Elena and said, "That term again. Guys?"

Back in the parking lot, David looked at Russ and Kim and said, "Well, congratulations."

"For what?" Russ said.

"Becoming first time homeowners, and not just a starter place. I know the house: an English, Tudor-style manor home with a turret."

"Hey. You gotta start somewhere," Russ said. "Even if we move, we can at least get it fixed up for your new neighbors."

CHAPTER 48

INTERLUDE

David remembered a cartoon he once tacked on a cubicle wall. It showed a fish swimming in a blender that was plugged in, and the fish's caption read, "I can't stand the tension!"

That feeling was growing with the tangle of ideas they were digesting. The Kingdom was to start momentarily, but yet they were on hold. They now had both a guide and a judge ruling over their township, superseding all other authority. They were no longer considered Christians, even though they were there because they had faith in God the Son, Jesus Christ...but now he was their King. Not to mention the devastation on an epic scale that needed restoration. They were going to use a lunar calendar, worship in some unfamiliar pattern, live for centuries, and expected to be an example to future generations.

Where to start?

They nibbled at the concepts, savoring ideas and implications like a campfire discussion, but sensed they couldn't grasp it all until the Kingdom actually began...if then. And when they asked about the timing, Elena the guide could only say 'soon'.

By now the remnant of the township population seemed fixed, so they had no qualms about taking over empty houses, one of the prerogatives of a pioneer generation. Having marked their choices on the township planning map, the two couples began work in the evenings to renovate their new homes. David and Vera began in the house next door to Irene's, and Russ and Kim did the same across the street. They were becoming a colony and could even include the O'Neill's up the street if they stayed. After Chris's death, they were considering settling somewhere else to ease the memory.

Neither house had suffered significant external damage from the bombardments or earthquakes. One huge tree collapsed, but it fell between David's house and Irene's, and only required a determined chain saw effort to remove. The walled patios and decorative outside walls for both houses suffered only minor damage. Squatters had holed up inside, and all areas of the house needed major cleaning from food waste and other debris. Carpets cleaned. Walls scrubbed. The beds and furniture were mostly intact, but the mattresses were soiled and scattered about the floors, so they went to a mattress warehouse and picked up replacements.

Angela tagged along and did what she could with Russ and Kim, feeling her way with her adoptive parents who, themselves, were unsure how to bring her emotionally into this new household. As work neared completion on their new place, Kim and Russ faced the inevitable task of taking Angela to her old house to collect whatever personal items and clothing she might like to keep. They postponed the visit as long as they dared, hoping her memories would fade a bit and soften the impact. No one knew how she would respond. Russ went ahead and removed all pictures of her parents and family so that at least that much of their memory would not be present.

When the day came, they took her over in the morning when she would be fresh from a night's sleep. It wasn't just her parents that might concern her. She had older siblings who also perished. They commented on the big age difference, and Angela confided that her parents called her 'a mistake', which no doubt affected their spiritual outlook and contributed to their nasty attitude toward her.

Angela handled the visit well, only breaking down in the bedroom of an older sister who apparently had favored her. Kim inquired about her whereabouts, but Angela said she had been killed in one of the bombardments when they were hiding out in a cabin in southern New Jersey. She might have been a believer, so they suggested she might see her again. Kim held her tight and let her tears run dry before they left the room, promising her that, with God's help, she would have more brothers and sisters, and now she would be the eldest.

As they worked, their guide, Elena, would often stop by to encourage them and praise their effort. When they confided that they were really not sure what they were doing and whether they were on the right track, she reassured them that everyone felt the same way, and until the Kingdom started, just carry on doing what they were familiar with.

When they asked on the timing, she would only say, "Soon now."

"How will we know it?"

"It will be obvious."

Once Ezra the judge learned that Walter was a civil engineer, he was given a team of six men to survey the road, bridge and building damage in the township. His protests that he didn't feel qualified were ignored. Ezra went so far as to cite the case of Hiram in ancient Israel, the pagan whose abilities were supernaturally enhanced to help build Solomon's temple in ancient Israel.

At the end of the first week, Irene asked how it was going, and he said, "Funny. It's coming back."

"Had you done this before?" she said.

"No. That's what's funny about it."

The wanderlust still stirred within Russ and Kim, and on one of Ezra's appearances, they asked him about opportunities to move elsewhere, either in the country or in the world.

"The whole earth is to be repopulated, so that would be acceptable.

You could even move to Israel. If you move earlier, there will be more housing opportunities such as you have here."

"Should we do it before this Kingdom starts...if we did it?" Russ said.

"I do not believe you would have enough time, unless you are not moving far."

"Well, we were thinking of either the Pacific Northwest, or even South America. But we don't speak Spanish."

"Language will not be a concern once the Kingdom starts. Was that mentioned to you earlier?"

"Oh yeah. It was," Kim said. "Forgot about that. That would make things easier."

"Does the little girl know that you might do this?" Ezra said.

"Yes. She's up for the adventure."

"Do you have contacts in other places?" Russ said.

"Contacts?"

"You know. People or judges we could talk to and ask about places to settle."

"If you tell me a specific area, I will ask who will judge in that area. You could meet the judge and speak with him."

"We'll let you know," Russ said.

One lingering question was what they would do for a living in this Kingdom. Would there be money, and salaries, and savings...things they were used to. Ezra reminded them that he was not omniscient, and could not say what might develop with time, through the centuries.

"In the beginning, you will work at whatever careers are necessary, and not be concerned with personal income. Your needs will be met by the King. That will seem odd to you, but you will learn to depend on him, and to serve each other. Think of it as a basic training period where you will learn to be a community rather than individuals competing with each other."

Only Walter had any military background, and he said, "Basic training seems reasonable. Strange, but reasonable."

Ezra went on. "With time, such a life would not be profitable for you, however. I believe you will find that contentment will be the result of useful work in the service of the King. You will each have a specialty in which to serve him, or perhaps a variety of specialties since you will live to be quite old."

"Will these specialties be something we've done in the past?" David said.

"Most likely not. In a new world there will be new requirements, and you will learn new skills. It will be an adventure for you."

CHAPTER 49

∽∞∽

AVI AND MICHELLE ROUTINE

The new Israel was a busy place. Work continued on the new Temple complex, and each tribe set up a council, led by judges, to reconstruct their own territory. They needed to clear debris and military wreckage, salvage what they could, and bury the bodies of dead combatants, and develop a plan for the multitudes of new inhabitants.

Part of the plan was to stake out homesteading locations for the pioneers. Even before Michelle arrived, Avi Sharon and the Cohens had haunted any official voice they could find who might be able to assign them home building locations. Others wanted the Sea or the Jordan Valley, but true to his word, Avi sought a plot within sight of the Temple Mountain to their north. And persistence paid off; he and the Cohens snagged an ideal location, along the edge of the mountain corridor, just below the Temple mountain area itself. They might not be able to actually spot it from other buildings on the mount, but they would know it was there.

This was all new to Michelle, but in two weeks of Settlement Number 28 life, Michelle had adopted a routine. It was temporary, as Avi said, but productive. They were not just hanging around, doing nothing. From walking and jogging, she learned the territory, and from talking with mortals and guides, she learned the lay of the land. She even ran into other non-Jewish wives; some were even blonde like her.

Sheila Cohen helped in the food supply warehouse and did what she could to teach Michelle kosher cooking. Then again, they really didn't know how many of her Jewish traditions were just that: traditions. Would the law teachings of the Kingdom be the same? No one knew.

Avi and Michelle didn't want to be on the same rebuilding tasks and spend twenty-four hours a day together, so they chose separate work details. Avi had volunteered for the body recovery and burial detail in their Benjamin tribal area. Not just local Israelites, but multitudes of enemy soldiers that perished during the King's return. For many they followed flocks of scavenger birds, others they found in searches, and still more were marked by passersby who set up markers to alert the body detail. For disposal, mass graves were the only option.

With her nervous energy, Michelle asked the local judge for outdoor-type work. Landscaping was out; there was nothing to landscape. It was all temporary. So, she volunteered for the fuel recovery detail that would drain unused fuel from ruined military vehicles and collect it in a tanker truck.

"Would an Israeli woman do such a job?" she said to Avi.

"Of course. They were in the army...with weapons."

This presented one problem. Ability was not an issue, but Michelle could not look plain if she tried. Even in a military jump suit and fatigue cap she was a potential distraction to her fellow workers. To maintain some semblance of propriety, Michael Cohen volunteered for the same detail as a chaperone. He told his fellow workers that she was his daughter, like the ugly duckling from the old fairy tale. Who knew she would grow up to look like that?

When Avi walked into the apartment, Michelle sat on their balcony, staring into the distance at nothing in particular. Now past the summer solstice, the balmy sunsets stretched long shadows from the ruined military vehicles strewn across the landscape opposite their apartment.

The dry air had cooled from the afternoon heat; not that she cared since the temperature was immaterial at the moment.

She was still wearing the oil-stained jump suit she used for her job. As he pulled the other chair beside hers, he noticed there were still grease stains on her face and dried tears on her cheeks.

"What has happened?" he said, rubbing her cheek with his fingers.

She didn't answer right away, just pointed straight out, north, toward the Temple Mountain and the judgment area.

"What?"

She broke her stare and looked at him and reached over to grasp his hand. "God himself is there, and you know, when the wind is right, I can still hear that awful wail from the judgment area. I'll never forget that sound. The people we saw who are no longer with us."

"Did you know many?" Avi said.

"A few. Angela's parents. A guy I went to college with that I met on the ship. Some thugs we ran into on the ship...them and their girlfriends."

"It was the same with our judgment. Different location, same result for some."

She studied his face. "Did the screams bother you?"

"Very much, but maybe I became used to them. There was so much suffering here in Israel before I was chosen. The Arabs and their friends were attacking us constantly, so we always heard the noise. Guns, rockets, screams. It was a bad neighborhood. You do not like it, but you learn to accept that life. But we had the promise that the King was coming, and that it would end."

"But it ended horribly for so many people," she said.

Avi looked out across the landscape, pausing for a moment. Then he shrugged and said, "Yes, it did. They had the same chance to trust the King, but they chose not to."

She squeezed his hand again and stared at his face, as if she hadn't heard him. "I keep asking myself: why me? Why am I still here? Why are my parents and my brothers gone? What's so special about me...or any one of us really?"

He reached over and stroked her cheek again, savoring the tender beauty of her face. Absorbed in this view, his eyes welled up, and finally he said, "I wish I had some great knowledge, my princess, like one of these guides. Why was *I* chosen as one of the twelve thousand from my tribe of Benjamin? And chosen even before the troubles really started. I think God knows something about me that I do not know. He saw potential in me to tell others about our great King, and to help rebuild our lovely land and our Kingdom. He knew he could trust me."

"But how do you know if you really trust him?" she said, searching his face. "I don't feel like I have great faith in God...or in the King. I'm pretty basic, really. I feel like I'm just along for the ride."

"Ah. I wish I could answer that with some great authority." He continued to stroke her cheek, and then kissed his fingers and touched them to her lips. "Why has God trusted me to love you and take care of you? Why did you trust me enough to accept my proposal and come to me in Israel?"

She didn't respond, so he slid his chair closer and put an arm around her and she leaned her head on his shoulder. If he only knew the doubts she had harbored.

"Let me tell you my simple view of what has happened. When we were in the bunker, your Uncle David played CDs of bible teaching, and he had books. In one of the books, I recall reading that faith means acting as if something is true."

"I'm not sure I understand," she said.

"I mean, that you trusted your uncle and your grandmother enough to go with them to the bunker, right?"

"Yeah."

"And at that time, the troubles had not even started yet. You only had your uncle's word that they were coming and that we should all go away and hide."

"That too."

"As I see it, your uncle had faith in God, and you had faith in your uncle...that he was not a crazy man for wanting to go away. You trusted him. You acted as if David was correct in what he wanted to do."

She didn't respond right away, but grasped his hand and finally said, "Go on."

"That is it. As I understand it, faith is as simple as that. Do you trust the King now that you have seen him?"

"Well, yeah. It's easier when you can see him. And these guides and judges. Is that really faith?"

"No. I don't think so. I think faith is when you *cannot* see him, and you still trust him."

"What are we supposed to be trusting Him about now?" she said.

He squeezed her shoulder and smiled at her, kissing the top of her head. "Oh, my princess, I think we must trust Him for many things now. That Israel will be the greatest country on earth now. That we can raise a family who will honor the great King. That we can be a blessing to all the other countries in the world. That we will be able to honor the King all of our long lives, and honor him even when we have everything we could ever want to live a happy and peaceful lives."

"We don't become spoiled?" she said.

"Exactly. I think that would be easy for us. And we will learn to worship him in strange ways that do not make sense, especially for you because you had a Christian background."

"I wasn't very much into church."

"I know. I know. But you know something about Christian worship ways. How do you say it: their 'liturgy'?"

"I think so," she said.

"Well, this will be a different liturgy. Or maybe none at all. We have to trust that, if it is important to the King, we will do it whether we understand or not."

"Oh, I hope you're right. It's just all so confusing right now. Has this Kingdom even started yet?"

"Not officially. I spoke with a guide today, and he said, "Soon. Very soon."

"How will we know?" she said.

"I asked him that and he said, "You will know. It will be obvious."

She lifted her head to look at his face and leaned forward to kiss him. Once he kissed her back, she put her arm around him, leaned her head on his shoulder again, and said, "If God gave me my prince, I guess he can give me whatever else I need."

"Whatever *we* need," he said.

"Right. We."

"Maybe it will start tonight," Avi said.

"Should I wash up then?" she said.

He squeezed her shoulder and smiled.

CHAPTER 50

THE VISITOR

It was a pleasant mid-July morning, and Irene was puttering around her yard, watering plants, pruning, weeding, planting seeds and new seedlings. From time to time, she stood back to visualize a decorative garden suitable for a kingdom.

Walter and the other adults were off on their various work details. Angela even rode in the garbage truck with Russ and Kim, sharing in the adventure of cleaning up this new home area.

Joshua stayed behind for the day. She left him in the house, reading, but he walked out to find her in the yard and said, "Gran. There's a man here to see you."

"Who is it?"

"I don't know. He says you know him."

"Where is he?"

"In the kitchen."

"Really? I don't recall seeing anyone walk up."

Joshua put his hands out and said, "He was standing there when I went into the kitchen. He has those bathrobe things on."

"You mean like Ezra and Elena, who talk with us?"

"Yeah."

She put her hand on his shoulder, and said, "Well. Shall we go and meet him then."

They circled around in front of the house, then along the driveway to the back mud room entrance. She slipped out of her clogs to keep the floor clean and stepped into the kitchen.

"Oh my God," she said, stopping dead and holding her hands over her mouth.

"Hello, Irene."

"Daniel? Oh my God…oh my God," she said, reaching out for a chair back to steady herself.

He walked toward her and put his hands on her shoulders to give her strength. When he did, she grabbed him and hugged him and wept quietly for a few minutes.

Joshua looked totally confused, staring at the two of them for clues as to how to respond.

When she composed herself, she said, "I need to sit down."

"Of course. I can see this is quite a shock. I did not know what to expect."

"Where have you been and why are you here? I have so many questions now."

"Take your time," he said.

She stepped back and looked at him for a few seconds, staring at the white robe. "What are you now? One of these guides?"

"I am one of the judges."

"Are you going to be our judge? What about this Ezra fellow?"

"I will not be your judge. I will be far away, but I asked permission to visit you one last time."

"I won't see you again?"

"Not in the Kingdom; only afterwards. Then it will be forever," he said.

She and Daniel sat opposite each other at the kitchen table, and he slid a chair out next to him for Joshua and patted it for him to sit down.

"Is this my grandson?" he said.

"Yes. Joshua was born about a year into the troubles, after you and Katherine and her family all disappeared."

Daniel reached out and stroked his hair. "So, he is six. A fine-looking boy."

"If you hadn't left that note for us predicting what would happen if you disappeared, I don't know if we would have survived. You can be proud of David. He believed you and worked with Russ…I don't know if you knew him."

Daniel shook his head no.

"Anyway, he enlisted help and built a bunker upstate that we hid out in for four years. He was our rock. He and Avi Sharon."

"Avi Sharon?"

"One of those hundred and forty-four thousand witnesses from Israel. He came over here and spoke to Michael and Sylvia Cohen, and they joined us."

"I remember Michael. We played golf and were on the school board together."

"They moved to Israel, along with Avi and our granddaughter, Michelle. Avi married Michelle, by the way."

"Seriously? Michelle married a witness and moved to Israel?"

"It was hard for me to believe as well. I don't know how they're doing because there is no mail or phone service yet," she said.

Irene stared at the tabletop for a few seconds, her head wavering side to side. "Did you hear about Abigail and Michael and the two boys? We don't know what happened to them. Michelle and Avi went to their house but only found a note saying they were going away to hide."

"You do not know whether they were saved?"

"No. We think it's unlikely."

Daniel stared across at her, and then reached out to squeeze her hand. "I am so sorry. I always hoped they might believe."

She shrugged and said, "I was no better than them, but I had the advantage of David and Avi's faith and wisdom. And afterword, I began to recall some of the things you used to tell me."

"Well, I believe there will be a purpose in all of this. You are a pioneer, and you have a strong group around you. You will do well. It will be a very special time for this world."

"So we've been told."

"And I understand you have met someone?"

She looked up at him. "My, word gets around. Yes, his name is Walter Petersen and he's staying here. David and Vera moved next door."

"Well, for what it is worth, I believe you and he should stay together. I am told he is a good match for you."

She squinted at him. "Who is telling you these things? And where do you live, by the way?"

Daniel looked around the kitchen, as if composing his thoughts. "Our superiors tell us things, which is how I know about Walter. I cannot say how they get the information."

She studied his face but didn't say anything.

Getting no follow up questions, Daniel said, "As to where we live, I cannot explain that either. It is not a physical location as you might think it. I suppose you would say it is a different dimension. It is paradise, where the Lord Jesus Christ lives when not on earth as your King. It is beautiful beyond any description that I might try to give you. The colors, aromas, the citizens, mortal and spirit…it is indescribable."

"So how do you travel here?

"I cannot really explain that either. We are like angels now. They are all around, by the way. We just think of a place, and we are there," he said.

Irene cocked her head and stared at him. "But you look so lifelike."

He chuckled and said, "I should. I am as alive as you are. I just have a different type of body. You will have one like it one day."

"Do you see Katherine and Stephen and the children? Would I know them?"

"Yes. And my brother Dennis; I know you were not fond of him."

"I am over those feelings," she said.

"I thought as much. Katherine and the others are around, although they have different assignments. The children are grownups now, of course."

"Grownups?"

"Yes. Once they were translated…when we were taken away…they became the adults they would have become if they had remained on earth to grow up slowly."

She broke into a smile, and Daniel said, "What are you thinking about?

"So, you can't read minds. I was thinking of Katherine's first son, Adam, and what a chatterbox he was. Is he still that way?"

"Somewhat. It fits his assignment."

"Which is…?"

"He is a guide in a minor province in what used to be Mongolia. There are not many people there now, but when it blossoms and the population explodes, he will be at the forefront."

They sat silently for a minute, then Daniel looked down at Joshua and said, "How are you, and do you have any questions? You are not as talkative as Adam when he was your age."

"Who was Adam?" Joshua said.

"He is your cousin. But you will not get to meet him for a long time. But when you do, you will like him, and you will be with him forever. And he has two sisters and a younger brother as well."

"And you're my grandfather?" Joshua said.

"Yes. And I am very glad that I got to meet you. You see, I went away to live with Jesus before you were born."

Joshua gave him a weak smile, and then looked up at Irene.

"Is this really weird for you?" Irene said.

He looked up at Daniel and then back at her and shook his head 'yes'.

"It is weird for me, Joshua. Daniel and I knew each other for over fifty years before all the troubles started. Before we hid out in the bunker. And now he will help other people, just like Ezra will help us."

"But we won't see him anymore?"

Irene looked at Daniel, and he shook his head 'no'.

Joshua said, "Don't go anywhere," and left the kitchen. They chatted for a few minutes while he was gone, and when Joshua came back he had a camera.

"I want to take your picture, Grandpa," he said. "And when I see you again, I will show it to you."

"How about the two of us?" Daniel said, standing up and drawing Irene to his side.

"Okay," he said, and snapped three quick shots.

The three of them looked at the images in the camera window. There he was, physical enough for a picture.

"Will you stay around to see David and Vera?"

"No. I must go," he said.

"Can I tell them I saw you?"

"If you wish. And they can see the picture. I will always look the same...even when you see me again after the Kingdom. We do not age."

"But we will," Irene said.

"Yes. But you will always be my beauty, even after 900 years. And when the Kingdom is over and the new earth comes, you will look young again. Forever."

She looked at him and then hugged him, holding on tightly. "I'm glad you came. We're all so confused right now. We don't know what to expect. Only that this Kingdom is coming soon. But these guides can't tell us when."

"I cannot either I am afraid."

She released him and backed up, wiping her eyes. "I feel like a schoolgirl again."

"That is the girl I married."

"Yes. It was, wasn't it? So long ago now." She stroked his head and shoulders and arms. "You are real, aren't you. This isn't a dream."

"I am very real. But I have noticed that mortals get uneasy when I appear and disappear suddenly. So perhaps it would be best if you took my grandson and walked outside again."

Irene pursed her lips and shook her head yes. "Come on, Josh," she said, and turned toward the kitchen door. As she reached for the doorknob, a last question occurred to her, and she turned back to ask him.

But he was gone.

CHAPTER 51

COMMENCEMENT

Long days of physical labor followed by house renovations in the evening made for deep and restful sleep. The nights were longer now as they passed mid-summer, but they could still barely sleep past dawn.

Vera opened one eye and squinted at the light in the room. It seemed unusual, and she poked David. *"Awaken."*

"What...?" he said, fighting sleep cobwebs.

"Look at the window."

David peered at the light that crept in around the edges of the drapes. It looked as if a spotlight was focused on their window. It was so bright that the drapes were almost translucent.

"My God," he said, and shot upright in bed. He stared at the drapes for a few seconds, and then got out of bed and walked over and peeked through a crack. As he did so he covered his eyes, then turned back to Vera and motioned for her to join him.

When she walked over, he put his arm around her and said, *"Ready?"*

"For what?"

"This," he said, and slid open the drapes. They had to shield their eyes for a few seconds, and when they adjusted to the brightness, they looked at each other and said in unison, *"This is it."*

They could see Russ, Kim and Angela in their yard across the street, so they slipped into shorts and tee shirts and walked out to meet them.

As they did so, Walter and Irene emerged as well, and they all gathered at the end of Irene's driveway.

"*Ezra said we would know,*" Russ said, "*so this must be it. The Kingdom has started. What do you think?*"

"*That would be my thought,*" Walter said.

They were transfixed and words failed the situation. The sky was a cloudless, electric blue that enhanced saturated colors with a richness they had never seen before. Irene's flowers seemed to glow, and even the drab barberry hedge around her yard shimmered in a vibrant satin green.

The light had awoken Joshua as well, and he wandered out from next door with his dog Phoenix in tow. He walked up to his parents, rubbing his eyes, and said, "*What is happening?*"

"*We believe the Kingdom has just begun, son,*" David said. "*This is the very first day.*"

As Joshua looked around with the rest of the group, Phoenix's ears popped up and he wandered down toward the corner. One of the neighborhood deer caught his attention, and where the animal would normally bolt with the dog in pursuit, they met on the street and nuzzled each other. Then the deer wandered up to them and let Angela and Joshua pet him for a minute before he seemed to tire of it and wandered off.

"*That was strange,*" Vera said. "*Is that part of life now?*"

"*I think so,*" David said. "*I believe animals will behave differently now. We will have to ask Ezra or Elena.*"

Walter wandered toward the house and then turned back to the group. He gestured at the yard and said, "*Look at that. I just cut this grass yesterday, and it looks like it has a week's growth already.*"

"*It does at that,*" Irene said, walking up and scanning the yard with him. Then she moved toward her plantings and beckoned for the group to follow her. The daylily shoots were now full grown, bright orange bells cheering from the side of the house. The peonies and hostas fully matured overnight as well. The group trailed along behind her as she pointed out two-inch seedlings she had planted yesterday that were already a foot tall. And seeds she planted two days ago were now six inches tall.

While they marveled at the plant growth, Irene studied Walter for a minute and finally realized what was different.

"Walter," she said, pointing to her eyes.

"What?"

"Where are your glasses?"

He felt his eyes, and with a startled look said, *"Ohmygosh. They're inside. I don't need them."* He stared at Irene and said, *"And look at you."*

"I do not wear glasses outside," she said.

"No. Not that. Your face. All your wrinkles are gone."

Vera wandered over to stare at both of them and said, *"Walter. Yours are gone, too. You look like you both are in your twenties again. Amazing."*

They looked at each other, then at their hands, seeing smooth skin and no age spots, and burst out laughing.

"You know," Walter said. *"We used to joke that we would like to be back in college, knowing what we know now. But this is really happening. I can start training for that marathon, now."*

"I would not go that far," Irene said.

"Hm. I can see the problem here," Walter said. *"Usually, the mind is young but the body is old. Now it's the other way around. This will take some adjusting."*

By the time they wandered around to the front of the house again, the O'Neill's had walked down in their bathrobes, with Elena the guide trailing behind them. They all looked at her as she walked up, and David said, *"So is this it now?"*

"This is it."

"What day is it?" Walter said.

"The First of Elul," Elena said. *"You are now using the lunar calendar."*

"What is supposed to happen now?" he said.

She looked around the group for a few seconds before answering. *"For the moment, you will all continue with your current tasks. In a few days you will receive a teacher who will instruct you in more detail about the Kingdom."*

"Like what?" David said.

"Many things. Teaching about the King's law, both for worship and for civil government since they will be one and the same now. The new calendar. New careers."

"How long will that take?" Vera said. "And is this teacher a rabbi?"

"The teacher will not be a rabbi in the sense that you may have experienced prior to the Kingdom. He will not just be officiating in religious ceremonies. He will have much to teach you, and it will take a long time to absorb and practice the details. But then you have a long time, so the teacher will proceed at a slow pace."

"Will he be a resurrected person like you?" David said.

"No. He will be a mortal."

A car drove by and stopped at the corner. The driver was one of the Korean men David had met during their workdays but had difficulty in conversation due to his thick accent. The man yelled out," Is this it?"

"Yes," they said in unison. He gave the thumbs up sign and drove on.

"Strange. His...," David started to say.

"His what?" Vera said.

"I was going to say I could barely understand him before in whatever his language was...I cannot remember the name...."

"It was called Korean," Elena said. "He is not speaking that now."

"What? What do you mean? What are we speaking?" Russ said.

"You are speaking the King's language. Everyone is. That is how you could understand him."

As they stared at each other, Vera said, *"Does it have a name?"*

"No. Just the King's language."

As they let this sink in, still absorbing the colors and the sense of the day, a cricket sound broke the silence. It came from Kim's direction, and she looked startled and then said, *"Oh, man...my cell phone. A text message. Guess they finally fixed it. I kept it charged just in case,"* she said, fumbling in her pocket.

They stared at her as she unlocked the phone and read the message.

"Well?" Vera said.

"*I cannot read it...in whatever this language is.*"

"*Let me see,*" Elena said.

The guide read the message and said, "*It is from someone named Michelle. She says the Kingdom has started.*"

"*We knew that,*" Vera said.

"*She also says she is pregnant.*"

"*Oh my,*" Irene said as the group broke into a collective smile.

Irene looked at the guide and said, "*Michelle is in Israel, you know. Do they have working hospitals in Israel now?*"

"*She will not need one. They will use a midwife.*"

"*But what if there is a complication?*" Walter said.

"*There will not be a complication.*"

"*Are you sure?*" he said.

"*Of course. You are in the Kingdom now. There will be no physical problems in childbirth, and the child will be healthy. The King will see to that.*"

Russ winked at Kim and put an arm around her shoulder. "*That was pretty quick. Looks like we have some catching up to do.*"

EPILOGUE

So it will begin.

For those with ears to hear, the King promises that history *can* be written before it happens. As promised to the patriarch Abraham four thousand years ago, all nations of the world will be blessed through Israel. Their long-promised Kingdom for Israel will begin and she shall be the crown of nations for a thousand years.

For those who *believed* in the Lord Jesus Christ for salvation *before* the troubles, they will be immortal participants, resurrected with new bodies. For those who *disbelieved* and survived by their newfound trust in the King, they needed to endure the seven years of tribulation. But if they survived, they would enter a wondrous Kingdom.

For the disbelieving who *reject* the King, their eternal fate will be horrendous.

Imagine living for a thousand years in an ideal world, ruled by a Benevolent King, undertaking the task to rebuild a just and moral society in a near perfect world. No malevolent spirits will torment you. No poverty, crime, wars, disease, or natural disasters to stifle your efforts. When help is needed, immortal beings and angels can give advice and ensure order.

What could possibly go wrong?

The answer: never underestimate the ability of our sinful human natures to create chaos. Given enough time, the human capacity for greed, lust, and pride can ruin even the most idyllic conditions.

But that's in the future, centuries ahead. For now, imagine following our three families, fueled with adventure, and join them as they begin their journey of many lifetimes in Cascadia, New Columbia, and Israel.

ABOUT THE AUTHOR

Like many authors, Ben Owens has had various careers that add to the sense of adventure in writing. This includes the Air Force security service, an industrial chemist, a foreign missionary, a customer service supervisor in the transportation industry, and currently a consultant fund raising for schools and libraries. He has a BS in Chemistry and an MBA from Drexel University, plus a Bible certificate from Lancaster Bible College.

Printed in the United States
by Baker & Taylor Publisher Services